GUNSMOKE™:
THE DAY OF
THE GUNFIGHTER

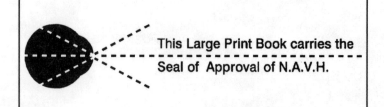

GUNSMOKE™: THE DAY OF THE GUNFIGHTER

JOSEPH A. WEST
FOREWORD BY JAMES ARNESS

WHEELER PUBLISHING
An imprint of Thomson Gale, a part of The Thomson Corporation

Detroit • New York • San Francisco • New Haven, Conn. • Waterville, Maine • London

Trade™ and copyright © 2007 by CBS Inc.

Foreword copyright © Penguin Group (USA) Inc., 2007

Thomson Gale is part of The Thomson Corporation.

Thomson and Star Logo and Wheeler are trademarks and Gale is a registered trademark used herein under license.

Wheeler Publishing Large Print Western.

The text of this Large Print edition is unabridged.

Other aspects of the book may vary from the original edition.

Set in 16 pt. Plantin.

LIBRARY OF CONGRESS CATALOGING-IN-PUBLICATION DATA

West, Joseph A.
 The day of the gunfighter / by Joseph A. West; foreword by James Arness.
  p. cm. — (Gunsmoke)
  ISBN-13: 978-1-59722-577-9 (pbk. : alk. paper)
  ISBN-10: 1-59722-577-0 (pbk. : alk. paper)
  1. Holliday, John Henry, 1851–1887 — Fiction. 2. Dillon, Matt (Fictitious character) — Fiction. 3. United States marshals — Fiction. 4. Large type books. I. Title.
PS3573.E8224D39 2007
813'.54—dc22   2007015811

Published in 2007 by arrangement with NAL Signet, a member of Penguin Group (USA) Inc.

Printed in the United States of America on permanent paper
10 9 8 7 6 5 4 3 2 1

FOREWORD

We celebrated the fifty-first year of *Gunsmoke* on September 10, 2006. The very first show was "Matt Gets It" in 1955 and the last show was "The Sharecroppers" in 1975. Due to the fine cast we had, *Gunsmoke* had fifteen Emmy nominations. It reminds me that *Gunsmoke* was a show that was fortunate enough to have many many excellent actors on the show.

Of course Amanda Blake was an integral part of the show. She was also a wonderful person and a very dear friend. Working with Amanda was always a joy. The fans always wanted a commitment from Matt Dillon to Miss Kitty, but being the lawman in Dodge City, he had a higher commitment to keeping law and order. And then there was Doc. Milburn Stone was a true professional. He grew up in Kansas and could remember hearing the stories of the real cowboys when he was a little boy. Everything on the set had to be authentic or he would let us know that it had to be changed. Dennis Weaver created his part of Chester during his original audition for the show. They wanted something special, and he did it. We are truly sorry to have lost Dennis last year. He was a friend for the last fifty years. When Dennis left the show, we were all concerned about his replacement, but we shouldn't have worried because Ken Curtis as Festus was perfect. Ken took to the part like a duck to water. From day one he fit in with the cast, and the fans loved him. Burt Reynolds was our resident blacksmith, Quint. Burt still says that doing *Gunsmoke* was "the best of times." Buck Taylor was our gunsmith, and we have stayed close over the years. He turned out to be just as great an artist as he was an actor. In our very last show, Bruce Boxleitner was again part of our cast, and I went on to do other movies with him. Glenn Strange played the part of the bartender and he also played Frankenstein's monster in some sequels to the original movie.

I also had the pleasure of working with Jack Albertson, Jenny Arness, Jean Arthur, Ed Asner, Jim Backus, Ben Bates, Ralph Bellamy, Dan Blocker, Bruce Boxleitner, Beau Bridges, Charles Bronson, Ellen Burstyn, Gary Busey, Dyan Cannon, Harry

Carey Jr., William Conrad, Lee J. Cobb, Iron Eyes Cody, Betty Davis, Angie Dickinson, Richard Dreyfus, Barbara Eden, Buddy Ebsen, Harrison Ford, Steve Forrest, Jodie Foster, Victor French, Melissa Gilbert, Mariette Hartley, Earl Holliman, Dennis Hopper, Ron Howard, George Kennedy, Michael Learned, June Lockhart, Lee Majors, Vera Miles, Ricardo Montalban, Leonard Nimoy, Carroll O'Connor, Slim Pickens, Suzanne Pleshette, Pernell Roberts, Kurt Russell, William Shatner, Aaron Spelling, Loretta Swit, Jon Voight, Leslie Ann Warren and Morgan Woodward, to name a few. I bet there are some surprises in there for you. Some of these actors had their first part on the show, and others were already seasoned professionals. I remember Ron Howard and Jodie Foster playing on the set as little kids. Jodie played the part of a young girl in three shows. Jodie and Ron played their parts to perfection and went on to be fine actors. Ron Howard's father, Rance, also played on *Gunsmoke*. You can imagine all our excitement when Betty Davis agreed to be in the show called "The Jailer." If you haven't seen that one, she was fantastic. You would truly have believed that she hated me. Bruce Dern played her son.

Many of the actors are still friends of mine

today, like Burt Reynolds, Buck Taylor, Harry Carey Jr., Mariette Hartley, Ricardo Montalban, Morgan Woodward, Michael Learned, and Angie Dickinson. It is hard to believe all the friends from the show who have left us.

There were so many other actors who played on the show that brought a great quality to *Gunsmoke* that it's impossible to name all of them. These are just a few, and I thank each and every actor who appeared on the show. They all contributed to its success and its longevity. During the twenty years of *Gunsmoke,* we made 633 episodes, and I don't think that any other show had or will have the opportunity to promote new actors and feature as guest stars so many established actors. It was a great joy for me, and I truly enjoyed making *Gunsmoke* and meeting so many wonderful friends. I thank all the fans who have remained loyal to the show and still enjoy hearing from them. How many people can say that after fifty-one years?

— James Arness
"Marshal Matt Dillon"

CHAPTER 1
GUNFIGHTER
TROUBLE

United States marshal Matt Dillon looked out his office window at the rider in the rain and knew the man shaped up to be big trouble.

That he knew this with certainty was understandable, because Matt had once ridden trails with this man, way back when, in another place and time.

The rider drew rein on his rangy Appaloosa and sat his saddle, both hands on the horn, studying the marshal's office. Rain ran off his slicker and hat in rivulets, and above him thunder banged, lightning forking across a sullen black sky.

Matt did not move from the window, his face tight and drawn as his mind worked. What was Ed Flynn, of all people, doing in Dodge?

From what he could see of the man's face under the wide brim of his hat, Matt decided that Flynn hadn't changed much over the years. Gray showed at his temples, but his long, narrow face, split by a sweeping dragoon mustache, was weather-beaten, burned brown by sun, wind and winter cold and seemed ageless. He was still lean and angular, his shoulders a shade too narrow for his large head, and by the way he slumped in the saddle, he had the look of a tired man who had traveled fast and far.

Lashed by the downpour, horse and rider were as unmoving as an equestrian statue in a town square and even Flynn's crossed hands on the saddle horn were still. Only the man's cold green eyes were restless, traveling over the front of the office, lingering finally on the window where Matt stood.

It was not yet noon, but the marshal had lit a lamp against the gloom of the day and he was sure Flynn saw him only in silhouette, yet the man suddenly smiled and swung out of the saddle.

"I'd recognize those shoulders of yours anywhere, Matt," Flynn said as he settled himself into a chair and accepted a cup of coffee from the marshal. "You're the only man I know who stands three ax handles tall and one accrost the chest."

Flynn's cool eyes took measure of Matt. " 'Course, you've filled out since I last saw you, put meat on them shoulders and arms."

"I was a skinny-enough kid back then," Matt said. "A man grows up and then out I guess."

Flynn sipped from his cup and made a face. "Your coffee hasn't changed, though. Still as bad as ever."

Flynn's slicker and hat were hung on the rack near the door, runoff water already pooling on the pine floor. The man sprawled, seemingly relaxed and at ease, but Matt sensed his inner tenseness, the coiled spring ready to unwind. He remembered Flynn, and the man's looseness was deceptive. If he took the notion, he could move out of the chair as fast as a striking rattler, a gun appearing like magic in his hand.

After a few moments of silence stretched between them, Matt, keeping any hint of welcome out of his voice, asked: "What brings you to Dodge, Ed?"

Giving time for Flynn to answer, the marshal drank from his own cup. He thought the coffee tasted just fine.

"They got me treed, Matt," Flynn finally answered. "I'm all through running and I reckoned you were the only one who could help me." He set his cup carefully on the desk and tilted his head, studying the steam rising from the coffee as though it was suddenly a matter of great interest. "I heard you was marshaling out of Dodge, and I came here."

Thunder rumbled across the sky and rain hammered on the glass of the office window, driven by a gusting prairie wind.

Matt's eyes dropped to Flynn's gun belt. Unusual at that time in the West, Flynn carried two guns, a long-barreled Colt on his thigh, the other, with a shorter barrel, in a cross-draw holster. He was lightning-fast on the draw and shoot with either.

"Who's got you treed, Ed?" the marshal asked. "I'd have thought you were too savvy an ol' coon for that."

Flynn shrugged. "Savvy don't come in to it, Matt. I guess my luck started to run out about three weeks ago down in the Chickasaw Nation at a settlement they call Murray. As settlements go, it wasn't much, just a combination saloon and general store and a scattering of shacks and tents along a creek.

"Me, I was studying on riding further west, maybe all the way to Californy, when I come on that place. It had started into heavy rain, a real gully washer, kind of like what it's doing outside right now, and I figured maybe I'd stop for a drink and a bite to eat."

Flynn picked up his cup again, looked at

the dregs and Matt refilled it for him. "Obliged," he said. His eyes lifted to the marshal's. "Ever been to Californy, Matt?"

"Can't say as I have."

"Me, neither. When I was down there in the Nation, I reckoned I wanted to take a look at the ocean-sea before I got too old. I've seen some mighty pretty lakes, but never the big water." Flynn smiled, making him look ten years younger than his forty-odd years. "Hell, but now when I study on it, maybe I didn't really want to see the ocean. Maybe I just had a hankering to ride the high country again for a spell, and spread my blankets above the aspen, where the junipers meet the timberline. One time I mind when I followed an Indian trail over the San Pedro and there were rimfire places where a man could fall for two miles if'n he got even a mite careless. But I loved that country, wild and untamed it was, with raw-boned peaks that scraped the sky and a solemn silence lying around me like I was in church."

Suddenly Flynn looked mildly embarrassed. "Hell, listen to me go on. I sound like a Sunday school preacher. But, Matt, I'm a traveling, long-riding man, and I've got no kin to speak of. My whole life no one has ever waited on my coming or cared about my going. Unless" — Flynn tapped the butt of his crossdraw Colt — "they'd hired me for this. I'm getting no younger and before I cash in, I have a hankering to cross over the blue mountains and maybe sure enough head all the way to the big water."

Flynn sighed deep in his chest. "Well, all what I've been telling you was on my mind as I rode into Murray and stepped into the saloon.

"I'll make it short from there, Matt. I'd just tasted my first rye when I was braced by a man who seemed to take exception to my being there, or my even being alive. I'd met his kind before, and so have you, just a four-flushing tinhorn on the prod, trying to build himself a rep. I learned later his name was Mick Feeney and that he was half-Irish, half-Chickasaw and all son of a bitch.

"He'd killed a couple of men in the past and fancied himself fast on the draw. Now he wanted to nail my hide to the wall and cut another notch in the handle of his gun."

Matt stirred in his chair. "Feeney . . . that name seems familiar."

Flynn nodded. "I reckon it will come back to you when I tell you the rest." He hesitated a few moments, remembering, then said: "Well, Feeney and me, we had words and I told him to back off, that he was sure enough bucking a stacked deck."

Shaking his head, Flynn said: "Some people just don't listen and they can't read the sign. Feeney made some more war talk. Then he drew down on me. I shot him just once, in the belly, and by the time he joined his shadow on the ground, I could see in his eyes that he didn't want to be a fast gun no more.

"It took Mick Feeney five hours to die, and all that time he screamed in agony and cussed me, the day he was born and the mother that bore him." Flynn's eyes were bleak. "He died hard. That's for damn sure."

Thunder roared louder than before, and a searing lightning flash lit up the dark corners of the office. The door rattled on its hinges, battered by the boisterous wind, and a steady leak plopped from the ceiling, forming a puddle near the entrance to the cells.

"Seems like a fair fight to me," Matt said. "What happened to make you cut and run?"

"Comin' to that," Flynn answered. He took time to build a smoke, thumbed a match into flame and lit the cigarette. He dropped the burning match into his cup, where it sizzled and went out. "Mick's brother is Lee Feeney," he said.

Now Matt remembered where he had

heard the name. Lee Feeney had been arrested in Texas three months before, suspected of killing a conductor during a robbery of the Katy Flier. He'd been put on trial, but had been quickly acquitted because of a lack of evidence. The only eyewitness, a middle-aged woman traveling home to Austin after visiting her sister in Philadelphia, had mysteriously disappeared.

Matt had heard that Feeney rode with up to twenty hardcases at a time, and was suspected of robbing trains, banks and stagecoaches all over Texas and into the Nations, but he'd always covered his tracks so well that nothing could be proved. He was said to be fast on the draw and had killed seven men, the last the long-haired Laredo gunfighter Bucky Logan, whom fellow shootists ranked among the very elite.

That Logan had been shot in the back was neither here nor there. At that time in the West, getting the drop on a man didn't mean shucking your gun faster. It meant shooting him any way you could and when he least expected it, preferably while he was asleep, drunk, unarmed or singing a hymn in church.

By all accounts Feeney was a born killer, and cold-blooded murder did not weigh on his conscience or keep him up at night.

"And Feeney came after you," Matt said.

Flynn's smile was thin and faded fast. "Matt, Lee Feeney I could have handled, but he's got twenty riding with him, all hard men and good with the iron."

"How did they manage to track you from the Nation?" Matt asked. He grinned, taking the sting out of what he was about to say. "You've covered your trail before and lost men who'd taken a notion to hang you."

Flynn nodded. "I have at that, but Feeney's got an Apache breed riding for him, a killer they call the Jicarilla Kid. That damn breed will cut any man, woman or child in half with a shotgun for fifty dollars. He can also track a minnow across a swamp."

Matt felt a pang of unease. "Where are Feeney and his men?" he asked.

"Close," Flynn answered. "I figured they were no more'n three, four hours behind me when I rode into Dodge" — he shrugged — "unless they've holed up somewheres on account of the rain."

Thunder grumbled like a grouchy old man and the air held the ozone tang of lightning. Beyond the window the rain looked like a steel curtain billowing in the wind, and a woman ran past the office, head bent against the storm, her heels drumming on the boardwalk.

A wordless silence stretched taut between the two men until finally Flynn said: "Matt, I'm surrounded by hundreds of miles of flat prairie, where a man on horseback can be seen forever." He shook his head. "I'm trapped like a yearling in a cattle pen and you're my only hope."

The gunfighter's eyes were pleading. "You owe me, Matt. You owe me from way back when."

"I don't need you to remind me of that, Ed," Matt said a little too sharply. "You saved my life and that's a thing a man doesn't forget, not now, not ever." He moved in his chair, hearing it complain under his weight. "What do you want from me, Ed?"

"Protect me, Matt. I can't take on twenty men by myself." Flynn's stiff-necked pride was hurting and it showed in his mouth, tight and white-lipped under his mustache. "Don't ask me to beg, Matt. Until today, I never asked a favor of no man, but now I'm asking one of you. Please . . . don't let them run me down and kill me in the street like a dog."

Matt's lifted his eyes to Flynn's face, then looked quickly away. He knew what it was taking for the aging gunfighter to swallow his pride and humble himself this way. But what distressed him more was the look in Flynn's eyes. They were the eyes of a trapped animal, haunted with fear.

Matt forced himself to again meet the man's gaze. "I'll do all I can for you, Ed," he said. "Lee Feeney won't kill you, not in my town."

"Thank you, Matt," Flynn said. "From the bottom of my heart, thank you." The man smiled. "Just like old times, huh? You and me."

Matt nodded, a cold unease riding him. "Yes," he said, "just like old times."

Chapter 2
Apache Gold

After Flynn left, Matt rose from his desk and stepped to the window. It had now rained for three days without letup and Front Street was a sea of thick yellow mud. A freight wagon drawn by six mules trundled past, the driver up on the spring seat bundled inside a glistening slicker, rain running off his hat brim.

Over to the Long Branch, a scrap of red, white and blue bunting left over from the cattle season flapped and curled in the wind. A man in black broadcloth stepped out of the door, glanced at the sky, then stepped inside again, shaking his head.

Matt's mind was on Ed Flynn.

The gunfighter was a legend, a named man who was mentioned in the same breath as Hickok, Hardin and Ben Thompson, and was said by most to be faster with the Colt than any of them.

He had been a cow town marshal, a

shotgun guard for Wells Fargo, hauling gold shipments out of Aurora in what was then the Nevada Territory. For a spell he'd been a hard-rock miner, but when his claim played out, Flynn had looked around for an easier way to make money and had begun to sell his gun to the highest bidder. He'd killed a couple of men in the early years of the savage Sutton-Taylor feud and had later drifted to Montana, where he'd worked as a range detective for an English cattle outfit. He'd done the same in Wyoming.

The last Matt had heard, Flynn was drawing gun wages from a big rancher in Texas who wanted to be bigger and was pushing out the smaller spreads. Called by some Lawson, others Layton, the rancher was apparently a hard, ambitious man hell-bent on building an empire. Those who dug in their heels and pushed back were referred to Ed Flynn, usually with fatal consequences.

The talk was that Flynn had killed sixty men, a figure Matt doubted. But over the years, he had killed more than his share and he was a bad man to tangle with.

Feared gunfighter though he was, Flynn had his limits, and taking on odds of twenty to one was too much even for him.

Matt watched rain run down the panes of the window, bleak as a widow woman's tears, and his memory moved back through the shadowed corridors of time, to another place and a land much harsher than the fair green plains of Kansas. . . .

Around Matt Dillon, in all directions of the compass, lay a godforsaken landscape of dust and alkali, an unending succession of arid mesas and rocky canyons. He was surrounded by a vast silence and only the occasional scurrying lizard brought any sign of life.

The sun was very hot and the rocks where he lay were as scorching as flatirons, his palms and fingers already blistered by his climb up a low sandstone ridge after his horse had been shot out from under him.

How many of them were out there?

Matt had no way of knowing. Five, maybe six, but then even one Apache was a force to be reckoned with. The Apache warrior was tough, patient and enduring, reared to survive in a hard and unforgiving land. He was fearless and resilient, a first-class fighting man as cunning as he was dangerous.

And now they were all around him, waiting. But for what?

They must know that his canteen was down there on the sandy flat, still looped to his saddle horn. It was not a fact an Apache would miss.

Water is the life of the desert country of Arizona. Without it nothing would exist but the rocks. But far from being an empty, barren place, the desert teems with life, nurturing a wide variety of animals, flowers, birds and insects, and it gives birth to a dry, whistling wind that now and then blows.

But there was no wind and, for young Matt Dillon, no water.

He knew that somewhere to his west, after emerging from the Huachuca and Mule ranges, ran the San Pedro river, where mint green frogs kicked through water cold as snowmelt. But he was far from there. Nor would the Apaches let him venture in that direction.

And he had no rifle. That too was down there with his horse.

Earlier the Apaches had fired a few probing shots around the shallow depression where he lay, a flat area about eight feet by six, scooped out of the slope just below the crest of the ridge. Matt guessed that a boulder had once hung there and had rolled down the slope during some ancient earth shake, leaving behind the hollow where it had rested.

The firing had stopped an hour ago, and since then he had not seen or heard a thing, just the occasional fleeting shadow that raced across the land when a white cloud sailed past the face of the sun.

Matt was tormented by thirst, and as the day wore on to noon, the heat was relentless, burning through the thin stuff of his shirt onto his back and shoulders. He tried sucking a pebble to generate some moisture in his dry mouth, but soon spat it out as useless. His lips were already cracked and split, and stinging sweat ran into his reddened eyes.

How long had he lain here?

The Apaches had hit them an hour after sunup as they were riding through the narrow ravine thirty feet below him.

Old Adam Barnes, the man who had led them here, and his son, Len, had tumbled dead out of their saddles at the first shattering volley. Matt's horse had gone down and he'd rolled clear, then scrambled up the slope, bullets kicking around him. He'd climbed fast, his breath coming in tormented gasps, anything to get away from the death in the ravine.

Big, laughing Tom Reuben had tried to make a run for it. But the Apaches had sealed off both ends of the arroyo and he'd run into a hail of gunfire. High Pockets Heelan, a lanky cowboy out of the Canadian

River country, had tried to make a fight of it, but he too had been soon cut down. Heelan had been more dead than alive when the Apaches dragged him away, but he'd found the strength to scream for two hours before death mercifully took him.

Only one man had been able to ride out of that hell, a former cow town marshal who called himself Ed Flynn. But Matt had no idea if he'd gotten clear or not. The Apaches had done a lot of firing in Flynn's direction, and when Matt last saw him, the man had been bent over the saddle as though he'd taken a hit.

Below Matt, the bodies of the dead were already beginning to swell and stink, and cold-eyed vultures were gliding in circles against the blue denim sky, waiting with infinite patience for the feast they knew must come.

It was not supposed to have been like this.

Adam Barnes had recruited Matt at Fort Stockton, Texas, a sprawling bulwark of adobe built to discourage Apaches raiding into the settled Comanche Springs country. Eighteen-year-old Matt had been scouting for General Edward Hatch's Ninth Cavalry for six months but was now anxious to try his hand at something else.

Barnes offered him that something else.

The man was small, brown and dusty, with bright, good-humored blue eyes. He had the rolling gait of the seafaring man, a fact he confirmed when he told Matt that three months before he'd jumped ship in San Francisco.

"Later I got into a poker game in a dive along the waterfront and won big," he said. "And included in me winnings was this." With a flourish Adam reached into his coat and produced a folded piece of yellow paper. "Know what this is, boy?"

Matt shrugged, only half interested. "I have no idea. A letter, maybe."

"No letter, boy. It's a treasure map. The key to a fortune in gold buried by old Spanish men a hundred years ago." He waved to the others who were with him. "None of us know the Arizona country to the northwest of here, but you do. I want you to scout a trail for us." Seeing Matt open his mouth to speak, and perhaps turn him down, Barnes held up a quieting hand and forged ahead. "I'll pay you sixty dollars now and one-tenth of the value of any gold we find, and that could stack up to be a tidy sum."

The man spread his arms wide. "I surely can't say fairer than that." He turned and looked at the five other men. "It sure beats working for the Army for fifty a month, don't it, boys?"

The others murmured agreement, except for a silent man who was taking Matt's measure with hard green eyes. Later Matt learned that his name was Ed Flynn and that he was good with a gun and had already earned a reputation as a man to step wide around.

Matt asked to see the map, studied it intently for long moments, then said, "According to this, the treasure is stashed under a rock cairn in an arroyo at the southern base of Mount Graham."

Barnes nodded, his mouth stretched in a wide grin. "You got it right, boy. Damn it all, I knowed I liked the cut of your jib the very minute I first set eyes on you. You're gold dust, boy, gold dust."

Matt ignored the compliments, and said: "The Apaches call that mountain *Dzil n'chaa si an.* It's sacred to them because they believe the peak is home to four powerful mountain spirits."

Disappointment clouded Barnes' weather-beaten face. "You telling me you're scared o' ha'ants an' such, boy?"

When a man is eighteen, he thinks he's indestructible, and to young Matt Dillon, the treasure hunt sounded like a great adventure and it was already in his mind to agree to Barnes' proposition. "I'm not scared of much, Barnes," he said, a statement that made Flynn look at him again. "But there and back, we have eight hundred miles of rough country to cross. I know the location of most of the water holes and we can shoot our own chuck along the trail, but you'll still need coffee, flour and bacon for a month at least."

Barnes beamed. "Already taken care of, Matt me boy. I've loaded up two packmules with all the stuff we'll need, including plenty of ammunition." The man rubbed his hands together and grinned. "This is going to be great. A couple of weeks from now we'll all be rich men."

But Adam Barnes, his useless map still in his pocket, was now a dead man, and the others with him.

When the merciless sun began to drop lower in the sky, the Apaches came for Matt Dillon. They came in a rush, a dozen dusky warriors, appearing like demons from among the talus rocks scattered at the base of the slope.

Matt rose to his feet, drew his bowie knife and held it in his left hand. In his right, his Colt was already up and shooting. An Apache fell and another. Then they were right on top of him. He emptied his gun, then went to his knife, slashing out at men who were coming at him from every direction.

A bullet grazed his leg and another thudded into his left shoulder. He dropped to one knee, knowing it was all over, but determined not to be taken alive.

Guns blazed and an Apache went down, followed by a second. Startled, the warriors drew off for an instant, looking around them.

Ed Flynn, mounted on his wiry paint mustang, was charging up the slope, a hammering Colt in each hand. Two more Indians dropped, one gut shot and screaming, then a third.

Surprised, the Apaches drew back, a few firing at Flynn as they retreated. But the man seemed to have a charmed life. Bullets kicked up Vs of dust around his horse, but he was not hit. He had holstered his revolvers and gone to his Winchester, firing aimed shots with amazing rapidity.

But the Apache had taken enough. Five of their number lay dead or dying on the slope, and they'd decided this was not a good day to fight. Like ghosts, they melted into the landscape and were gone. There would be another day when the odds were more in their favor. Like the dogged, circling vultures, they would wait.

When Flynn swung out of the saddle and stepped toward him, Matt smiled and said: "You came back."

"Of course I came back, just as soon as I heard the shooting," Flynn said. "A man doesn't cut and run when an hombre who ate out of the same skillet as he did is in trouble."

"You saved my life, Ed," Matt said.

The gunman nodded. "Maybe, if you survive that shoulder wound. If you do, I might ask you to do a favor for me one day." He glanced up at the sky and the scorching fireball of the sun. "Now let's get out of here before them 'Paches take a notion to come back."

"Know where I'm headed?" Matt said, rising unsteadily to his feet. "Somewhere far from here, somewhere it rains."

Matt Dillon stood at the window of his office and listened to the driving rain rattle relentlessly on the tar-paper roof, starting other leaks to join the one at the door to the cells.

He'd thought it through. Ed Flynn had saved his life and he owed the man. Now he must return the favor, no matter the consequences.

Matt could not step around the problem — he had to do it.

CHAPTER 3
AN OUTLAW DRAWS
THE LINE

The gray day shaded into a grayer evening, and still the rain fell. The lamps had been lit along Front Street but their light did little to penetrate the gloom. To the north, out on the plains, thunder rumbled and banged, cowing the coyotes into a sullen silence.

Festus stepped into the office, rain running down his slicker. He stood his rifle in the gun rack, shucked the slicker and stepped to Matt's desk.

"Still thundering out there, Festus," Matt observed.

The deputy nodded. "Sure is. My pappy always said that lightning does the work, but thunder takes the credit." He shook his head. "Why are you sitting in the dark, Matthew? It's so downright dark in here it's getting to where a man can't see his hand in front of his face."

Festus thumbed a match into flame and lit the oil lamp above the desk. "There," he said, "that's better. Now I can see your face when I tell you who's in town, got himself a room at the Dodge House, as mean-looking as ever an' bold as brass."

Matt's smile was faint and quickly fled his lips. "Let me guess. It's a feller by the name of Ed Flynn."

Looking crushed, Festus sat on a corner of the desk. "How did you know, Matthew? I only seen him because I met him at the livery and walked to the hotel with him."

"He paid me a visit," Matt said, his face now set and unsmiling. "He wants me to return a favor I owe him."

A slow-thinking man, Festus looked puzzled. "I don't catch your drift, Matthew. How could you owe ol' Ed a favor, an' him always tippytoeing along the line between what's legal and what ain't?"

"He saved my life once, Festus. Ed is a cold-blooded killer with the conscience of a rattlesnake, but, like it or not, I'm beholden to him."

The bewildered expression had not left the deputy's face. "But . . . but how come, Matthew? How did you ever hook up with a killer for hire like Ed Flynn?"

"It was years ago, when I was a lot younger."

Using as few words as possible, Matt told

Festus how Flynn had saved him from Apaches in the Arizona Territory. Then he described the gunfighter's visit to the office and how he'd begged for help.

When Matt had finished talking, the deputy thought for a few moments, then said: "Matthew, seems to me you're the one that's treed. You mought have told Ed that sometimes it's safer to pull freight than your gun."

"Where would he go? If Lee Feeney and his boys catch him out in the open on the plains, Flynn is a dead man."

"You could put him on a train, Matthew, him and his hoss. A train to anywhere, just so he's out of Dodge."

Matt nodded. "I thought about that, but Feeney is smart. I guarantee you he's already got men watching the station and the stage depot."

Festus' right eyebrow crawled up his forehead like a hairy black caterpillar. "What you gonna do, Matthew?"

"Talk to Lee Feeney as soon as possible, maybe smooth things over. I don't want to wait, because hate is like water in a dry gulch. The longer it runs, the deeper it digs, and by all accounts, Feeney is a hating man."

Festus crossed to the stove, poured himself

coffee and stepped back to Matt's desk. A steady drip from the roof thudded onto his hat as he asked: "Is Ed Flynn as good as folks say he is, Matthew? You reckon he's really killed sixty men?"

"I don't know about that, Festus, but he's killed his share. And yes, he's as good with a gun as folks say. Maybe he's the best there is or ever will be."

Festus snorted. "Then if he's that good with the iron, how come he's sceered o' a two-bit outlaw like Feeney?"

Matt shook his head. "He's not scared of Feeney. He's scared of the twenty hardcases riding behind him. No man, no matter how slick he is with a black-eyed Susan, can buck those kind of odds."

Matt stood. At six-foot-nine in his two-inch-heeled boots, he towered over his deputy. "And, Festus, Feeney isn't a two-bit outlaw. He knows how to cover his tracks and so far the law hasn't been able to touch him. He's also a dangerous man, real fast with the Colt, and like Ed Flynn, he's killed more than his share."

Thunder rolled across the sky and lightning flared searing white in the office, then flickered and died into darkness. When the thunderclap faded to an ill-tempered growl, Matt glanced out of the window and saw a rider sitting his horse at the hitching rail.

"Damn it all, didn't you hear me yell?" the rider snapped when Matt and Festus stepped onto the boardwalk. "A man can get hisself killed sitting a hoss in a lightning storm."

"Man can also get himself killed if he doesn't take his hand out of his slicker," Matt said mildly.

The rider read something in the tall, grim marshal that he didn't like, and he said quickly: "I got a note in here from Lee Feeney. I was keeping it dry, like."

"Then take it out real slow," Matt said. "I'm not what you might call a trusting man."

His hand moving like molasses in winter, the rider brought out the note, leaned forward in the saddle and passed it to the marshal.

"Here," the rider said, "Lee will want to know. What's your name, mister?"

"Tell him it's Matt Dillon. United States marshal Matt Dillon."

The name obviously meant something to the rider, because recognition dawned in his eyes and with it a flicker of doubt. "I'll tell him," he said. He swung his horse away from the hitching rail and cantered south along Front Street, mud from his mount's hooves spattering the tails of his yellow slicker.

Matt sat at his desk and read Feeney's note. It was exactly what he'd expected of the man.

TO WHO IT MAY CONCERN
I KNOW THAT ED FLYNN IS IN DODGE AND I RECKON HE TALKED TO THE LAW. WHOEVER WEARS THE STAR COME MEET ME TERMORROW MORNING AT THE BIG WILLOW POND ON THE CREEK DUE SOUTH OF TOWN. IF YOU DON'T COME HAR I'LL RIDE INTO DODGE AND THERE WILL BE A HELL OF AN EXCITEMENT.
    P.S. MY BOYS AINT SITTIN ON THERE GUN HANDS
                        LEE FEENEY ESQ.

Matt read the note to Festus and the deputy asked: "You gonna talk to him, Matthew?"

"The sooner the better. Feeney is talking about Mulberry Creek. I'll ride down there at first light and hear what he has to say."

"Want me to come with you?"

Matt shook his head. "No, Festus, this is

37

something I have to do alone."

Matt Dillon rode across rolling prairie lashed by a cold, driving rain. Around him the grama grass was green, watered well enough to survive the frosts and snows of the coming winter. Only the tufted switch-grass was brown and would remain so until spring. Here and there spread wide swaths of late-blooming fall wildflowers, the yellow of dandelion, sunflowers and sweet clover and the pink blossoms of wild onion, devil's claw and hollyhock.

The wind hammered rain against the front of Matt's slicker, and water dripped steadily from his hat, now and then an icy drop finding its way down the back of his neck.

Thankfully the thunder was gone, at least for the present. A man on a horse, sitting a wet saddle, was the highest object on the plains and lightning was always a danger.

After an hour, through the shifting steel curtain of the rain, Matt made out the cottonwoods and willows lining Mulberry Creek. The pond Feeney had spoken of in his note lay off to his right. Years past, during a drought, an enormous buffalo herd had crossed the dry creek and broken down both banks. Thousands of hooves had dug a wide channel in the sandy bottom and when the water returned it followed the new contours of the creek, forming a deep pool.

Later willows had grown around the place along with cottonwoods and a few stunted oaks.

Feeney had chosen a good spot to make camp since there was water aplenty, and the trees would shelter him and his men from the worst of the wind and rain.

Matt eased his Winchester in the scabbard under his knee and took time to thumb a cartridge into the empty chamber under the hammer of his Colt. If things went bad during his meeting with Feeney, he might need that extra round.

When he was a hundred yards from the creek, men appeared from among the trees, watching him. All wore slickers and carried rifles. A thin ribbon of smoke rose from the bank, the wind busily tying it into bowknots, and among the cottonwoods stood picketed horses.

A man doesn't ride into a camp uninvited, especially an outlaw camp, and when he was a dozen yards from the nearest man, Matt drew rein and waited.

"Come on ahead," a man said. He was small and wiry, a shock of black hair showing under his hat. As Matt drew nearer, he added: "You must be Matt Dillon."

The marshal nodded. "That's the name."

"Heard o' you," the man said. "I'm Lee Feeney."

"Heard of you too," Matt said. Then, unwilling to compromise his position as a lawman, he added: "None of it good."

To Matt's surprise, Feeney laughed. "Forget half of what you've heard and you'll come closer to the truth. Now light and have some coffee and a bit o' grub. Man, you look as wet as a rooster under a drain spout."

It was in Matt's mind to refuse, but the coffee smelled good and so did the frying bacon. He hadn't had either that morning.

The marshal swung out of the saddle, sliding his rifle free of the scabbard as he did, and led his bay into the trees. He eased the cinch and pretended to watch as the horse wandered off to graze. But he was observing Feeney and the men who were with him out of the corner of his eye.

The outlaw was not what he'd expected. The man's blue eyes were mild and humorous, as though he was smiling inwardly at a secret joke, and his slicker was buttoned over his gun.

Feeney was an easy man to underestimate, Matt decided, and he vowed not to make that mistake. As for the others, they came in a variety of shapes and sizes.

But all shared in common hard, watchful eyes and mouths that were a little too thin, revealing a pitiless, violent past. When the outlaws moved, they were aware of everything: Matt, their surroundings, the closeness of their rifles.

When men ride moonlit trails, they develop an instinct for any possible danger, and these were no exception. They pretended to be absorbed in their tasks around camp, but they saw and heard everything.

These were tough, hard-riding men and, like their boss, not men to be taken lightly. They'd be hell on wheels in a fight, and when the shooting was over, they would leave the ground covered with dead men.

But one man stood out from the rest. He was short and stocky, with a wide swarthy face, and his long hair hung over his shoulders. He studied Matt with glittering black eyes that held a challenge, and his slicker was open, the engraved silver buckles of crossed gun belts showing at his lean belly. This could only be the man Flynn had called the Jicarilla Kid. The man was on the prod, and Matt knew that if there was to be shooting, the Kid would be the one to start it.

Feeney stepped beside Matt and slapped

him on the shoulder. "Take a seat, Marshal, and have some coffee."

The outlaw waved Matt to a sheltered spot at the base of a cottonwood. The marshal sat, but laid his Winchester across his knees, a move that made Feeney's smile widen. "Careful man, ain't you, Marshal Dillon?"

"Live longer that way," Matt said.

"So be it. Have some breakfast and then we'll talk."

Somebody brought Matt a thick sandwich of bread and bacon and laid a tin cup of coffee beside him. Feeney squatted next to the marshal but didn't eat. He drank coffee, his eyes wandering constantly beyond the fringe of trees to the prairie and the direction Matt had come from.

"I don't have a posse following me, Feeney," Matt said, smiling slightly, "if that sets your mind at rest."

The outlaw nodded. "It do. Like you say, Marshal, a man can't be too careful."

When Matt finished his sandwich and picked up his coffee, Feeney told him to hold on. He got up and returned with a bottle and held it up where Matt could see it. "Hennessy brandy, Marshal. Let me splash some into your cup against the cold and rain."

As the outlaw poured the liquor into

Matt's coffee, he said: "Feeney, you're a right hospitable man."

Feeney nodded, his words coming from a dark place in his mind. "I'm always amicable to a man I might have to kill one day."

He had made Matt aware of the iron fist in the velvet glove, but the marshal nerved himself to show no reaction. He tested his coffee and nodded. "Real good. Makes a man forget the rain."

All the humor was gone from Feeney's eyes and now they hardened into seriousness. "Is there a lowlife by the name of Ed Flynn in Dodge?"

"You know he's there." Matt nodded in the direction of Jicarilla Kid, who was looking at him with open dislike. "He led you here."

"You know that Flynn killed my brother?" Feeney asked.

"He told me. He said Mick drew down on him. Sounds like a fair fight to me."

Feeney scowled and waved a dismissive hand. "Fair fight, unfair fight, it don't matter a damn. Flynn killed one of my blood and he has to pay for it. I want him dead. It's a reckoning."

"Ed Flynn saved my life once" — Matt pointed at the Kid, knowing that what he was about to say would irritate the gunman

— "from Apaches that were maybe some of his kinfolk. I owe him."

Feeney let that go and asked: "Do you plan on protecting him?"

"I reckon I do. Like I said, Feeney, I owe Flynn my life and I'm not one to forget my debt to a man."

For a few moments, the outlaw thought that through, the muscles bunching in his jaw. Then he said: "You got a watch, lawman?"

"I have a watch."

"Then take a look at the time and tell me what it is."

Matt reached into his slicker, found his watch in his vest pocket and glanced at it. "The time is eleven thirty."

"So be it," Feeney said. "Three days from now, at eleven thirty, bring Ed Flynn here to me."

"And if I don't?"

"Then I'll ride into Dodge and take him." Feeney's eyes locked on Matt's, about as cold as the muzzles of a Greener scattergun. "It's no small thing to kill a United States marshal, but if I have to, I will."

Matt nodded. He drained his coffee cup and rose to his feet. "You've stated your case plain, Feeney, and you've drawn the line. Take my advice and don't cross over it by riding into Dodge."

The Jicarilla Kid, who been watching the two men intently, took a couple steps toward Matt and stopped. He brushed his slicker away from his guns and spoke to Feeney. "Hell, Lee, I don't mind gunning a marshal. How about I take him right now?"

Matt's rifle lifted almost casually until it was centered on the Kid's belly. His voice icy, he said: "Make a move toward your guns and I'll blow those fancy belt buckles right through your backbone."

There was a reckless look in the Kid's eyes. But, no matter how fast he is, a man facing a .44-.40 Winchester at a range of a few yards will often find cause for reflection, and the Jicarilla Kid was obviously one of them.

Even so, the breed was just wild enough to have made a play, Matt decided later, but Feeney ended it.

"Let it go, Kid," he said. "I offered the marshal the hospitality of my camp and he will leave unharmed."

Like many who had fought on the losing side in the War Between the States, Feeney had an ingrained sense of chivalry, and the code of Southern hospitality dictated that a guest was safe under his host's roof. That Feeney had only the canopy of the trees for a roof did not matter. The principle held.

"Some other time then" — the Kid hesitated a second, his eyes ugly with malice — "United States marshal."

Matt ignored the breed. Then somebody brought him his horse, and he swung into the saddle.

Feeney caught hold of the bay's bridle. "I'm a reasonable man, Marshal. You've got three days from now. Plenty of time to surrender Flynn." He waved a hand, taking in the twenty men crowding around him. "These boys are my bona fides. Every man jack of them rode with Quantrell or Bloody Bill Anderson during the late unpleasantness. If we have to come for Flynn, we'll come shooting."

Matt's talking was done, and he said only: "I'll bear that in mind."

His eyes on the Kid, he backed away from the camp, then turned his horse to the north. The rain was pounding even heavier and thunder rumbled closer.

The marshal glanced over his shoulder at Feeney's camp. The Jicarilla Kid was standing away from the trees, the rain falling hard around him, his eyes never leaving Matt's back.

CHAPTER 4
DEATH ON THE NOON STAGE

Matt Dillon rode to the livery stable in Dodge, unsaddled his horse and rubbed it down with a piece of sacking. He forked the bay some hay and a good bit of oats, then returned to the office.

Festus was sitting in his chair, his booted feet on the desk, snoring under a newspaper that he couldn't read spread over his face.

Matt made some unnecessary noise as he hung up his slicker, hat and gun belt, and Festus woke immediately, snatching the paper from his face.

"Oh, it's you, Matthew. I must have dozed off." Festus swung out of the chair and rose to his feet. Apparently believing that an explanation was called for, he stretched into a yawn. "Patrollin' the lace-curtain side of town all night can tire a man, you know."

"I reckon it can, old-timer," Matt said, holding back a smile. He knew that his deputy's idea of patrolling was to sit in comfortable parlors drinking bonded bourbon while regaling the fashionable belles of Dodge and their mothers with a string of whizzers about his Indian-fighting days.

Deciding that he had the marshal's understanding, Festus asked: "You talk to ol' Lee down there by the creek?"

Matt nodded. "He wants Ed Flynn, and he's given me three days to surrender him."

Festus whistled though his teeth. "What will he do if'n you don't, Matthew?"

"He says he'll ride into Dodge with his boys and take him."

Matt was trying to walk a difficult path and Festus knew it. "What you gonna do?"

The marshal shrugged and took the chair recently vacated by his deputy. "Right now I reckon the train is my best option. That is, if I can get Flynn on board without him being seen."

Festus scratched his jaw, deep in thought. "Night might be the best time, Matthew," he said finally. "There's a train pulls out just after eleven. Ol' Ed can ride the cushions all the way to Boston town if he has the notion."

"I'll study on it some, Festus," Matt said. He picked up the discarded newspaper and began to scan the headlines.

"New feller in town," the deputy said, by

48

way of conversation. "Came in last night. I met him at the Long Branch afore I left on my patrollin'."

Visitors were rare after the cattle season and Matt looked up in vague surprise. "Oh, really? Who?"

"English feller, call himself Charles T. Granville. He says he's a poet, and he looks it too, all pale and quiet like." Festus grinned. "He's a sight to see, Matthew, wears a funny kind of tweed overcoat and one of them hats with earflaps tied up on top an' a brim front an' back." The deputy hesitated. "What do you call them kind o' hats, Matthew?"

"Deerstalker?"

"Yeah, that's it, a deerstalker. I mind when Bat Masterson wore one, but he threw it away right quick after some drunk punchers threatened to shoot it right off'n his head."

"What's an English poet doing in Dodge?" Matt wondered more to himself than Festus.

The deputy shrugged. "Maybe he's gonna make up some poems about the town, Matthew. Kinda like 'O Dodge it is a real nice place, where an outlaw don't dare show his face, an' if he does, he'll get arrested by Matt, quicker'n scat.' " Festus grinned, pleased. "How's that?"

Matt groaned. "Festus, stick to being a deputy, and please don't tell me any more poems."

An offended look crossed the deputy's face, quickly replaced by excitement. "Matthew, I was so busy talkin' about that English feller's hat, I plumb forgot about what Big Bill Hansen done when he seen him."

"Did he threaten to shoot off the hat?" Matt asked, smiling despite the fact that he had no liking for Hansen, whom he suspected of riding outlaw trails.

"No, he didn't, Matt. The strangest thing happened. Ol' Bill, he took one look at that Englishman, his eyes poppin' out of his head like he was seeing a ghost. Then he saddled up an' left town in a hurry."

Now Matt was puzzled. Hansen was an arrogant bully with a vague reputation as a gunman and not a man to scare easily.

"Did you speak to Hansen?" he asked.

Festus nodded. "Sure did, Matthew. I caught up to him in the street and asked why he was leaving town in sich an all-fired rush. All he'd say was for me to take nothin' at face value 'cause nothin' is ever as it seems. Then he skedaddled out of Dodge so fast his pony cut a hole in the wind."

Matt was intrigued. Why would a hardcase like Hansen be afraid of a mild-mannered poet?

He had no time to ponder that question as running feet pounded on the boardwalk and the office door burst wide open.

Jim Taylor, the Lee-Reynolds stage company agent, rushed inside, accompanied by a gust of wind and rain. "Marshal, the noon stage has been robbed!" he yelled, his eyes wild. "We got a dead guard and a wounded passenger who ain't likely to last the night."

Matt rose to his feet, aware of Festus turning questioning eyes to him. "Lee Feeney?"

"Could be," Matt answered. "If it was him, we're in for a fight."

The stage driver was a man Matt didn't know, a tough, bearded oldster who gave his name as Mark Freeman. Beside him on the box, the shotgun guard slumped in death, the front of his buckskin coat running red in the streaming rain.

"What happened?" Matt asked after Freeman climbed down and stood beside him. The grizzled old driver glanced at Doc Adams as the physician stepped into the coach. Then he spat a stream of tobacco juice into the mud of the street.

"They jumped us at Elm Creek, Marshal. Came a-hootin' and a-hollerin' out of the cottonwoods and didn't even ask a by your leave afore they started shootin'."

Freeman nodded toward the dead guard. "Lou Sadler up there didn't even get the hammers of his scattergun cocked afore they gunned him." The driver shook his head. "An' him with a wife an' a passel o' young'uns too. It's a right shame."

"What did they take?" Matt asked.

"Lifted the strongbox we were to drop off at Bodkin's Bank. I'd say five thousand in gold, silver and paper money. And they shot and robbed our passenger. He's a whiskey drummer we picked up in Newton. Name's Amos Garty. Kinda quiet, but a right nice feller."

Matt turned as Doc backed out of the stage, his face stiff. "How's the passenger, Doc?" the marshal asked.

"He just died, Matt. He told me the holdup men wanted his watch but he refused because his wife's picture was in it. So they just shot him and took it anyway."

A tight anger flared in Matt. "How many were there, Freeman?"

"Four, all of them wearing slickers, well-mounted and well-armed men."

"Recognize any of them?"

The driver shook his head. "Never seen their like before. Wait, Marshal. There's something I do recollect. One of them killers had a black mark about the size of a silver dollar" — Freeman's fingers strayed to his cheekbone — "right there. Looks like he got too close to a gun one time and it left a powder burn."

Matt thought back to Feeney's camp. He had studied the outlaw's men pretty closely but recalled no one who matched Freeman's description, unless he'd somehow missed it. In the teeming rain that was possible, especially if the man had kept his head turned away from him.

There was little to be gained by further talk. Matt turned to his deputy. "Saddle up, Festus. We're riding."

As Matt and Festus headed out of town, under a sky that lay gray and heavy on the plains, a man rode toward them from the direction of the Dodge House.

He was sitting a flat English saddle and was astride a rawboned buckskin. The man's caped coach coat and deerstalker hat were black with rain, and he held a white handkerchief to his red nose.

"Good afternoon, Marshal," he hailed Matt as he swung alongside him. "I heard about those bounders who robbed the stage and murdered the guard."

"And a passenger," Matt said, figuring this

had to be the poet Festus had told him about.

"My name is Charles T. Granville. I'd like to ride with you, Marshal," the man said, sounding as though his nose was stuffed. "It seems like an excellent opportunity to pick up some local color for my wretched verses."

"Granville, this is no fandango we're headed into," Matt said patiently. "We're going after four mighty dangerous outlaws, and when we choose partners, it will be for a shooting scrape."

"Fear not, Marshal," Granville said. He brushed his handkerchief across his nose, then reached inside his coat and produced a nickel-plated short-barreled Colt with an ivory handle. "As you can see, I'm armed to the teeth."

"Granville," Matt said, "it's a free country and you're welcome to ride with us. But when the shooting starts, you hit the ground and stay there until it's all over."

"Sound advice, Marshal," Granville said. "And be assured I shall heed it well."

Festus leaned over in the saddle, looking past Matt to the Englishman. "Hey, Charlie," he said, "I made up a poem about Dodge. You want to hear it?"

"No!" Matt said before Granville could

respond. "He doesn't, and neither do I, ever again."

Granville smiled. "Ah, Festus it was ever thus. As the Roman writer Horace said, *'Vesanum poetam qui sapient fugiunt.'* "

"What does that mean?" Festus asked, looking irritated. "Sounds like cussin' to me."

The Englishman laughed. "No, Festus, it's not cussin'. It means 'Anybody with half a brain flees a versifying poet.' "

Matt nodded, his eyes slanting to his deputy as a smile twitched at the corners of his mouth. "Wise man, that Roman."

The three riders left Dodge behind them, then swung east toward Elm Creek.

Matt recalled a few years before seeing a wooden marker on the creek's west bank, where three unidentified immigrants from a wagon train were buried. The rough piece of pine said only:

3 PEOPLE
CHOLERA
1849

As he rode head bent against a driving rain, he wondered if the marker was still there, or if it had fallen over in some winter blizzard and had then been blown away by the wind.

The rain showed no sign of slacking, drawing a steel mesh curtain across the prairie. Thunder crashed above the three men and lightning flickered inside low leaden clouds, filling them momentarily with an orange-and-gold glow.

The icy-cold wind was driving hard from the west, bringing with it the threat of winter and the big snows that were already on their way.

Festus kneed his mule alongside Matt's mount and asked: "Matthew, you reckon them four outlaws will be riding in this weather?"

As Granville inclined his head to listen, Matt answered: "I'm betting they headed east along the stage trail. If they are, they're bound to see an abandoned buffalo hunter's cabin that lies a couple of miles beyond the creek. They might decide to hole up there for the night, figuring a posse would search no further than the creek and then turn back."

"They could have gone north, toward the Santa Fe road," Festus said. "The way the darkness is crowding in and it's getting hard to see, all they'd have to do is follow the rails east and they'd eventually reach Newton or Wichita."

Matt nodded. "They've got five thousand dollars to spend on whiskey and women, so that's a real possibility."

"But you don't think those brigands will do that, do you, Marshal?" It was Granville's question.

"No, I don't. If I was one of them, I'd head due east and put as much ground between me and a posse as possible. I'd reckon that a bunch of married men wouldn't enjoy riding out in this weather with night coming down fast. I'd tell myself that they'll lose heart and turn back at the earliest opportunity. Then if I saw an abandoned cabin, I'd reckon it was a good place to spend the night."

"A great deal of supposition on your part, Marshal," Granville said, wiping his nose.

"Could be. Maybe it's all down to my hunting instinct, but I know those four are right ahead of us. I can smell them in the wind."

Granville smiled. "I agree with you totally, Marshal. You see, my own hunter's instinct is telling me the very same thing."

Matt looked sharply at the man. "You don't shape up to be a hunter, Granville."

The man's smile was as elusive as the expression on his face. "I shape up to be many things, Marshal Dillon . . . not all of them obvious."

CHAPTER 5
BLOOD ON THE PRAIRIE

Thirty minutes later, in a pounding rain, Matt and the others rode up on the abandoned cabin. It was empty.

Disappointed, the marshal sat his bay and looked around him. The prairie was lost in gloom, menacing clouds in the distance hanging so low they seemed to touch the ground. He figured there was maybe an hour of daylight left.

How far ahead were the stage robbers?

Festus helped answer that question. He had been scouting the area for tracks, and now he drew rein close to Matt. "Four riders headed east, Matthew. No more than an hour ahead of us, and maybe a lot less."

Festus could read sign like an Apache, a bent blade of grass or a scuffed rock telling him all he needed to know. For that reason it never entered the marshal's mind to doubt him.

Granville had been searching the cabin, a

one-room sod house with a broken-backed timber roof. He tried to push open the pine door, hanging aslant on its rawhide hinges, but the bottom ground on the flat rock that had been used as a step and stuck there. Finally he pushed on the door and it tore loose and fell flat on the ground.

"They were here all right, marshal," he said, looking up at Matt. "Used an old pack rat's nest to start a fire and boiled up coffee. The ashes are still warm."

Matt thought things through.

It would be real easy to stay here for the night, out of the rain and cold, and pick up the chase at first light. But by then the four outlaws could be long gone and there would be no catching up to them.

Festus said they were close. That meant they could track them down before it got too dark to see.

He knew there was no other choice. They would have to go after them. "Get mounted, Granville," he said. "We're riding."

The Englishman watched lightning fork across the sky like a skeletal hand. "A bit inclement for riding, don't you think, Marshal?"

Matt swung his horse around. "Then stay here. It's up to you."

He and Festus followed the tracks scarring the wet grass at a canter. When Matt looked back, Granville was already mounted and following.

Fifteen minutes later they saw four riders, barely visible in the rain-thrashed distance ahead of them.

Matt slowed his bay to a walk and the others did the same. He slid his rifle out of the scabbard and laid the butt on his thigh. He knew there would be no talk, no negotiating. The outlaws would go to their guns as soon as they spotted him and Festus.

"Granville," the marshal said, without taking his eyes off the four men, "you're out of it. Stop here, and if it goes real bad, hightail it back to Dodge without drawing rein between here and Front Street."

"Right you are, Marshal," the Englishman said. But he did not slow his horse, his jaw set and determined.

Matt did not have time to argue with the man. The distance between them and the stage robbers was closing fast.

Now that he was closer, Matt peered through the shifting curtain of the rain. Three of the outlaws were mounted and the fourth was bent over, examining his horse's leg.

"Lame hoss," Festus said out of the corner of his mouth, telling the marshal something

61

he already knew.

"Looks like," Matt said. "Get ready."

Festus already had his Greener across the saddle horn and now he thumbed back the hammers. "When do we have at it, Matthew?"

The marshal gauged the distance. "Let's do it!" he yelled.

He spurred the bay into a gallop, Festus just behind him and to his right. He had no idea where Granville was.

The outlaws saw them coming, and they were shooting.

Matt lifted his Winchester to his shoulder. Then it seemed like a sledgehammer drove out of the hammering rain and crashed into the side of his head.

Suddenly the sky rocked crazily, and he was falling, his rifle spinning away from him. He hit the ground hard and lay there stunned. Thunder exploded among the clouds and lightning flashed. Above the roar Matt heard the spiteful *pop-pop-pop* of a sixgun. He tried to rise but his head ached and spun wildly and he sank back to the wet grass. Fear spiked at him. Festus was battling four killers on his own.

Again Matt tried to get to his feet, but then a scarlet-streaked darkness took him and he knew no more. . . .

"Matthew, Matthew, are you all right?"

Matt opened his eyes and the hairy, concerned face of his deputy swam into his vision. "Where are we, Festus?" he asked, his thinking still muddled. "In hell?"

"No, Matthew, at least no closer to hell than Kansas."

Helped by his deputy, Matt struggled into a sitting position. "What happened?"

"It's all over, Matthew. Them four hardcases are as dead as they're ever gonna be."

Matt's fingers strayed to his head and came away bloody.

"You got grazed by a bullet afore the fight even got started, Matthew." Festus smiled. "But ol' Doc Adams will fix you up in no time."

Finally able to think through the pain in his head, Matt nodded. "You did good, Festus," he said, "taking on four men and getting the best of the bargain."

"Warn't me," the deputy said, his eyes holding something akin to wonder. "An' them boys were no bargain. Matthew, after you went down, I fired the Greener twicet, an' missed both times. Then I was almost on top of them and" — Festus made a gun of his thumb and forefinger, looking down at it in puzzlement — "I . . . I drawed my hogleg . . . but by then it was all over. All four o' them fellers was lying on the ground and a hoss was down."

"But who . . ."

"Ol' Charlie. He charged right among them. That fancy Colt o' his started firing faster than you can ever imagine an' one by one them outlaws bit the ground."

"Granville!" Matt exclaimed. "The poet gunned them?"

"Sure did. In my whole life I never seen a man get his work in that fast."

"Help me to my feet, Festus," Matt said.

The marshal was swaying unsteadily when Granville walked through the rain and stopped beside him. His eyes studied Matt's bloody head. "A flesh wound, I see, Marshal. Good because when I saw you fall I thought you were a goner for sure."

"Granville, I told you to stay out of it," Matt said, an edge to his voice. But then he smiled and added: "But I'm real glad you didn't."

The Englishman began to feed shells into his Colt. "Happy I could be of help."

"How come you rode into 'em, Charlie?" Festus asked. "It warn't your fight."

"Ah, but I think it was, Festus."

"How do you figure that, Granville?" Matt said. "Unless some of your money was in the stolen strongbox."

The Englishman shook his head. "I had no stake in that money."

"Then why?"

Granville again gave his small, mysterious smile. "Marshal, just call me Tancred."

"I don't —" Matt began, but a yell from Festus, who had wandered to the spot of the fight, cut him off.

"Matthew! One of these rannies is still alive."

"Really?" Granville said, surprised. "My aim must have been off a tad."

Matt threw the man a puzzled look, then stepped over to his deputy. Festus was looking down at a young man lying on his back on the ground, blood seeping though a hole in his slicker at the chest.

"What's your name, son?" Festus asked.

The man ignored the question and whispered: "I told 'em we should've kept on goin' an' not stopped to bile up coffee." He nodded to one of the bodies. "Jem Gault there was a coffee-drinking man."

Festus nodded, looking wise. "Boy, it's always better to say, 'Here's where he ran' than 'Here's where he died.' "

Matt looked around him and saw the

strongbox lying on the ground, where it had fallen. His eyes moved to the dying outlaw. "You have any kinfolk we can let know what happened?"

"No, nobody."

Despite the rain, Matt had opened his slicker, and for the first time, the outlaw saw the star on his chest. "Was the man who kilt me an' the rest a lawman like you?"

Matt shook his head. "No, he's a poet."

The outlaw looked like he'd been slapped. "Whoever heard of a poet who can shoot like that? What's his name?"

"Calls himself" — Matt hesitated, then added finally — "calls himself Tancred."

"What the hell kind of name is that?" The young outlaw took a shuddering breath as all the life that was in him began to drain away. "Me . . . kilt by a damn poet," he whispered, and the wonder was still in his eyes as death took him.

Matt walked around, checking on the other dead outlaws. One thing was sure. These were not Lee Feeney's men. He recognized one of them as a hardcase he'd seen hanging around the Long Branch a week before Ed Flynn rode into Dodge.

For the moment Feeney would be watching his step, unwilling to tangle with the law until it became necessary three days from now. In any case, if Feeney's men had held up the stage it would have been a neater job and they'd have gotten away clean. The robbery had been a messy holdup done by drifting amateurs.

But three of the dead men had a story to tell. Each had been shot only once, a .45 bullet to the middle of the forehead.

Firing off the back of a horse, Granville had gunned down four men in the space of a few seconds, three of them killed by difficult head shots. By any standard that was excellent shooting. Granville had demonstrated a revolver skill possessed by very few men. Ed Flynn and John Wesley Hardin could have matched it, and maybe Hickok and Longley.

Matt could think of no others, and he included himself in that category.

CHAPTER 6
AN INTERVIEW WITH
DOC HOLLIDAY

"Matthew, I just spoke with banker Bodkin, and he's right glad to get his money back," Festus said as he hung his dripping slicker on a hook. "He even offered ol' Charlie Granville a fifty-dollar reeward, but he wouldn't take it."

"Strange one, that Granville," Matt said. "Judging by what he did today, he shapes up to be as good with a gun as Ed Flynn."

"Maybe better," Festus said, pouring himself coffee. "He works that fancy Colt of his'n mighty slick."

The office clock stood at eleven, and rain hammered on the office window. Now that the cowboys were gone, Front Street was quiet — so quiet that even above the rattle of the rain Matt heard a bored saloon girl picking out the notes of a Chopin nocturne over at the Alamo.

"How are things across the tracks?" Matt asked, already knowing the answer.

"Right peaceful, Matthew. Seems like everybody's in bed because of the rain. Well, not everybody. I seen Doc Adams walking under an umbrella. Then he went into Uriah Scroggins' place. Seems like Mrs. Scroggins is keeping poorly again."

Matt had seen Uriah Scroggins around town. He was a small, thin, inoffensive man, the shoulders of his coat always stained with drool from the youngest of his brood of eight children. He'd arrived in Dodge at the start of the last cattle season, telling people he was looking for work.

As far as Matt knew, he hadn't found any, though he must have had some money saved because he'd rented a large house across the Deadline and kept a teenage servant to help his wife.

"Seems like Mrs. Scroggins is always ailing," Matt said, accepting coffee from Festus.

"Seems like," the deputy agreed. "Uriah says he was workin' as a teller in a bank in the Arizona Territory, but they left because the dry air played hob with his wife's chest."

Matt glanced at the window, where the rain was running down the panes. "Well, he made the right move. There's no dry air in Dodge."

Festus perched on the desk. "Matthew,

when do you plan on speakin' to Ed Flynn about the train?"

"I don't know. Tomorrow, I guess. I don't have much to say to him. I don't want him to stay, but I can't ask him to leave, and I have a feeling the station is being watched."

Festus grinned his enthusiasm. "Matthew, I got an idea. Maybe we can round up some men, arm them with rifles and show ol' Lee that it would be a bad idea for him and his boys to try an' hooraw this town."

"Festus, I saw those men of Feeney's. Most of them were guerrilla fighters during the war and they can take Dodge apart and cover the ground with dead men. There are only twenty of them, but when you face fighting men like those, that's an army."

"Matthew, there are plenty of men in Dodge who fought in the war."

"I know, and they're good men, men like Newly O'Brien and Quint Asper, men with sand who will step up when there's need. But ask yourself this — when the chips are down, will they be willing to die for Ed Flynn?"

The deputy scratched his jaw, his mind turning. Finally he said: "No, Matthew, I reckon not. Heck, I don't figure on dying for him my ownself."

"Well, there's your answer." Matt rose to

his feet. "When did you see Doc?"

Festus shrugged. "Oh, not long ago, just afore I came back here."

"Then I'll try and catch him before he heads for home," Matt said.

"Your wound paining you, Matthew?"

"No, it's fine. I just want to ask him if he's ever heard the name Tancred." Matt smiled. "Doc tends to know things like that."

As luck would have it, when Matt stepped onto the boards he saw Doc Adams and Uriah Scroggins walking toward him. Rain streamed from Doc's umbrella and the bottoms of his pants flapped wetly around his ankles.

"Matt, what are you doing out on a night like this?" Doc asked sourly. "I doubt if there are any desperate bandits abroad." His eyes lifted to the marshal's face. "How's the head?"

"Just fine, Doc. Seems to me that every time you paint on something that stings like the dickens, it usually cures what ails me. And speaking of that" — the marshal turned to Scroggins — "is the missus keeping better, Uriah?"

The man shook his head, his round glasses reflecting the orange light of the sputtering street lamps. "Alas, no, Marshal. My dear

Emily is still ailing."

"Balderdash, man," Doc snapped. "She has a little congestion of the chest, is all." The physician turned to Matt. "I'm taking Uriah back to my surgery to give him some medicine. His wife will be as right as rain in a few days."

"Doc, before you go," Matt said. "Does the name Tancred mean anything to you?"

"Should it?"

"Not really. I just thought you might have heard it somewhere."

"Sounds to me German or maybe French," Doc said. "Why don't you ask another of my patients, a very knowledgeable man?"

"Who's that?"

"Doc Holliday. He's sick and currently under my care — well, mine and his lady love, Kate Elder. At least, she brings him his whiskey and cigars. I don't think Miss Elder is much into nursing the infirm."

Rain pattered against Matt's slicker and ran steadily off the brim of his hat. He had heard from Festus that Holliday hadn't migrated with the rest of the gamblers after the cattle season and was holed up sick at the Dodge House.

Holliday was always a problem around the saloons, as was the fiery-tempered Kate, and although Matt didn't wish the man ill, he didn't exactly wish him well, either.

"I'll take a pass on that, Doc," he said. "I've never set much store by Holliday."

"Suit yourself, Matt," Doc said. "But he's quite a well-educated man and might be able to answer your question." The physician shivered as an icy gust of wind threatened to tear the umbrella from his hand. "Now I suggest we all get indoors before we catch our deaths of cold."

Matt watched Doc and Scroggins leave. He was about to open the office door, but stopped, his mind working.

Why would a gun-slinging English poet call himself a strange name like Tancred? And had the name, and its meaning, something to do with Bill Hansen's hasty exit from Dodge?

He could ask Granville, of course, but he doubted he'd get a straight answer. The Englishman seemed to go out of his way to portray himself as a man of mystery.

It would appear that Doc Holliday was Matt's only option.

The marshal looked through the sheeting rain to the Dodge House, where lamps were lit against the darkness in several rooms. It was still not yet midnight, early for Holliday, sick or well.

Reluctantly, Matt turned away from the door and walked along the boardwalk, then angled across the muddy street.

Against his better judgment, he would talk to Holliday.

Kate Elder, looking older than her years without her usual paint, let Matt into Doc's room. She drew her silk robe around her and said: "He's not a well man, Marshal. He keeps drifting in and out of consciousness, and he's coughing up blood."

A weak voice from the bed asked: "Kate, who the hell is there?"

"It's Marshal Dillon, Doc. He wants to talk to you."

Holliday's laugh was a painful cackle. "Kate, when the law comes calling, it's time to leave town."

Kate crossed to the bed. "You're not going anywhere, Doc. Not until you're well again."

Again Holliday laughed. "Damn it all, woman, I'm never well. At the moment I'm just dying a little faster than usual, is all."

Kate had turned down the lamp and the room was lost in shadow. Matt made out Doc's frail form lying on the bed, his head propped up with pillows. The heels of his boots thudding on the rough pine floor, the marshal stepped to the bed and Holliday waved a hand: "Pull up a chair and set, Marshal."

Picking up the comb and scissors that were lying on the patchwork quilt, Kate said: "I was just trimming Doc's mustache."

Holliday smiled. "We believe in keeping up appearances, Marshal. Kate is a fastidious woman." He raised a thin eyebrow. "I hardly think this is a social call, so to what do I owe the honor?"

Matt straddled a chair. "I have a question for you, Doc."

Before he answered, Holliday poured three fingers of whiskey into the glass at his bedside and downed it in a single gulp. He wiped his mouth with a blue-veined white hand and said: "Marshal, I make it a habit to never rat on members of my profession or the elusive gentry of my acquaintance who ride night trails where the owl hoots."

"I'm not asking you to rat on anyone," Matt said. "I want to know why a man would call himself by a certain name."

"Well, that sounds intriguing. And what name might that be?"

"Tancred."

Holliday lapsed into silence, his eyes closed, and an agitated Kate fluttered closer. "Please don't tire him, Marshal. He's very weak."

"I'm not asleep, Kate, my dear," Doc said. "Merely thinking." His cold blue eyes held humor as they lifted to Matt's face. "You never had the benefit of the Southern gentleman's education, did you, Marshal?"

Matt shook his head. "My ma taught me to read and do my ciphers."

"An admirable woman." Holiday struggled higher on the pillows.

"Marshal, when the War Between the States broke out, many a young Southern gallant rode off to battle astride his white charger, imagining himself to be a veritable Tancred. Very few of them rode back."

"Who was he, Doc?" Matt prompted.

"He was the greatest of the Crusader knights. On July 15, 1099, he was the first Christian to enter the holy city of Jerusalem after it was taken from the Turks." Holliday smiled. "That was a long time ago."

"A fair spell," Matt acknowledged, trying to make sense of what Holliday was telling him.

"Tancred, the perfect, gentle knight in shining armor, was famed as a great fighter. He was also quite the ladies' man, loved by many women, including the pagan warrior-maiden Clorinda and the fair Erminia, Princess of Antioch."

"So a man who calls himself Tancred would consider himself some kind of crusader," Matt said, his mind grappling with the mystery.

"Exactly so, Marshal. And he'd think of himself as the best of them."

"The question is," Matt said, more to himself than Holliday, "what would a man who gives himself that name figure he's crusading against?" He managed a slight smile. "There are no Turks in Dodge."

"Maybe your man is a preacher, crusading against the sinful like the unrighteous and unrepentant Kate and me."

"Earlier today I saw him kill the four men who robbed the Lee-Reynolds stage," Matt said. "It happened so fast, Festus drew his gun but didn't get off a shot."

"Ah, then he's a bounty hunter."

The marshal shook his head. "There was no bounty on those men, though Bodkin offered fifty dollars to —" Matt stumbled over the name — "Tancred. He refused to take it."

"Is he an outlaw, perhaps one of my acquaintances?"

"I don't think so."

Suddenly Doc seemed tired. His head sank lower into the pillow. "Then I'm afraid I can't help you any further."

Kate stepped beside the marshal. "Better let him rest now."

Matt rose to his feet, Holliday's wary eyes following him. "Get better soon, Doc," the marshal said.

"Your concern for my health is most touching."

"I just want to know when you'll be well enough to travel, Doc," Matt said.

He touched his hat to Kate, then stepped to the door, but froze as a single gunshot echoed through the hushed canyon of the night.

CHAPTER 7
MURDER IN THE
DARK

When Matt reached the boardwalk Festus was already standing in the middle of Front Street, looking north toward the Crystal Palace Saloon. The deputy, who had been sleeping in a cell in the marshal's office, was wearing his boots and hat, but had thrown a slicker over his long johns.

Matt waved Festus toward him and then crossed the street.

The bartender and another man were standing outside the saloon when Matt stepped beside them. The bartender, a barrel-chested man in a brocade vest, said: "The shot came from the alley, Marshal. Maybe somebody shooting at a coyote or stray dog."

Festus, shotgun in hand, peered into the angled shadows of the alley between the Crystal Palace and the hardware store next door. "I'll take a look, Matthew," he said.

"Step careful, Festus," Matt warned,

drawing his gun. "Don't get mistaken for a coyote."

The deputy had only been in the alley for a few moments when he yelled, "Matthew, you'd better come see this."

As the marshal walked toward him, Festus thumbed a match into flame. He was kneeling beside a man sprawled on the ground in death, a round bullet hole, leaking blood and brain, in the middle of his forehead. It was Uriah Scroggins.

Matt called out to the bartender, a man named Elliot, and told him to bring a lamp. A couple minutes later, Elliot appeared in the alley, holding high a red storm lantern.

As yellow light splashed over Scroggins' body, Matt asked: "Recognize him?"

Elliot nodded. "Sure do. For a while tonight, he was my only customer. He nursed a beer for about twenty minutes and then left. Come to think on it, I heard the shot a few minutes later."

"Then he must have talked to somebody before he was killed," Matt said. "He was lured into the alley and then murdered."

Matt took a knee beside the dead man. After a quick search of Scroggins' clothing, he handed Festus a green medicine bottle. "That was for his wife from Doc Adams," he said. He rose, opened the dead man's wallet and held it to the light of the lantern. "He must have close to five hundred dollars in here and he's still wearing his watch. Somebody wanted Scroggins dead, but not to rob him."

Elliot shook his head. "Who would want to kill the little man? He came into the saloon now and then, a meek, little fellow, not given to swearing and rough talk."

"Well," Festus said, "maybe he decided to get mad at whoever cut his suspenders."

"A puny man can't afford to get mad," Elliot said.

Matt had been casting around in the alley, looking for prints. But the rain was slanting in the light of the lantern and the ground under his feet was liquid mud. Any footprints the killer had left had been quickly washed away.

Finally the marshal said to Festus: "Let me have that medicine bottle. Then go bring Percy Crump here and have him take care of the body. I guess it's time I talked to Mrs. Scroggins."

"She'll be worried," Elliot said.

Matt's eyes held the bartender's in the darkness. "Don't you think she's got cause to be?"

A dark figure stood at the entrance of the alley, then said: "Don't anybody get an itchy trigger finger. It's only me, Ed Flynn."

Flynn stepped into the alley, his dark silhouette taking form as he emerged from darkness into the guttering lamplight. "I was out walking when I heard the commotion," he said.

"You always walk in the rain, Ed?" Matt asked.

The man was wearing a yellow slicker and had a long red scarf wound around his neck, the fringed ends falling to his waist. He smiled under his dripping mustache. "Matt, after that time we spent in the Arizona Territory, I took a notion to like the rain. It soothes a man, helps him think." Flynn looked down at the body. "Do I know him?"

"I doubt it," Matt said. "His name is Scroggins and he hasn't been in Dodge for very long."

"Scrawny little feller, ain't he?" Flynn took the lamp from Elliot and held it high, letting the light fall across the body. With the detachment of the professional gunfighter, he said: "Close-range head shot. That's real unusual. When you're at arm's length to a man in uncertain light and put a bullet into him, you aim for the belly, and then when he's falling, maybe try for a skull shot. Whoever killed this man was confident, and real good with the iron."

"Good like you, Ed?" Matt said, the dig obvious.

"Good like me, and maybe better." His eyes sought Matt's in the darkness. "I didn't kill this man, Matt, if that's what you're implying. Before tonight I'd never set eyes on him."

The marshal shook his head. "I know it wasn't you. Not your style to gun an unarmed man."

Flynn's smile was thin. "This man wasn't gunned. He was executed. And, Matt, that ain't my style either."

It was Elliot who spoke, his wet shirt clinging to his thick shoulders. "Why would somebody execute him? He didn't do nothing, except maybe breed young'uns."

Flynn shrugged. "Maybe it was payback for a thing he did before he arrived in Dodge." The gunfighter laughed. "Hell, I'm not the law. Ask the marshal why he was killed."

"I don't know, either," Matt said. "But I sure aim to find out."

"How did Mrs. Scroggins take it, Matthew?"

The marshal hung up his dripping slicker, then his hat and gun belt. "About how you'd expect a woman with eight kids to

83

take it when you tell her she's suddenly a widow."

"I'll get you some coffee," Festus said. "You look kinda used up."

Matt eased gratefully into his chair and glanced at the clock. It was almost two, and out on the dark plains, the rain-soaked coyotes were yipping their misery.

Festus laid a cup of coffee on the desk in front of Matt, then took the chair opposite. He had taken off his boots and slicker but was still wearing his hat and underwear.

"She have any idea who might have killed her husband?" he asked.

"No. She said they haven't been in Dodge long enough to make enemies and that she and her husband were not the kind to dispute with folks, anyway. Before they came here, Uriah was a clerk in a cow-town bank just north of the Mogollon Rim and was doing well until Mrs. Scroggins took poorly. They immediately packed up what they owned and headed east and ended up in Dodge."

"About that town in the Arizona Territory, Matthew. I once spent a summer punching cows in the high rim country. You recollect what the burg was called?"

"Why, is it important?"

Festus shrugged. "No, it's not important.

I just wondered if'n I knew the place, is all."

"War Bonnet, sits on the Little Colorado. Mrs. Scroggins said the town consisted of a stockman's bank, a few saloons and stores and a scattering of shacks and houses. But they had a church, a schoolhouse and a volunteer fire department."

"Too bad they had to leave in such a hurry. Sounds like a real nice place for a young family to settle."

"Mrs. Scroggins said the dry air didn't agree with her lungs."

Festus yawned and stretched. "Not so dry in that neck o' the words, though. The country north of the rim ain't like the desert further to the south, where it takes a hundred years for a nail to rust." Festus smiled. "Well, you know all about that, Matthew, on account of how you was there with Ed Flynn back in the olden days. Now north of the rim is different. Plenty of good grass and water up there, and all kinds of pine."

Matt looked puzzled. "Then why does Mrs. Scroggins claim it was so dry?"

Festus shrugged. "I guess if you've got a weak chest and are strugglin' to breathe, anyplace can feel like it's dry."

"I reckon so," Matt said. Tiredness was beginning to crowd him and he decided against walking in the rain to his room at the Dodge House. He got to his feet. "I'm going to catch some shut-eye in the other cell, Festus," he said. "Try not to snore."

Despite the fact that Festus' snoring had sounded like a ripsaw running through a pine knot, Matt felt refreshed when he woke in the morning. He rose and added coffee and water to the pot on the stove, and to his chagrin, it was still raining.

He stepped to the window and looked out on the gray dawn. The low clouds were the color of lead, shredding to black at the edges, and a rising wind was cartwheeling the driving rain along Front Street.

A brewery wagon rumbled past, then a surrey, the mud-spattered Morgan in the traces struggling. At this early hour, no one was as yet walking the boards, though the stores and banks had lamps lit against the gloom.

Dodge was a depressing sight, Matt decided. The gray-faced buildings looked like they were fading away in the half-light, as though being absorbed into the prairie as they melted in the rain.

"Coffee on the bile yet, Matthew?" Festus stood in the doorway to the cells in his sagging long johns, scratching his belly.

"It will be soon," Matt said. "It's still raining."

"Can see that," Festus said sourly. He found himself a cup and stood by the stove, intently watching the pot.

Matt smiled. "You know what they say, Festus. A watched pot never boils."

"We need some more wood in the stove, Matthew. That's what we need — if folks who spend the night here would just notice."

Later Festus' mood slowly improved as he poured his second cup of coffee and sat opposite Matt at the desk. After a few minutes of silence, the deputy scratched his jaw and said: "You know, Matthew, I've been thinking." He waited, drew no response from the marshal, then asked testily: "Don't you want to know what it is I'm thinking?"

Matt smiled. "I figured you'd get around to telling me."

"Well, I'm thinking that ol' Charlie Granville done for three of those stage robbers with shots to the head, just like what happened to Uriah Scroggins."

"I worried around that thought my ownself," Matt said. "But Granville had no reason to kill Scroggins. He's only just arrived in town and I doubt he even knows the man."

"I reckon so," Festus acknowledged. "But

it is strange. Unless there's somebody else in Dodge who can shoot like that."

"Ed Flynn is the only one."

"Ed didn't know Scroggins either, Matthew. He told you that his ownself."

"I don't think it was him."

"Then who?"

Matt shook his head. "Beats me, Festus. But it could be that the killer shot Scroggins as a warning. He murdered the man for no other reason than to warn me that he means business on some other matter."

It took Festus a few moments to absorb what Matt was saying. Finally he said: "You mean Lee Feeney pulled the trigger?"

"Him, or one of his boys," Matt answered.

CHAPTER 8
SHOWDOWN WITH THE JICARILLA KID

As Matt walked through the rain to the railroad station, he thought over what he'd told Festus. Deep inside him he doubted that Feeney was behind the killing of Scroggins, but as of now, everyone was a suspect.

Only three men had the gun skill to go for a head shot in the dark. Feeney was one of them, Granville another, and Ed Flynn the third.

Only Feeney had a motive, vague as it was, though Scroggins may have known something about one of the other two that made it necessary he be silenced.

The marshal realized he was clutching at some flimsy straws. All he had was supposition and, no matter who the guilty party was, that would not stand up in court.

When he reached the empty cattle pens, Matt stopped. He stood in the teeming rain and looked around him.

The feed sheds were locked and bolted

and so were the scattering of shacks where cattle buyers sometimes met with ranchers to discuss prices and herd counts.

A train stood at the passenger depot, the locomotive hissing steam into the gray morning, and a guard carried a carpetbag toward one of the coaches, a woman in a rain-soaked cloak and bonnet following behind him.

Were any of Feeney's men here?

Matt stepped away from the pens and walked closer to the depot. He rounded the front of a feed shed and saw three horses tethered under a dripping overhang at the side of the depot. Hay was scattered at their feet, and a battered zinc bathtub, enjoying a second career as a water trough, stood close to the wall. Nothing moved and there was no sound but the steady hiss of the torrential downpour.

Three of Feeney's riders were keeping an eye on the station — that much was clear. The outlaw was taking no chances on letting Flynn slip away from him.

Matt started to turn away and head back to the office, but the devil of mischief riding him, he changed his mind and headed for the depot.

It was time to let Lee Feeney know that

he wasn't intimidated — by him or his gunmen.

Two of Feeney's men were sharing a wooden bench on the station platform, sheltered from the rain by a wide overhang. The Jicarilla Kid was standing close by, building a smoke, and it was he who lifted his eyes to Matt as the tall marshal strode toward them, his spurs ringing.

The Kid's mouth twisted in a sneer. "Well, well, if it ain't the law. You come to arrest us?"

Matt made a show of opening his slicker, clearing his gun. "I could," he said. "Run you in for loitering on railroad property."

The train at the station pulled out, the clanking locomotive venting sooty black smoke from its stack. Voices could not be heard as the huge engine racketed along the rails, but when the caboose was almost lost to sight in the rain, one of the men on the bench grinned, a challenge in his pale eyes. "Maybe we're waiting on a train. The next one."

"Maybe," the marshal said. "But then I'd have to wait and see you all get safely on board. I wouldn't want to see you boys get lost."

"You'd like that, wouldn't you, Dillon?" the Kid said. He spread his legs and brushed his slicker away from his guns. "Only we ain't going anywhere. We're here to see you don't try to sneak that killer you're protecting out of town."

"Then you're loitering," Matt said. He did the last thing the Kid expected. The big marshal strode quickly toward the gunman and stopped when only a couple feet separated them. "Now all three of you climb on your ponies and be sure to tell Lee Feeney I put the skedaddle on you."

The Kid's face was black with rage but his eyes revealed the certainty that the lawman had backed him into a corner. At this close range, even if he got in the first shot, a man as big as Matt Dillon could take the hit and then kill him.

The gunman tried to back off a step, but Matt followed, crowding him close.

Aware that the two other men had gotten to their feet and were unbuttoning their slickers, the marshal snapped: "This is between the Kid and me. Back off!"

"That how you want to play it, Kid?" one of them asked.

"Hell, Jake" — the pale-eyed man grinned — "the Kid can take him any day of the week."

Matt's voice was ice cold. "How about that, Kid? You said once before you could take me. Like to choose partners and give it a whirl, like he says?"

The gunman knew he'd been called, but he hesitated and touched his tongue to his top lip, the closeness of the huge lawman weighing on him. "Not now," he said, his throat tight with frustrated fury. "Not today. I'll wait until I have six feet of ground between us."

"Hell," Matt said, his anger flaring as all his recent frustrations reached boiling point, "you're nothing but a yellow-bellied tinhorn pretending to be a right dangerous man."

And he slammed a fist into the Kid's chin. Taken by surprise, the gunman took the punch flat-footed. His head snapped back, sudden blood fanning into the air from his smashed mouth. Like a man falling backward down a flight of stairs, he staggered back a half dozen steps on rubber legs, his bootheels thudding on the pine boards of the platform. Then his feet left him and he crashed onto his back and lay still.

The man with the pale eyes was making a play, drawing fast.

Matt swung toward him, his Colt clearing leather with lightning speed. He fired, fired again. Hit hard, the gunman slammed back against the wall of the depot, then slid slowly to a sitting position, his eyes already glazing in death.

"No! Don't shoot!" the third outlaw yelled, his hands frantically clawing for the sky. "For God's sake, lawman, I'm out of it!"

Quickly Matt punched the spent shell from his gun, reloaded and slid the Colt back in the holster. His eyes cold, he said: "They call you Jake?"

The gunman nodded, his eye wild with fear. "Uhhuh, Marshal, that's right. That's what they call me. Jake Henry's the name."

"Well, Jake Henry" — Matt nodded to the still unconscious Kid — "take that and the dead man back to Lee Feeney. Tell him I won't be buffaloed and I won't be threatened in my own town." He nodded. "You tell him that."

"Sure thing, Marshal," Henry said. "I'll tell him, just like you say."

The rain falling around him, Matt watched Henry get the Kid to his feet. Blood was streaming from the breed's mouth and his eyes were half shut and unfocused.

"Kid," Henry said, talking close to the gunman's ear, "the lawman did for Higley. Beat him to the draw and shot him twicet right through the middle."

"Leave me the hell alone," the Kid snarled, pushing Henry away from him. "I don't give a damn about Higley."

Matt's hand dropped to his Colt, but the gunman wanted no part of him. His black eyes blazing with hate, he said: "Dillon, this ain't over, not by a long shot. The next time we meet, I'll kill you."

Matt smiled without humor. "Kid, if I ever let a threat from a tinhorn like you worry me, I'll know it's time to turn in my badge. Now get that dead man and yourself out of here."

Matt stepped into the street and watched as the Kid and Henry rode out of town, the man called Higley hanging facedown over his saddle.

The Jicarilla Kid had been right about one thing, Matt decided. This wasn't over. In fact, he had the feeling it was only beginning.

The question was, what would Lee Feeney do next?

CHAPTER 9
HOME TRUTHS

It's a hard thing to kill a man before breakfast, and Higley's death lay heavy on Matt
as he walked back to his office, head bent
against wind and rain.

Festus was gone, helping a widow woman
out on Saw Log Creek set a trap for a fox
that had been raiding her chicken house.
Matt doubted that his deputy would have
much success, since the average Kansas fox
had a sight more savvy than Festus.

The marshal had been plowing through
paperwork for an hour when the door
swung open and Mayor James Kelley
stepped inside, the shoulders of his gray
wool coat black with rain.

"Will this deluge never end, Matt?" he
asked as he hung his wet coat on the rack.
"Or will it rain for forty days and forty
nights like in the Good Book?"

"Maybe it's time to build an ark, Mayor."
The marshal smiled, setting down his pen.

"And start loading the animals two by two."

"It's shaping up that way," Kelley allowed. He stepped to the stove and poured himself coffee. "Poor Mrs. Kelley is all a-tremble because she can't get her laundry dry."

The mayor took a chair opposite Matt and the marshal could see by the man's face that he was thinking hard about what he was going to say next. Finally he came at it from an angle.

"Two killings in two days, and the cattle season done and gone," he said. "Makes a man wonder what's happening to his town, Matt."

"Uriah Scroggins was murdered by person or persons unknown," Matt said. He hesitated a moment, then added: "The man I killed this morning didn't give me much choice."

The mayor nodded. "I know. Sam Caulkins, the ticket agent, saw it happen. He says the man shucked iron on you but you were considerably faster." Kelley stirred in his chair and tried his coffee, his eyes on the marshal over the rim of his cup. "Want to tell me what's going on, Matt?"

By the time the marshal had finished talking, Kelley's face had grown pale. "Matt, you've made yourself a bad enemy. Lee Feeney's name is a byword for lawlessness down in the Nations and elsewhere." The man's shrewd Irish eyes locked with Matt's as he tried to sum up how he felt. "Is saving the life of a notorious gunslinger and paid assassin like Ed Flynn worth the risk to the town?"

Matt answered without hesitation. "No, Mayor, it's not. But as I told you, Flynn saved my life once and I owe him."

"You're an honorable man, Matt," Kelley said, his statement tinged slightly by sarcasm.

"I try to be," Matt answered, irritated.

Kelley obviously did not like the direction the conversation was taking, so he steered it in another. "Now you've killed one of Feeney's men and put the crawl on two others, what will he do next?"

Matt shook his head. "I don't know, Mayor. He may wait until tomorrow morning to see if I turn Flynn over to him. Or he may not. In that case he and his boys will ride into Dodge with their guns blazing."

"I don't want that to happen, Matt," Kelley said.

"Nor do I, Mayor."

Kelley showed his unease. He did not have the authority to give a United States marshal a direct order, yet he obviously feared for his town and had decided to throw caution to the winds.

"Matt, I want Flynn out of Dodge. And the sooner the better."

"I plan to, Mayor," the marshal answered, the determination in his voice surprising even himself. "One way or another, Ed Flynn will be gone by tonight."

It did not occur to Kelley to doubt the marshal's word, knowing from past experience that when Matt Dillon promised something he'd make good on it.

"So be it," the mayor said. "In the meantime, I'll have some of the solid citizens in town stand by their arms, just in case."

"I hope it won't come to that," Matt said.

"Holy Mother of God, so do I," Kelley said, his face troubled.

Ed Flynn opened the door of his room at the Dodge House a crack. When he saw it was the marshal, he lowered the hammer of his gun and opened the door wider.

"Come in, Matt," he said. "What are you doing out on a morning like this?"

Matt stepped inside, his slicker dripping onto the rough pine floor. "I have to talk to you, Ed."

"Is it about Feeney?"

"Yes, about Feeney and other things. I killed one of his men earlier this morning down at the rail depot." The marshal looked around the untidy room. "I reckon that's a thing he won't forget and forgive."

"So where does it leave me?"

"I'm getting you out of Dodge, right after dark."

Flynn sat on the edge of the bed, the iron springs screeching under him. "What's happening with Feeney?"

"He's given me until tomorrow morning to hand you over to him."

"And if you don't?"

"Then he'll come for you. If he tries to hooraw the town, there will be men killed in Dodge, men I know and like, and I don't intend to let that happen."

Flynn looked stricken. "Where will I go?"

"There's a place to the north of town called Horse Thief Canyon, up on the fork of Buckner Creek. I'll hide you there. I'll tell Feeney you lit out, and I don't know where you've gone. He'll have a lot of ground to search and the chances are good he won't find you. After Feeney gives up the hunt, you can burn the breeze west to the mountains like you intended."

Flynn shook his head. "It's thin, Matt, mighty thin. I don't like the idea of being among the willows while Feeney searches for me."

"You don't have any choice in the matter," Matt said. "As it is, when Feeney doesn't find you he may decide to take his frustration out on the town and bullets will start flying and people will die."

Flynn sat lost in thought for a few moments, then seemed to accept the inevitable. "I'll do what you ask, Matt. I'll be ready as soon as it gets dark."

"There are no guarantees in all this, Ed. I may not even be able to get you out of town. I suspect that some of Feeney's men are already here."

The gunfighter smiled. "Then there had better be plenty of them. If they tangle with you and me, they'll have a couple of cougars by the tails."

Matt shook his head. "That's not how it's going to be, Ed. I've already killed a man because of you, and I don't plan on killing another."

Flynn sprang to his feet. "Don't you worry yourself about that. They're outlaws, all of them. Feeney and his boys have robbed and murdered and raped since the end of the war. They're trash, Matt, worthless trash."

A cold hardness crept into Matt's soul. His voice flat, he said: "Ed, I don't think you are any better than the worst of Feeney's men. You're a hired gun who'll kill

101

any man for fifty dollars. You got no call to be preaching to me about how bad other men who do the same as you are."

Flynn looked like he'd been slapped. "That's what you think of me, the man who saved your life? You're comparing me to Feeney's tramps?"

"Yes, I am, Ed, and if you hadn't saved my life, I would have run you out of town the minute you arrived. As it is, after this is over, we're even. As far as I'm concerned, the slate will be wiped clean."

Flynn's green eyes were like flint. "Later, if it turns out all right, I'll thank you for helping me. But from that moment on, if our trails ever cross, we'll meet as enemies."

"Ed," Matt said, knowing he was burning yet another bridge to his past, "I wouldn't have it any other way."

CHAPTER 10
MISS KITTY
ATTENDS A FUNERAL

It was not yet noon, but Mayor Kelley had ordered the lamps lit along Front Street in a vain attempt to banish the murkiness of the day.

Heavy gray clouds squatted on the roofs of the buildings and merciless rain sprung leaks everywhere, driving through the chinks of the warped pine boards that formed the walls of the saloons and stores. The wind was cold, blowing off the plains with cruel ferocity, a chilling portent of an iron winter.

Matt added more wood to the office stove and spread his hands to the heat, the cherry red glow of the iron reflecting on the lean planes of his face. He turned as the door opened and Kitty Russell stepped inside, rain cartwheeling around her, billowing the skirts of her coat.

"What a day!" she said as she vigorously shook her umbrella, causing a little rainstorm in the office.

"Why are you out walking?" Matt asked, smiling. "I didn't think you'd venture out of the Long Branch."

"Poor Mrs. Scroggins buried her husband this morning," Kitty said, hooking the handle of her umbrella on the rack. "Percy Crump told her it was for the best, before the ground got any more waterlogged." Kitty tried for a smile, didn't quite manage it, and said, "I went to the funeral because Uriah was a customer of mine. Not a big spender, but regular." She shrugged. "Just as well. There was only the widow and Percy and me at the graveside."

Kitty accepted Matt's offer of coffee and sat at the desk. "Mrs. Scroggins is leaving town tomorrow, she and her kids. I just walked with her to Bodkin's bank. She said she planned on withdrawing her husband's savings. I guess they're little enough, poor thing that she is."

Matt eased into his chair. "Oh, I don't know, Uriah was able to rent a pretty big house, and he kept a servant to help his wife with the children."

"Matt," Kitty said, scolding gently, "her husband was a bank clerk. How much does a bank clerk earn?" She saw Matt shrug, and said: "Not much, I can tell you that."

Thunder rumbled and rain was loud on

the roof. Kitty sipped her coffee, set down the cup and lifted her eyes to Matt's. "Mayor Kelley met me as I was walking to your office. He told me what happened this morning."

Matt nodded. "I'll tell you what I told him — I didn't have much choice."

"It was three against one, Matt. You take too many chances." Before the marshal could respond, Kitty pressed on: "Is that man Ed Flynn still in Dodge?"

"Yes, at the moment. He's pulling his freight tonight."

"Will the Feeney person go after him and leave the town alone?"

"I don't know, Kitty. I hope so. But whatever way it shakes out, Feeney will have to go through me first."

Kitty gave an exasperated little sigh. "Matt, do you always have to be so all-fired brave?"

The marshal laughed. "It's not a question of bravery, Kitty. I'm the one wearing the star, so I've got it to do."

Kitty was silent for a moment. Then she said: "When the mayor mentioned Flynn's name, I remembered hearing it before. You know Tom Beamis, the rancher who brought in a big herd of Herefords last season?"

Matt nodded.

"Well, Tom told me that he saw a man called Ed Flynn kill three men in a saloon in Tucson one time. The men were brothers, nesters by all accounts, and Flynn drew down on them and killed all three in a heartbeat. Being a rancher, Beamis approved of course, but I remember thinking what a cold-blooded act that must have been."

"Sounds like Ed all right. He's fast on the draw."

"Beamis said there was some question as to whether the men were armed or not. But Tucson is in cattle country, so nobody much cared."

Matt shrugged. "Like a lot of professional gunfighters, Ed Flynn kills any way he can and at the least risk to himself."

"Well" — Kitty sniffed — "I'm glad he's leaving. We certainly don't need his kind in Dodge."

Matt's eyes angled beyond Kitty to the window, where movement had caught his attention. Two riders bundled up in slickers, their hats pulled low against the rain, were passing, one of them holding his jaw as though in great pain. Matt couldn't see their faces, but it seemed that the taller of the two had a real bad toothache. They were probably heading to Doc Adams' place, since in the absence of a dentist he extracted teeth.

The riders were probably drifters passing though, Matt guessed. But he made a mental note to check on them after Kitty left. It was unlikely, but they could be Feeney's men, since even outlaws get tooth-aches.

Kitty was talking to him again, and for the moment, Matt put the riders out of his mind.

"I have to be going, Matt. I need to get out of these wet clothes."

She rose, stepped to the door and took her coat from the rack. When she turned, she was smiling. "I know you'll be busy tonight, but can we meet for breakfast tomorrow, say around ten?"

Matt nodded, matching her smile with one of his own. "That's the best offer I've had all day. Of course, we'll have breakfast together." He helped Kitty into her coat and took down her umbrella. "Festus tells me Ma Smalley just got in some sides of smoked bacon all the way from New York City."

"Then good for Ma Smalley," Kitty said. She opened the door, letting in a cold blast of wind and rain. "I'll see you tomorrow morning then."

Matt looked doubtfully outside at the river of mud that was Front Street. "Let me help you back to the Long Branch," he said.

The woman shook her head. "Thank you, Matt, but I've got an appointment at the hat shop." She smiled. "Besides, I've learned how to cross muddy streets. A lady just hikes up her skirts and off she goes. Of course, the mud plays all kinds of hob with her boots and bloomers."

A restlessness in him, Matt buckled on his gun belt, settled his hat on his head and buttoned into his slicker. It was time to check on the two riders who had come into town, and then he'd head out and see if Lee Feeney was still camped on Mulberry Creek.

It could be the man would wait until his deadline was up before making any kind of move against Dodge.

A pair of field glasses hung on their leather strap from a hook on the hat rack and Matt put them around his neck before he opened the door and stepped outside.

There had been no letup in the rain and it hammered hard against him as he walked along the boardwalk to Doc Adams' surgery. The boards were scattered with thick gobs of mud, and the people who hurried past him did not look up, their heads bent against the wind and flurrying rain. The marshal had to weave around the lucky few who had umbrellas, pushed out in front of them like giant black bats.

Two horses were at the hitching rail outside Doc's surgery. Matt stopped near the door, and from within, he heard a man bellow in pain, followed by a string of curses. The man bawled again, louder this time, and Matt smiled.

It seemed that Doc was contending with a mighty stubborn molar.

Now was not the time to interrupt, so the marshal turned on his heel and headed for the livery stable.

It was time to check on Lee Feeney.

Ahead of Matt the prairie was shrouded by the downpour. There was no horizon, land and sky merging into a solid wall of gray. The wind whipped at him, driving sheets of rain into his face, and above him thunder growled, testy that a mere mortal would defy its might by riding out on such a day.

The long grass tossed like a green sea in a storm and the uncaring wind shredded the blossoms of the fall wildflowers, throwing up tiny petals of pink, yellow and blue that stuck to the front of Matt's slicker.

Once, a small herd of antelope moved ahead of him, crossing the prairie like gray ghosts before vanishing into distance and mist.

The cottonwoods lining Mulberry Creek came into sight as a smear of smoky green, half hidden in the haze of lowering clouds. Matt drew rein and studied the land around him. A tall rider wearing a yellow slicker could be seen for a long way, and Matt swung out of the saddle and reluctantly draped the coat over his saddle horn.

Ahead of him, and about a hundred yards to his left, lay a shallow rise, tufts of buffalo grass covering its humpbacked crest. From there he would get a better view of the creek and Feeney's camp.

Crouching low, the marshal made his way to the rise. Within a few steps his shirt and pants were soaked, the pounding rain like drumming fingers on his hat. Lightning split the sky, thunder roared and the air crackled with electricity, smelling of ozone and scorched earth.

Matt lay on his belly at the top of the rise, trusting to the buffalo grass to break up the shape of his head and shoulders. He raised the field glasses and focused on Feeney's camp. Despite the rain, men were moving about, and several horses stood saddled and ready.

The marshal counted four mounts, and as he watched, their riders swung into the saddle. The remainder of Feeney's men were huddled under shelters they'd rigged from tree branches and tarps, and a string of smoke rose from a small fire.

It seemed like the outlaw was staying put, at least for now. The four men who were now riding out of the trees could be a hunting party.

Matt swung his glasses on the riders. They were strung out in a line, and the man in the lead had a slump-shouldered posture in the saddle, the way the Jicarilla Kid rode. And that made sense to Matt. Antelope and deer are reluctant to move around in rain, and it would take a skilled tracker like the Apache breed to hunt them down.

The four men had been heading north. Now they angled east, following the Kid, who was bending over, reading the wet ground as it passed beneath him.

Alarm spiked in Matt. The riders were heading right for the spot where he'd left his horse and they were closing fast.

Right then he knew he was in big trouble.

CHAPTER 11
A BOLT FROM THE BLUE

Matt backed away from the top of the rise, then got to his feet, knowing that as soon as he did, the sharp eyes of the Jicarilla Kid would spot the movement.

The Kid saw him immediately. He drew rein on his horse and pointed, yelling to the others.

Matt made a run for it.

A bullet kicked up dirt at his feet and another split the air next to his ear. The marshal stopped, turned to face the oncoming horsemen and drew his Colt. He fired, fired again, and missed both times. But his shots had the effect of slowing Feeney's men. They pulled up their mounts and grabbed for their rifles.

The marshal heard the Kid curse at the others. Then the gunman savagely dug spurs into his horse's flanks, his revolver flaring orange in the dim light as he charged.

Bullets sang around Matt as he ran. His

horse was close, only forty yards away, the Winchester ready in the scabbard. He heard the pounding of his feet on the grass and the sound of his own labored breathing in his ears as he quickened his pace.

Behind him there was a hammer of hooves as the Kid galloped closer. Matt stopped and turned, his Colt coming up. Too late. The Kid's horse slammed into him, knocking him flat on his back. The animal suddenly reared and bucked in fright and the gunman fought to get it under control. Stunned, Matt struggled to rise. The Kid had quieted his mount and he was grinning. His gun came down, leveled at the marshal's chest. . . .

And fire fell from the sky.

There was a blinding flash as a searing column of stark white stabbed into the soaked ground a few feet from the Kid's horse, accompanied by a deafening roar of thunder. The gunman's horse screamed as the lightning bolt blasted the animal on its side. The Kid was lifted from the saddle and thrown clear, but he landed hard, his gun spinning from his hand.

Groggy, his ears ringing, half blinded by the dazzling glare of the lightning, Matt saw a rider charging toward him, a rifle at his shoulder. Matt's fingers closed on the wet walnut handle of his Colt and he rose up on his left elbow and fired. The rider jerked in the saddle and swung away, his face gray with shock, and his rifle thudded onto the grass.

Matt got to his feet. The two other riders were still a ways off and seemed reluctant to get closer, apparently not wanting any part of what the big lawman could give them.

The Kid was also standing, but he was looking around with glassy eyes, stunned into a daze by the near-miss of the lightning bolt.

Matt staggered to his horse, but the bay, scared by the thunder, got up on its toes and danced away from him, white arcs showing in its rolling eyes. A bullet cracked past the marshal, then another. The two outlaws were sitting their horses, shooting at him. Matt emptied his Colt in their direction. He scored no hits, but the riders stayed their distance. Holstering his gun, he tried for the bay again. This time the horse had calmed down a little and stood and Matt climbed into the saddle. He swung around and spurred the big horse into a fast gallop. Behind him he heard the Kid cursing, and a few probing shots followed him. But the strong-running bay quickly carried him out of rifle range and only the empty rain-lashed prairie stretched away in the distance.

Matt put up his horse at the livery, then changed into a dry shirt and pants in the room he kept at the Dodge House. Once more wearing his wet slicker, he walked to his office as the dark day was shading into a murky late afternoon.

Festus was already in the office when Matt stepped inside and the deputy's eyes widened in surprise when he saw him.

"Matthew, what happened to you?" Festus asked. His fingers strayed to his right cheek.

"You're red as a mortified Injun all down this side."

Matt stepped to the scrap of mirror kept on a shelf near the door to the cells and studied his cheek. The whole side of his face was bright scarlet and it was tender to the touch.

He turned away from the mirror and smiled at his deputy. "I was struck by lightning, or close enough" — he waved a hand — "out there on the prairie."

Festus' face revealed his shock. "Matthew, you know better than to ride on the plains when it's thunderin'. A man can get hisself kilt that way."

Matt nodded. "I know, but it seemed a right good idea at the time."

Matt sat at his desk and recounted his brush with the Jicarilla Kid and the other Feeney men.

After he'd finished talking, Festus shook his head and said: "That's twicet in one day you've bested the Kid. It seems that boy just never learns."

"And I reckon Feeney has another dead man on his hands. That outlaw I shot was hit hard."

"That's gonna make ol' Lee tetchy as a teased snake, Matthew. He's already lost two men and him no nearer to gettin' aholt o' Ed Flynn than he was when all this started."

Matt wanted to tell Festus about how he planned to spirit Flynn out of Dodge as soon as it got dark. But first he asked about the widow Johnson's fox trap, since, minor as it was, that was also police business.

"Got it all set up real good, Matthew." The deputy grinned. "See, ol' Mr. Fox, he'll come a-sneakin' up to the hen house an' he'll spot a chicken all plucked an' ready to go in a box by the door. 'Mmm . . . mmm . . . but that looks like good eatin',' he'll say, an' then he'll step right in there. But I set up a doodad that will lower a door behind him jes' as soon as he trips a wire. He'll get trapped in the box an' by an' by be mad enough to bite the sights off'n a six-gun."

Matt nodded. "Sounds like a good arrangement to me, Festus. What does the widow Johnson plan to do with the critter?"

Festus shrugged. "Don't rightly know, Matthew. She's got herself a scattergun, so I reckon she'll shoot him. Ain't much else you can do with a fox that's got hisself a taste for a body's chickens."

"Mighty hard on the fox, though."

"Well, Matthew, Mr. Fox mought have thought o' that afore he became a chicken thief." Festus stepped to the window and glanced outside. "I can't recollect it rainin' this hard for this long, can you?"

"We had a real dry summer. That usually means a rainy fall and a hard winter." The marshal eased back in his chair. "Festus, we're getting Ed Flynn out of town tonight."

"The train?"

"No, we'll take him to Horse Thief Canyon and leave him enough grub and coffee to last a week. When Lee Feeney gives up looking for him, Flynn can then ride west like he originally planned. He says he wants to see the big ocean, and that's just fine with me. He'll be a long ways from Dodge."

Without turning, Festus said: "A man can

lose hisself in Hoss Thief Canyon an' that's a natural fact. But, Matthew, gettin' him there might be a lot more toilsome than you think."

The marshal looked up in surprise. "Why do you say that?"

Festus nodded to the street outside. "Take a look-see."

Matt rose and stepped beside the deputy. Six riders were swinging out of their saddles at the Long Branch hitching rail, and there was no question that they were Feeney's men.

"Hardcases, every man jack of them, Matthew," Festus said, "including four that kept on riding toward the Alamo. None of them boys shaped up to be pilgrims, either."

Matt swore under his breath. Feeney's men were staking out the town, and what better place to watch and wait than the saloons? He couldn't run men out of Dodge for loitering over a beer at the bar.

Despite all that had happened, Feeney was keeping his word. He wouldn't act until his deadline had passed. But his men were already in place, and after Matt's watch ticked past eleven thirty tomorrow morning, all hell could break loose.

Matt turned away from the window, his mind made up. Tomorrow he'd ride out to

Feeney's camp, but he'd be by himself.

Maybe when he told the outlaw that Flynn had cut and run and was somewhere out on the plains Feeney would search for him and leave Dodge alone.

It was a long shot, but it was all he had. If it all went bad and Feeney threatened to vent his spleen on the town, then he'd draw and kill the man.

Matt knew it would be the final, despairing act of his life.

But he wanted to save his town . . . and there might be no other way.

CHAPTER 12
AN UNHOLY
ALLIANCE

Matt Dillon's carefully laid plans hit a major snag just as night was crowding into Dodge. The light of the reflector lamps stained the mud on Front Street like spilled yellow paint, and the alleys between the buildings were angled with shadow.

A rider drew rein outside the office and yelled: "You in the jail! I have a message from Lee Feeney."

Matt and Festus exchanged glances. Then the deputy took down the ten-gauge Greener from the rack and said: "Behind you to your left, Matthew."

The marshal nodded, threw his slicker over his shoulders and stepped onto the boardwalk. A tall man sat his horse in the rain, his face shadowed by the wide brim of his hat. Aware of Festus taking up his position, Matt asked: "What does Feeney want?"

Teeth flashed white as the rider smiled. "As to that question, you already know what he wants, lawman."

"Then what did he send you here to tell me?"

"He don't want me to tell you anything. He can speak for his ownself." The outlaw's hands had been crossed on top of his saddle horn, and now he raised his right to his chest. "I have a note for you. It's in my shirt pocket under the slicker."

"Move real slow, like an old coon dog in summer," Matt said. "I see you move any quicker, I'll shoot you right off the back of that pony."

Beside him the marshal heard a *click-click,* as Festus eared back the hammers of the shotgun.

The rider's teeth again gleamed white in his shadowed face. "Marshal, my mama didn't raise no pretty boy, but she didn't raise a dumb one either. Do you think I'd make a play with the muzzles of that there scattergun looking right at me like a stepmother's eyes?"

"Then real slow, just like I told it to you," Matt said.

After the man handed the note to the marshal, he touched his hat and grinned. "See you around, star strutter." Then he touched spurs to his horse and left town at a gallop.

Matt took the penciled note inside before he opened it, fearing that the pelting rain would shred it in his hands. It was curt and right to the point:

I GOT DOC ADAMS. FAIR EX-
CHANGE IS NO ROBBERY.
YOU GET THE DOC BACK WHEN I
GET ED FLYNN.
   P.S. IF I DON'T GET FLYNN THE
DOC GETS SHOT.

Matt angrily crumpled the note in his hands and Festus asked: "What does it say, Matthew?"

"Lee Feeney has Doc Adams. He says if he doesn't get Ed Flynn, he'll kill Doc."

"But . . . but how . . ."

"I saw it, Festus," Matt said bitterly. "I stood by, watched it happen and did nothing."

The deputy's stricken face showed his confusion. "Matthew, I don't —"

"I saw two men ride into Dodge earlier today," Matt interrupted. "One of them was holding his jaw, like he had a real bad toothache. I figured he was on his way to get Doc to pull it for him. Later I walked past Doc's surgery and I heard a man hollering as though his bad tooth was being yanked, so I figured I'd best leave Doc alone and let him have at it."

The marshal shook his head. "All that hollering was for my benefit. They probably had Doc at gunpoint and tied up by that time and one of the two was acting the part of a hurting man."

"Can't blame yourself for that, Matthew," Festus said. "I would have figured the same thing."

"I had those two pegged as drifters," Matt said. "I should have realized they were Feeney's men."

Festus sat on a corner of the desk and studied the marshal. "Matthew, when a man finds hisself in a hole, the first thing he has to do is stop diggin'. Maybe it's time to tell Flynn he ain't welcome in Dodge no more and run him out of town. Then you can tell them boys over to the Long Branch that he's makin' a run for it." The deputy shrugged. "After that, it's up to Flynn to get away clean or die out there on the long grass."

The deputy's words hit Matt like a blow to the stomach. He knew that what Festus said made sense, but if he threw Flynn to the wolves, he'd be turning his back on the very principle he held dear: that a man never forgets a favor.

He owed Ed Flynn his life and that

counted for something. But did Doc have to die to repay his debt? No, the cost was too high — something Matt would never accept.

There had to be some other way . . . if only he could find it.

Festus thumbed a lucifer match into flame and lifted it to the lamp over the marshal's desk.

"No, leave it, Festus," Matt said. He was sitting in his chair, his head bent, and he did not stir as he spoke.

"But, Matthew, it's pitch-dark in here an' you haven't even twitched a muscle in an hour."

"I've been thinking. I've been trying to find a way."

Festus blew out the match and the office went from flickering orange light and angled shadow to darkness again. "Maybe the only way is like I told it to you, Matthew. Run ol' Ed out of town."

"It's a way, all right," the marshal said, "but it's not my way."

A silence stretched between the two men and the *tick-tick-tick* of the office clock was the only sound, soft and steady, like water dripping from a leaky tap. Outside, in the distance, thunder rumbled and the coyotes were talking, their heads lifted to the flashing sky.

"Rain's stopped," Festus said from the window. "At least for now."

Matt did not answer, his mind working.

Six of Feeney's men were at the Long Branch, another four at the Alamo. There was a chance he had a man watching the station, and he'd lost two to the marshal's gun. Including Feeney himself, that left seven or eight men guarding Doc back at the creek.

It was still long odds, but not impossible, especially if . . .

Matt had one of the deadliest shootists in the West right here in Dodge. Ed Flynn was a gun for hire, a paid assassin, but he was a first-class fighting man and he had sand. He would stand in a fight, especially when his own life was at stake.

And there was someone else.

Charles Granville had proved himself in the fight with the stage robbers. He was good with a gun, maybe as good as Flynn, and there seemed to be no backup in him, either.

If Festus, Flynn and Granville rode with him, Matt believed he could free Doc Adams and maybe make Lee Feeney see the light. *No, not Festus,* he decided. His deputy would have to stay in Dodge and keep an eye on Feeney's men. There was always the chance they'd mount up and head back to the creek, and Festus could head them off on his long-riding mule. Ruth had a stubborn streak, and more than once, Matt had seen her keep on going after his own strong bay had faltered to a halt on the trail.

Matt rose to his feet and lit the lamp.

"You thunk o' something, Matthew?" Festus asked, grinning expectantly.

"Maybe, but it's thin, Festus, real thin. I want you to round up Ed Flynn and Charles Granville. Tell them to arm themselves and come here."

Festus' face frowned a question and Matt outlined his plan.

After the marshal was through talking, Festus said: "I'd feel better if I was riding with you, Matthew."

Matt nodded. "Me too, Festus, but I need you here. Keep Ruth saddled and handy, and at the first sign those Feeney boys are leaving town, hightail it after us."

"Think Granville and Flynn will play along?" the deputy asked as he shrugged into his slicker. "From all I've heard, Lee Feeney is a mighty dangerous man, and I'd guess them two have heard that as well."

"All I can do is ask them," Matt said.

Festus returned ten minutes later, Granville and Flynn walking into the office behind him.

"Were you seen?" Matt asked.

The deputy shook his head and grinned. "Look at our boots, Matthew. We took to the alleys and back ways wherever we could."

"And deuced hard walking it was," Granville complained. "I almost tripped and fell a dozen times." The Englishman's eyes held a question. "Why did you bring us here?"

Matt glanced from Granville to Flynn. The gunfighter looked sullen, as though he was still smarting from the talk he'd had with Matt earlier. "If I'm not mistaken we're headed for a place called Horse Thief Canyon," he said, his voice flat.

"That plan has changed, at least for now," Matt said.

Quickly he told about the kidnapping of Doc Adams and his plan to free him from Feeney.

When the marshal finished, Granville asked: "This Lee Feeney chap, is he an outlaw?"

"One of the worst there is," the marshal

answered. "Robbery, murder, rape, you name it, but somehow he always manages to stay one step ahead of the law."

Granville didn't hesitate. "Then I'm in," he said.

"You?" Matt asked Flynn.

"That damned Mick dogged my trail for months until he finally got me treed," Flynn said. "I'd love to put a bullet into him. Count me in as well."

Matt saw the bulk of Flynn's guns under his slicker. Granville wore his usual caped tweed coat and deerstalker hat. "Are you armed, Granville?" Matt asked.

The man pulled back his coat, revealing his fancy Colt in a shoulder holster. "All loaded and ready to go, Marshal," he said.

Matt nodded. "We have to get out of town unnoticed, so we can't ride down Front Street. We'll saddle up at the livery, then walk our horses out of town to the north. After we're clear, we'll saddle up and loop around town and cross the Arkansas. On account of all this rain, I don't know how high the river will be, but I think we can get across without getting our feet wet."

Flynn's face showed his irritation. "Wet feet, dry feet, who cares? Let's get it done."

"My sentiments entirely, old boy," Granville said, smiling.

But the Englishman's eyes were like ice.

Chapter 13
At the Outlaw Camp

Matt took the point, riding a hundred yards ahead of the others as they neared the Arkansas, trusting to his instincts and knowledge of the terrain that he could find an easy crossing in the darkness.

It was raining heavily again, and now and then the plains were illuminated in stark detail by the sheet lightning that flashed in the sky. The wind sent ripples through the vast sea of grass, adding a constant rustle to the night sounds.

The river had not recovered from the summer drought and the heavy rain of the past few days had added little to its level.

Matt waited for the others, then rode his bay down a shallow bank that had been broken down by the passage of a cattle herd. The horse splashed into two feet of water, and then onto a sandbar littered with white limbs of driftwood that had washed downstream during the spring melt. Once he reached the opposite bank, the marshal rode through a stand of cottonwoods and swung to the southeast in the direction of Feeney's camp.

For an hour the three horsemen rode abreast through a worsening downpour, the surrounding prairie flaring constantly from dark to a shimmering light that gleamed wetly on their slickers. Thunder boomed, rolling across the sky like a gigantic boulder being bowled along a marble hall, and the wind smashed the hard rain against them.

"How far, Marshal?" Granville asked, shouting above the din.

"We're getting close," Matt answered. "And I hope Feeney has managed to keep a fire going or we could ride right past his camp."

A few minutes later, Matt smelled smoke. He drew rein and called out for the others to do the same.

"There's smoke in the wind," the marshal said. "The camp has got to be close."

They sat their horses and stared into the night, their eyes searching for the telltale flicker of a campfire.

It was Flynn who saw it. "Off to our left, a glow among the trees."

Matt scanned the darkness. He saw it

then, just a pinprick of red light in the gloom.

"Well, how do we play this . . . Marshal?" Flynn asked, putting a mocking emphasis on the last word of his question.

Matt let that go. Now was not the time to let Flynn irritate him. "We dismount here and walk right up on them. We'll try and take them without a fight, but if they grab for their guns, then I'll open the ball."

"Or I will," Flynn said, his face hidden in the darkness.

Matt sensed rather than saw Granville glance up warily at the black arch of the sky. "Then we'll hope that there's not a flash of lightning when we're only halfway there," he said. "That could be dashed awkward, not to say fatal."

"And that," Matt said, "is a chance we'll just have to take."

"I say we ride into them," Flynn said. "Hit them hard before they know what's happening."

Matt opened his mouth to speak, but Granville snatched the reply from his lips. "My dear fellow, those men will be sleeping light. One never hears the snores of the righteous arising from an outlaw camp. They'd hear our horses and cut us to pieces before we even got close."

Signaling that he would listen to no more argument, Matt slid his Winchester from the scabbard and said: "All right, let's get it done."

Crouching low, the three men started to cross the open ground between themselves and the outlaws. After a few steps, they hugged the ground as lightning lit up the clouds and thunder crashed. But they had not been seen, and Matt rose and waved the other two forward.

A hundred yards to go, Matt guessed. *No more than that.*

They crossed the flat, open ground, hidden by the darkness and a slanting wall of rain. When twenty yards separated him from the camp, Matt took a knee and the others crouched beside him.

The outlaws were sleeping under the cottonwoods, sheltered by canopies of tree boughs and a few oilskin groundsheets. A small anger rose in the marshal when he spotted Doc Adams lying out in the open, his feet and hands bound with rope.

As he watched, a night guard stepped beside Doc, bent over and tested the knots at his ankles and wrists. Doc, no doubt his usual grouchy self, looked up and said something Matt couldn't hear. The guard laughed, then slammed the butt of his rifle into the physician's belly.

The outlaw was wearing a battered black hat with a concho band, and Matt marked him. In a few moments, he and that man would have words.

Beside him, the marshal heard Flynn whisper: "I'm through skulking around out here." He rose to his feet. "Time to get it over with."

Flynn walked toward the camp and Matt and Granville followed. The three men were almost in the middle of the camp before the guard wearing the black hat saw them.

"Stay right where you are!" Matt yelled. "You're all under arrest."

Beside him, Flynn's Colt roared and the guard screamed and fell back, his rifle dropping from his hands.

Men were rolling out of their blankets, and guns flashed and banged. A bullet sang past Matt's head and he fired at a kneeling man with a rifle to his shoulder. His bullet slammed into the receiver of the outlaw's Henry and ranged upward, hitting him under the chin. The outlaw doubled over, then stretched his length in the mud.

The camp was in chaos. Men were running and firing, tripping over roots and fallen branches. Granville and Flynn were firing steadily. A tall outlaw in a yellow slicker was hit, and he fell backward into the fire, sending the coffeepot clanking across the ground, spilling grounds and brown liquid. Another man went down near the picketed horses, and off to Matt's left, he saw an outlaw take one of Flynn's bullets in the belly. The man was screaming when he hit the dirt.

Pounding hooves sounded from the other side of the camp and Matt searched for a target. But he saw only darkness and the hammering rain.

As quickly as it had begun, it was over.

Five men lay sprawled on the ground, the gut-shot man groaning and cursing, and the hoofbeats of the fleeing outlaws were fading into the distance.

"Did we get Feeney?" Flynn asked, looking around him as he loaded fresh rounds into the cylinder of his Colt. Then, more urgently: "Did we get Feeney?"

"I don't know," Matt answered. "He may have cut and run."

The marshal stepped over to the dead man in the yellow slicker and pulled him out of the fire. He did not recognize him.

A shot slammed into the sudden silence of the night and Matt turned, his gun coming up fast.

Granville was standing over the body of

an outlaw, a wisp of smoke drifting from the muzzle of his Colt. He saw Matt striding toward him and he said, a half smile on his lips: "Poor fellow was shot in the belly and could not live. I put him out of his misery."

The outlaw had a neat hole in the middle of his forehead. Flynn stepped close, looked down at the man without compassion and said: "His miseries are over now — that's for damn sure."

Matt opened his mouth to speak, stunned by Granville's callousness, but a call from Doc made the words flee his lips. "Do you think one of you gentlemen might take the time to untie me?"

After Matt had cut him free, Doc stood and rubbed his wrists. "I wondered when you'd get here, Matt," he said. "What took you so long?"

"Bad weather, Doc. How are you feeling?"

"I'm all right, but I'm soaked through. If I don't get double pneumonia, it will be a miracle."

The physician looked around him. "Five men down. Are any still alive?"

Matt shook his head. "They're all dead. Lee Feeney isn't one of them."

"What about that Jicarilla Kid?" Doc asked, his face flushing with anger.

"He skedaddled as well."

"He's the one who wanted to kill me if you didn't deliver Ed Flynn. He said he'd fix it so it took me three days to die, and I'd scream like a woman for the last two."

"He's half Apache, Doc," Matt said. "He wasn't making any empty promises."

"Pity you missed him. I'd have shot that man myself."

Matt found a slicker for Doc, draped it over his shoulders, then picked up the spilled coffeepot. "Ed, look around and see if you can find some coffee," he said. "I'll go fill this at the creek."

"That might be difficult," the gunfighter said. He sat down hard on the ground, his face twisting in pain. His eyes lifted to Matt, who was standing over him. "I've been hit."

Matt kneeled beside the man. "Where? Is it bad?"

Flynn opened his slicker. The right side of his shirt was black with blood. "Took a bullet in the ribs. I can't tell if it's still inside me or not."

Matt turned his head and yelled for Doc.

After a few minutes' examination of Flynn, Doc rose to his feet. Matt standing close to him. "The bullet passed between his ribs and ranged downward into his lower back. I can feel it, close to the spine."

Flynn looked frightened. "Can you cut it out of there, Doc?"

"I can, but I'll have to do it here. I'll lay it on the line for you, Flynn. I can't risk the bullet moving any closer to the spinal cord. If it did, I wouldn't have the surgical skill to remove it. I'd have to cut really close to the spine, and I could paralyze you for life."

The gunfighter swallowed hard. "Do you have your doctoring tools here?"

Doc shook his head. "When Feeney's men kidnapped me, they didn't bring my bag."

"Then how . . . ?"

"With Matt's folding knife," Doc said. "And an anesthetic."

Granville, smiling, was holding up a bottle. "Hennessy brandy, and the bottle is half full. That ought to do the trick."

"When does the cutting start, Doc?" Flynn asked.

"Just as soon as I can get some sort of shelter rigged over you," the physician answered. "You're not moving from this spot until I get the bullet out."

Flynn stretched a hand to Granville. "Then give me that damned bottle. I got the feeling I'm going to need it."

CHAPTER 14
THE PINKERTON'S TALE

"He'll be all right, Matt," Doc Adams said, helping himself to coffee by the sputtering fire. "But once we get him back to Dodge, he'll have to spend a few days in bed."

"When can he ride, Doc?" Matt asked, the realization that he'd left Festus alone with a bunch of Feeney's men weighing on him.

"We should wait until first light. He won't be comfortable up on his horse, but he's strong and he'll make it to town."

Flynn was sleeping under a shelter of cottonwood branches and oilskins, the empty bottle of brandy by his side. Doc had cut deep and the bullet had been wedged hard against the man's spine, but apart from a groan that now and then escaped between his clenched teeth, the gunfighter had borne the surgery well.

He even earned the grudging admiration of Granville, who stepped close to Matt and said: "He's a tough man, but his kind usually are. They're very hard to kill."

Lightning flashed, flaring on Granville's pale face, his eye sockets deep in shadow. "I suspect Lee Feeney will die just as hard."

"You know, Granville, for a poet, you sure know a lot about killing," Matt said, the memory of the bullet he'd put into the dying outlaw still lingering.

The Englishman shrugged. "But there's no conflict, Marshal. Bertrand du Born, Sir Walter Raleigh, Francois Villon, just to name a few, were all famous poets. But they were also fighters and brawlers who had killed more than their share."

"And Tancred," Matt said, watching how the man would react. "What about him?"

Granville smiled. "Ah, but he was not a poet. He was a crusader knight who used his sword to battle lawlessness no matter where he found it. It is said he rode about the desert country of the Holy Land righting many wrongs, and that he mercilessly punished the wicked and the oppressors, often with a single stroke of his mighty battle-ax."

"So he set himself up as judge, jury and executioner," Matt said.

Granville shrugged. "In a lawless land, that is sometimes necessary."

"Not in Dodge, it isn't," the marshal said.

"Really? Then if Tancred rode his white charger into your town, he would not be welcome."

"He'd be welcome, but I'd sure keep an eye on him," the marshal said, his meaning clear. And for some reason that he could not understand, he suddenly remembered the dead white face of Uriah Scroggins. It was as though the man had come back to haunt him.

A gloomy dawn broke over the plains, and one by one the coyotes fell silent. Clouds the color of iron hung so low that in places they touched the grasslands, and the creek that ran behind the camp was lost in an eddying mist. Matt and the others shared the last of the coffee; then Granville left and brought the horses into camp.

"Sorry it took so long," he said. "But Flynn's horse had wandered for quite a distance."

Matt and Granville got Flynn to his feet, Doc fluttering around them like a mother hen, his concern for his patient obvious. "Gently, Matt," he said. "Be careful getting him up on his horse."

Flynn's smile was a pained grimace. "Doc, with you around, it's almost a pleasure to get shot."

When he was safely in the saddle, Flynn gathered up the reins and Matt asked him: "Are you feeling all right?"

The gunfighter nodded. "I can make it. Back is paining me some, though."

"That is a nasty wound," Doc said, his face full of concern. "Just take it slow and easy."

With Doc up on one of the outlaw horses, Matt led the way across the plains, the rain battering at him. He raised hopeful eyes to the sky, but from horizon to horizon, there was no break in the clouds, and it looked like the sun would never shine again.

But the fall wildflowers were prospering, and the marshal's bay walked through a carpet of blossoms that tinted the air with a fleeting delicate perfume. Flynn seemed to be holding up well, but the man was no longer a youngster, and Doc's rough-and-ready surgery had obviously taken its toll on him. He dozed often, his head nodding in the saddle.

It was Doc who helped Flynn into his room at the Dodge House while Matt and Granville put up the horses at the livery.

It was still not yet eight, but to the marshal's surprise when he returned to his office, Festus was already dressed, his Colt buckled around his waist.

"Coffee's ready, Matthew," Festus said, lifting the pot from the stove.

"I could use some," Matt said. He found a cup and stepped to the door, where he threw an inch of dregs into the street. Thick grounds remained, so he held the cup under runoff from the roof, rinsed it out and went back inside.

"Feeney's men still in town?" he asked as Festus poured for him.

"Pulled out real early, Matthew. Must have been two, three in the morning."

Matt nodded, his face stiff. "Then Feeney or the Kid rode directly here and rounded them up." He tried his coffee. "It's good."

"What happened out there, Matthew? How is Doc?"

Matt described the gunfight at Feeney's camp and the wounding of Ed Flynn. "Feeney and the Kid got away clean," he concluded. "They'd kept their horses saddled and ready. I guess they didn't trust me too much."

Festus thought through what Matt had just told him. "So ol' Ed is at the Dodge House, all shot up, an' Feeney is still out there someplace."

"That's about the size of it. Doc says we can't move Flynn for a couple of days, so my plan to stash him in Horse Thief Canyon will have to wait."

"If Lee Feeney will give us that long, Matthew."

"I have a feeling he won't. He probably knows that Flynn helped me shoot up his camp. In fact, it could have been Feeney that plugged him. He's lost half his men, and by now he'll be good and mad."

Festus drank his coffee, the faraway look in his eyes showing over the rim of his cup revealing that he was thinking. After a few moments, he gave up the struggle and asked: "What you reckon ol' Lee will do next?"

Matt shook his head. "I don't know, Festus. I reckon he'll come after Flynn and maybe me. But I think he'll leave that part up to the Kid. He may be angry as hell, but he still won't want the killing of a U.S. marshal laying on his back trail."

"Could be he thinks he done for Flynn."

"Could be, but I doubt it. Flynn was still on his feet and shooting when Feeney lit a shuck."

"How did ol' Charlie Granville do?" Festus asked.

Matt's face hardened. "He done his part, killed his man."

"You don't cotton to that Englishman

much, do you, Matthew?"

"I don't cotton to a man who calls himself a poet, yet thinks nothing of shooting a gut-shot man like a dog. Sure, the man was in agony and would die soon, but what Granville did doesn't set right with me. He said it was an act of mercy, and maybe it was, but it still looked a lot like murder to me."

"You plannin' to call him on it, Matthew?"

"I am. But right now it can wait. I've got Feeney to deal with first."

The office door opened and Kitty Russell stepped inside. Despite the early hour she looked fresh and beautiful and she gave the two lawmen a dazzling smile. "I know I'm early, but I'm here for that breakfast date, Matt."

The marshal rose to his feet. "You're not early, Kitty. You're right on time. I'm hungry for that smoked bacon Festus mentioned and maybe half a dozen eggs and twice that many biscuits."

Kitty laughed. "After all that, I'll have to roll you back to your office."

The restaurant was busy when Kitty and Matt stepped inside, the place cluttered with umbrellas and steaming wet coats slung over the backs of chairs.

They found a table near the window and

Matt removed his slicker and helped Kitty off with her cloak. They had just ordered when a small, thin man in a ankle-length brown coat and derby hat of the same color got up from his seat and walked to the table.

"My apologies," he said, "but I just now caught sight of the badge on your vest. You must be Marshal Matt Dillon." The man stuck out his hand. "My name is Silas Vernon. By profession, I'm a Pinkerton detective."

Matt shook hands with the man; then Vernon pulled out a chair. "May I?" The man saw the doubt in the tall lawman's eyes, and he smiled. "This won't take but a few moments. I have no desire to interrupt your breakfast, especially with such a beautiful companion at your side."

Kitty, well used to compliments from men, smiled in acknowledgment as Vernon sat. The Pinkerton got right to the point.

"Marshal I just got in on the morning cannonball. I'm from Texas, you know, but was assigned a case here in Kansas that might interest you."

Matt smiled. "I was once told to never ask a man where he's from. If he's from Texas, he'll tell you. If he's not, you'll just embarrass him."

Vernon's stiff face did not change. "Yes,

that's very amusing, I'm sure." He hesitated a moment and said: "I am trying to establish the whereabouts of a man named Uriah Scroggins. I have reason to believe he and his wife and their eight children are here in Dodge City."

"Scroggins was here, but he's dead, murdered," Matt said.

The Pinkerton's face registered neither shock nor disappointment. "And his wife?"

"She left town early yesterday," Kitty supplied. "She said she was going east to live with her sister."

"By train?"

"Yes, by the Santa Fe. She was headed for Boston."

Vernon suddenly seemed to shrink inside his heavy wool coat. "Then I'm too late."

"What's your interest in Scroggins?" Matt asked.

The man sighed. "Mr. Scroggins was a clerk at a bank in a town called Broken Bow, in the Arizona Territory. By all accounts he was a steady and industrious employee, but, alas, he yielded to temptation and embezzled funds to the sum of more than thirty thousand dollars. Then he and his family immediately skipped town."

Vernon's hang-dog eyes lifted to Matt's. "Marshal, you know that when a bank is robbed, it's not the bank's money that's taken, it's the hard-earned savings of the investors. That was cattle country around Broken Bow, and the ranchers were stretched financially, trying to recover from three bad years, first a drought, then two years of low beef prices.

"People were wiped out when their bank was robbed, and there was at least one suicide. Broken Bow never recovered and soon died. Now I'm told that it's a ghost town and none of the surrounding ranches are still in business."

A harried young waitress brought Kitty and Matt their food, and Vernon rose to his feet. "I'll leave you to enjoy your meal. I must catch the next train east and catch up with Mrs. Scroggins. If I can get the stolen money back, perhaps something can be salvaged, though I very much doubt it."

Vernon touched his hat to Kitty and turned to go, but Matt's voice stopped him. "Mr. Vernon, do you recall the name of the suicide?"

The Pinkerton shook his head. "I believe I was told, but right now the name escapes me. If I remember, I'll send you a wire." Vernon looked puzzled. "Marshal, do you think remembering the name might help me recover the money?"

"No, I don't," Matt said. "But I've got a hunch it might help bring the killer of Uriah Scroggins to justice."

CHAPTER 15
A STOLEN HORSE
HERD

"Marshal, depending on the circumstances, I can tolerate a certain amount of slick-eared calf poaching, but horse stealing is a hanging offense."

Big John Farnborough stood at Matt Dillon's desk, his face black with anger. "Hell, they run off sixteen head of my best stock, including an American stud I paid two hundred dollars for at the Wichita horse fair not three months ago."

Farnborough, a tall, heavyset rancher with a handlebar mustache and spiky gray eyebrows, was normally an easygoing man, but right now he was ready to spit nails.

"When did it happen, John?" Matt asked.

"Early this morning, as near as I can tell. The horses were lifted from the east fork of the Pawnee and trailed southwest. I figure seven, eight riders, maybe more. Me and my hands went after them, but we lost their tracks at the Arkansas."

Matt felt a pang of unease. This sounded like the work of Lee Feeney. Was the man trying to pressure him to give up Flynn? It was possible. No, it was more than just possible — it was very likely.

The marshal's eyes moved beyond Farnborough to the window. It was not yet three, but the low clouds and falling rain had cast the gloom of night over Dodge.

"Well, what you going to do about it, Marshal?" the rancher demanded.

Matt rose to his feet. "There's maybe a couple of hours of daylight left, such as it is," he said. "I'll scout along the river and maybe find the spot where they crossed." He looked into Farnborough's blazing eyes. "John, right now I'm not promising much."

The big rancher visibly forced himself to relax. "Hell, I know that, what with this rain an' all. But I sure set store by that stud. Marshal, I'll ride with you."

"We may have to hole up somewhere after dark, John," Matt said. "That set all right with you?"

"How many times have I done that before?" The man grinned. "Mrs. Farnborough put coffee and grub in a sack for me, on the chance I might have to overnight on the trail somewhere on account of the weather. Still, she said she'd keep a candle burning in the window for me to guide me home. Good woman, my wife."

Matt smiled. "I reckon she is, John." He was already buckling on his gun belt.

The marshal and Farnborough rode along the north bank of the Arkansas, across flat country cut through by innumerable narrow creeks and streams running off the river. It was pouring without letup, the only sounds the dragon hiss of the rain, the fall of their horse's hooves on wet grass and the creak of saddle leather.

A jackrabbit, soaked and miserable, bounded away from them, bouncing like a rubber ball, and once they saw a huge lobo wolf regarding them with scant interest from behind the trunk of a wild plum tree.

To the north of the hunched riders stretched a wilderness of grama grass and prickly pear and here and there a solitary stand of yucca. Across the river the land looked much the same, though in the distance it was shrouded in low cloud the color of wood smoke.

The day was shading into night when Farnborough turned in the saddle and said, "Marshal, I figure we're just about due south of my place on the Pawnee. We should keep our eyes skinned. They may have crossed close to here."

Matt scouted the bank as he rode, the waning light making it difficult to see. Just ahead of him, visible through a heavy curtain of rain, was a stand of cottonwoods and a few willows. Here a bend on the Arkansas narrowed to a shallow channel about thirty feet wide, confined by broad sandbanks.

Matt stopped short of the cottonwoods and studied the ground. During spring snow melts the action of the river in flood had cut a deep arc about fifty yards long into the bank. The sand had piled up here into a shelf that slanted gradually to the water, an ideal crossing for the stolen horse herd.

With a word to Farnborough to stay mounted, Matt swung out of the saddle and stepped to the bank. He dropped down to the sandy ledge but its entire surface was smooth from the rain. And any tracks that might have been there had long since been washed away.

The marshal regained the bank and walked closer to the cottonwoods. The embankment was not as broken here, but was much less deep, about knee-high to a man. But again rain and wind had done their work. The grass around the top of the bank was flattened, the sand leading to the water smooth.

But then Matt found what he'd been looking for.

A fist-sized rock had tumbled from the top of the rise and come to rest close to the water's edge. Matt picked up the rock and turned it over in his hand. There was a raw scar about an inch long on one side.

He looked up at Farnborough, who was sitting his mount under the lean shelter of a cottonwood. "John, are all your horses shod?"

The man nodded and Matt scrambled up the bank and stepped beside him. He showed Farnborough the white scar on the rock's smooth black surface. "The hoof of a shod horse did this and not too long since. This must be where they crossed the river all right."

The day was rapidly dying around the two men and the clouded sky was shading to black. Rain hammered on Matt's hat and the shoulders of his slicker and thunder slammed in the distance.

"Now I'm wishing I'd brought my hands with me," Farnborough said, his face gloomy. "We counted at least eight of them rustlers."

Matt nodded. "That's why we won't ride

up on them tonight in the dark. I have a feeling they'll stash those horses somewhere pretty quick and leave a couple of men to guard them. Lee Feeney won't stay close to a stolen horse herd for long. He's too clever for that and he's got more important things on his mind."

Farnborough showed his surprise. "Lee Feeney, the famous outlaw? He's the one who stole my horses?"

"I believe so."

The rancher shook his head. "I guess in a kind of perverse way I should be honored. But why would a big-time outlaw like Feeney bother himself with my pony string? The only hoss I have that's worth more than twenty-five dollars is the American stud."

Matt's bay had wandered close and he gathered up the reins. "It's not about you, John. It's about me. I think Feeney is trying to push me into a corner, maybe by stirring up the ranchers and settlers around Dodge. If he can turn public opinion against me, and do it quickly, he reckons I'll be glad to give him what he wants.

"My guess is you'd soon have gotten a ransom note demanding money for the safe return of your horses. And Feeney would explain why your string was stolen in the first place — because Marshal Dillon is refusing to hand over the man who killed his brother."

In answer to the question on Farnborough's face, Matt quickly told him about Ed Flynn and the shooting scrapes he'd already had with Feeney and his men.

When Matt was through talking, the rancher's lips stretched in a grim smile under his mustache. "And I thought I had problems. Marshal, you've sure got a hair in the butter. Most folks will reckon a gunslinger like Ed Flynn is no better than Feeney himself and that it's not worth climbing out onto a limb to save him. So how do you aim to get out of this fix?"

"The first thing to do is get your horses back," Matt said. "Show Feeney that I won't be buffaloed and I won't be pushed around." The marshal shrugged. "And after that . . . well, John, your guess is as good as mine."

But Matt did have a plan, or at least a hope, that he did not share with Farnborough.

If he was lucky enough to catch Feeney with the stolen herd, he would arrest him. Feeney might beat a charge of kidnapping, but as Farnborough himself had said, horse theft was a hanging offense in Kansas.

So far in his outlaw career, none of

Feeney's crimes could be laid at his doorstep. Witnesses, including lawmen, often refused to testify or simply disappeared, and on the few occasions he'd appeared before a judge, his expensive lawyers had quickly got him acquitted.

But Matt could not be railroaded, and if Feeney was caught red-handed with stolen horses, the best lawyer in the world might not be able to save him.

Matt and Farnborough made an uncomfortable camp under the cottonwoods. They shared the thick beef sandwiches the rancher's wife had packed for him, and after several attempts at lighting damp wood, they finally coaxed a small fire into life and had coffee.

They were saddled and riding at first light, tracking south across flat grassland under an ominous, surly sky.

Matt had no illusions about what would happen if Lee Feeney was still with the stolen horses. He wanted to take the outlaw without a fight, but that might be impossible. The Jicarilla Kid was a man to be reckoned with, and so were the others with him. They were fighting men, not the kind to throw up their hands and meekly surrender.

The marshal knew that somehow he had to get the drop on Feeney and convince the man that if it came to shooting, he would be the first to die. What happened next would depend on the outlaw. But Matt would need more than his share of luck, because the whole thing could go real bad, real fast.

John Farnborough was a solid, steady man and he'd stand his ground. But he wasn't gun handy like Feeney and his men, and the marshal realized he and the rancher would be facing a stacked deck.

Of course he could swing his horse around, head for Dodge and round up a posse. But by then Feeney would be long gone. A lesser lawman would have done that, turned tail and run, and who would have blamed him?

But under Matt Dillon's slicker, pinned to the leather vest he wore over his blue wool shirt, was the star of a federally appointed United States marshal. That star told him he had it to do. There was no one else.

CHAPTER 16
AN OUTLAW FINDS
REDEMPTION

After two hours of riding through teeming rain, Matt caught sight of a small antelope herd in the distance. Led by a young buck, the animals picked their way across the wet grass toward a half-mile-long saddle-backed rise that at its highest point swelled about ten feet above the flat. At the last moment the pronghorns veered away, and led by the buck, they trotted to the east, their heads up as they read the gusting wind.

Matt drew rein and Farnborough did the same. Had the antelope caught man scent?

"Saw that my ownself," the rancher said, nodding toward the departing herd. "What you reckon, Marshal?"

"If I'm remembering right, the other side of that rise slopes down to a stream. There are a few trees and a shelf of red sandstone rock sticking out of the ground at a fairly sharp angle. If I was guarding horses in the rain, I'd make my camp under the shelter of that rock."

Farnborough's eyes were suddenly worried. "What are we riding into, Marshal? When we top the rise, there could be eight, nine outlaws waiting on the other side."

Matt glanced at the gray sky, the rain falling on his face. When he turned to the rancher, his eyes held no trace of accusation. "John, I would not think any less of you if you were to turn around and head home."

Farnborough nodded. "No, I don't reckon you would." He eased himself in the saddle, leather creaking under him. "Marshal, it's taken me four hard years to build up my spread. First the Cheyenne and Blackfoot tried to take it away from me, but I wouldn't let them. Cost me, though. I lost five men in as many fights and once my Chinese cook had to cut a three-inch iron arrowhead out of my thigh. I fought rustlers before there was any law in Dodge and hanged three of them."

The rancher opened his slicker and slid his holster around on the gun belt where it would be handy. "Those are my horses Lee Feeney stole. I reckon I'll stick."

"I never figured it otherwise, John," Matt said. He smiled. "You'll do."

"Just so you know," the rancher said.

The two riders topped the rise through a shifting wall of rain. There were only two men with the stolen horses, and as Matt had predicted, they were sheltering in the lee of the rock shelf. Both were drinking coffee, but they set their cups down and rose to their feet as the tall lawman and Farnborough drew closer.

When he was ten feet away, Matt drew rein. One of the outlaws was a youngster, and he'd already pulled his slicker away from his gun. The other man had a lot of hard years on him that showed in his heavily lined face, gray mustache and faded blue eyes.

"Howdy, boys." Matt smiled. "We're looking for a string of horses that wandered away from up on the Pawnee." The smile grew into a grin. "But I see you found them for us, and I'm much obliged to you."

It was the youngster who spoke. "Well, as to that you're mistaken, mister. See, these ponies belong to our boss, feller by the name of Lee Feeney, and he told me his ownself that he's took a real liking to them."

Moving his left hand slowly, Matt drew back his slicker and uncovered the star on his chest. "Mistakes happen," he said. "Now, if you'll just let me see a bill of sale, we'll be on our way."

The young outlaw's face was suddenly ugly. He tapped the handle of the holstered Colt on his thigh. "Lawman, this right here is our bill of sale." He sneered. "I know you put the run on ol' Lee and the Jicarilla Kid, but you sure as hell won't do that to me."

"Let it go, Sam'l," the older man said, his wary eyes on Matt. "I ain't planning to die for Lee Feeney."

"You scared, Lem?" the younger man jeered.

"Yeah, I am." He nodded in the direction of the marshal. "I've lived this long because I've learned to step wide around fellers like him."

Matt cleared his slicker from his gun. "Sam'l, is that your name?" he said to the youngster.

"Yeah, that's my name. Sam'l Brewster, out of the Red River country."

"Well, Sam'l Brewster," Matt said "you're a young man with your whole life in front of you, and that's why I'm giving you a chance. Now mount your pony, head back to the Red River and never show your face again in Kansas."

"Damned if I will," Brewster yelled, getting up his nerve. "I've killed three men and now I aim to make it four."

And he went for his gun.

Matt's first bullet hit the man square in the middle of the chest, his second, a heartbeat later, just an inch to the left of the first.

A surprised expression on his face, Brewster stood on his toes, his mouth gaping, and then fell facedown on the wet grass.

Matt's gun swung on the older man, who was standing stock-still, like a stone statue. "He called it," the marshal said, "after he was notified. You agree with that?"

The man called Lem gulped down the lump in his throat and nodded. "I didn't see it no different from what you say." He hesitated, then asked: "That offer to ride out of here apply to me?"

"It does. Take what grub you can find, then get up on your horse and light a shuck."

The man made to turn away, but Farnborough's voice stopped him. "How old are you, feller?"

"Near as I can figure, I'm crowding fifty."

"About the same age as me," the rancher said. "You ever work cattle?"

The outlaw managed a smile. "Did some o' that for ol' Charlie Goodnight. But it was a fair spell back."

"I need help getting my horses back to my place near the Pawnee and one of my hands just quit on me. You're getting too old to be on the dodge all the time. How do you feel about honest work for a change? Thirty a month, and I've got the best Chinaman cook in Kansas."

"Name's Lem Anderson, an' if it sets right with the marshal, I'd like to take you up on your offer. I've been thinking about settling down somewheres and sleeping under a roof for a change."

Matt shrugged. "If Mr. Farnborough wants to take a chance on you, I won't stand in the way."

"One thing, though, Lem," the rancher said. "Steal another horse from me and I'll hang you."

Anderson's laugh was good, ringing with genuine humor. "Boss, you can't say it any plainer than that."

Matt parted ways with Farnborough at the Arkansas; then he swung east toward Dodge. There was just no accounting for people, Matt decided as he rode through the teeming rain. He had always pegged John Farnborough as a hard, unforgiving man, yet the rancher must have seen something in Lem Anderson that was worth saving. Or maybe the fact that they were close to the same age had made the difference.

Either way, the marshal was glad every-

thing had turned out the way it had —
because if Anderson had even twitched after
the shooting started, he would have killed
him.

CHAPTER 17
MERCY — OR
MURDER?

Matt Dillon walked to his office along the mudspattered boardwalk, the great belly of the scowling sky flashing orange and scarlet as it rumbled thunder. It was still afternoon, but the alleys were dark, and the buildings along Front Street cast no shadows. The hanging signs outside the storefronts dripped rain, and their rusting iron chains creaked and groaned in the gnawing wind.

The brown rivers of mud oozing along the streets were constantly churned up by passing freight wagons, so they bubbled and squelched, smelling of manure and a cloying dankness.

Dodge was hunched and bleak, mantled by gray rain, as though the town was wearing a dingy mourning garment, attending a funeral for the summer sunshine and the glorious cattle season now long gone.

Matt's boots thudded on the boards, his spurs ringing, as he quickened his pace, needful of coffee and a warm stove.

"I say, Marshal, hold up!"

Matt stopped and turned to see Charles Granville hurrying toward him. The man smiled. "I've been trying to catch up to you, but those long legs of yours were leaving me behind."

Matt was suddenly irritable. He was finding it increasingly difficult to like the Englishman. "What is it?" he asked.

"I'd like to talk to you, if I may, Marshal. It's about Ed Flynn."

Rain cascaded off Matt's hat brim as he nodded. "Fine, but not out here. Come to the office."

Once inside, the marshal removed his slicker and hat. Normally he would also have hung his gun belt on the rack, but some sixth sense about Granville nagging at him, he draped the rig over his shoulder. The Englishman took off his tweed coat and deerstalker, the first time Matt had ever seen him without it. To his surprise Granville was nearly bald, with just a narrow fringe of curly brown hair around his head.

Matt stepped to the stove. Festus had left coffee on the boil, and the marshal lifted the pot and motioned with it to Granville: "Want some?"

"No, thank you, Marshal. I'm a tea drinker

myself."

"Well, I don't have any of that."

Matt motioned the Englishman into a chair at the desk and sat in the other. He noticed that the bulge of Granville's Colt in its shoulder holster showed under his tight-fitting jacket.

The Englishman slid his hand under the coat and Matt tensed. But Granville produced a silver cigar case. "Care for one?" he asked.

Matt shook his head.

"Mind if I do?"

"Go right ahead."

Granville lit his cigar, then said: "I tried to find you earlier, but you were gone. Out of town, I presume."

"I was running down some horse thieves, south of the river."

"Did you find them?"

Matt nodded. "The rancher has his string back."

"Any trouble?"

"Some. One of the rustlers got shot and the other got religion."

"Feeney's men, I take it."

"Yes, they were Feeney's men. I think he's trying to stir things up to make me hand Ed Flynn over to him."

For a moment Granville's face was lost

behind a cloud of blue smoke. "Poor Mr. Flynn," he said. "I visited him today, you know. He's not doing well."

"Oh," Matt was surprised. "Doc said he'd be up and about in a couple of days."

"He's still very weak. That wound took a lot out of him. He's no youngster, you know."

"Flynn is tough," Matt said. "He'll be able to ride soon. Doc Adams will see to that."

Granville was silent for a few moments, as though he was collecting his thoughts. Then he said finally: "From what I've heard, Mr. Flynn is a fascinating man. What can you tell me about him, Marshal?" The Englishman waved his cigar. "Purely for research purposes, you understand. I may want to make him the hero of an epic poem someday."

Matt shrugged. "What is there to tell? Flynn was just a kid when he killed his first man, and he's killed a sight more since. He hires out his gun to the highest bidder and he's not real particular about who he shoots, just so long as the money is good."

"Then he's an outlaw?"

"Not really. A lot of people think the men Ed Flynn killed needed killing. He has some specialties, like hiring out to big ranchers who need to get rid of nesters and gunning down the opposition in range wars. He has a reputation of being death on sheep men. I've heard that when the wives of sheepherders want to frighten their young'uns, they'll say, 'Ed Flynn will get you.' "

"Women and children, has he killed those?"

Matt's face was stiff. "When Flynn takes money to wipe out nesters or sheep men, he finishes the job."

"And the law can't touch him?"

"He's like Lee Feeney in that respect. When he's been brought to trial, he's always had some mighty expensive lawyers behind him. The big cattlemen's associations don't want to see their best range detective hang, and they have both money and influence." Matt smiled without humor. "I'd say Ed Flynn would hardly make a hero for your epic poem."

"Yet you protect him."

"He saved my life. I can't forget that."

Granville smoked in silence for a while, then said, as though he'd suddenly come to a realization: "Marshal, I know how you feel about Flynn, but when all is said and done, I believe the man adds to the lawlessness of the West and holds back the march of civilization."

Matt smiled. "He isn't much on schools

and churches, if that's what you mean."

"This land needs more of those, Marshal, schools and churches."

"Men like Ed Flynn are already a vanishing breed," Matt said. "His world is disappearing fast. The buffalo are almost gone and soon the Indians with them. I hear that in Texas and other places ranchers are fencing their ranges and around them sodbusters are plowing the prairie and building those schools and churches you want so badly. The old ways are going, Granville, and maybe men like Flynn and Festus Haggen and me are destined to go with them."

The big marshal got up, filled his coffee cup and returned to the desk. "Not much call for straight-shooting lawmen in a farming town with a church and a school."

"You're right. There will be no need because the country will be free of the likes of Lee Feeney and Ed Flynn. I say good riddance to them both."

"Is that why you killed the gut-shot man at Feeney's camp, Granville? Just because he was an outlaw? You know, in my book that was just a hop, skip and jump away from murder."

Granville threw back his bald head and laughed. "Marshal, surely you jest?"

Matt shook his head. "I don't joke about a killing, legal or otherwise."

"The man was dying, for heaven's sake. We couldn't carry him. All we could have done was ride away from there and let him scream for hours. That's a terrible fate for any man, to die alone in the dark with his belly on fire."

"Maybe so, Granville, but the one thing that bothered me that night was the look on your face. I believed you enjoyed killing that man."

The Englishman shrugged. "Enjoyed? No, not really. But then again, I don't plan to lose any sleep over one more dead outlaw."

Matt carefully laid his cup on the desk, then lifted cold blue eyes to Granville. "This isn't over. I mean about the man you shot. I'm going to study on it some, and later you and I will have more words."

"And what will you do, Marshal? Charge me with murder? You killed your man that night, just as I did."

"I know, but he was coming at me with a gun in his hand. He wasn't down and out of the fight."

Granville sighed and rose to his feet, his flushed face revealing a trace of anger. "Then do what you must. But you'll never find a jury to convict me."

"I know that," Matt said, "but I can run you out of town and clear out of Kansas."

The Englishman smiled. "Now that would be a very interesting situation indeed."

After Granville left, Matt thought about that statement. But no matter how he came at it, the implied meaning stayed the same.

It had been a threat.

Matt rapped on the door of Ed Flynn's room at the Dodge House, and the man yelled: "Come in!"

When the marshal stepped inside, Flynn eased down the hammer of the Colt in his hand and laid it on the bedside table. "Oh, it's you," he said. "I figured it might have been Feeney or one of his men."

"How are you feeling?" Matt asked. "Do you need anything?"

Flynn shook his head. "The desk clerk brings me all I need: my grub, whiskey and the newspaper. I read where old Queen Vic is ailing, but I don't know about that." The gunfighter's hard eyes lifted to Matt's. "I don't reckon you're really interested in my health, any more than I'm interested in Queen Vic's misery."

"I need to know when you'll be fit to ride, Ed. I want to get you out of Dodge."

"Throwing me to the wolves, huh?"

"No, I gave you my word I wouldn't do that. Horse Thief Canyon is about half a day's ride, maybe less. You can stay there until I deal with Feeney, or he gives up and heads back to the Nations."

Flynn raised the pillow behind him and sat higher in the bed. "The desk clerk told me he heard you had a run-in with Feeney's men this morning. Gunned a couple, he says."

"I killed one of them. He'd been notified but went for his gun anyway."

"You're whittling them down. There can't be many of them left."

"There's enough, and even by themselves, Feeney and the Jicarilla Kid are no bargain."

The gunfighter nodded. "I'd heard about that breed before all this trouble happened. He made a name for himself right after he killed Windy Sinclair down Austin way. Windy was fast with his Remingtons and had killed his share. Right about then I should have tracked down the damned Kid and put a bullet into him. Might have saved you and me a world of grief."

"Getting back to it, when can you ride?"

Flynn moved his position in the bed and winced. "My back's still punishing me some, but I reckon I'll be able to fork my bronc tomorrow morning."

"I'll saddle your horse and meet you outside the hotel at first light," Matt said. "I'll sack up coffee and grub for a week."

"Maybe we should just go after them, Matt," Flynn said. "How many are left?"

"With Feeney and the Kid, maybe eight. That's more than we can handle."

"Then we can whittle 'em down some more."

Matt shook his head. "There's been enough killing already. I want to settle this thing without leaving more dead men behind me."

"Getting a conscience?" Flynn asked, a slight sneer on his lips.

"You can call it that." Something that Granville had said popped into Matt's head. "Ed, have you ever lived within the sound of a church bell?"

"Hell, no, never in my life."

Matt smiled. "I thought not."

CHAPTER 18
RIDERS FOR THE BRAND

Of all people, it was Doc Holliday and Kate Elder who first saw the dead man.

Holliday, gambler pale with deep black shadows under his eyes and in the hollows of his cheeks, was using a cane to support his frail weight, with Kate's substantial arm around his waist as they made their way along the boardwalk to the Long Branch.

"Doc says he'd never seen such a thing in all his born days, Matthew," Festus said. "I mean a dead man riding into Dodge at midnight."

Matt buttoned into his slicker, settled his hat on his head and followed his deputy from the office. It was not raining as hard, but the thunder was fierce, exploding like dynamite in a sky aflame from horizon to horizon.

Despite the weather, a crowd had gathered outside the saloon, and Matt saw Holliday, dressed in an ankle-length black oilskin and sou'wester, telling anyone who would listen that Kate was quite undone by nerves and shock.

A man sat his horse at the hitching rail, hatless, looking unnaturally upright and stiff in the saddle. He also seemed vaguely familiar.

Matt plodded through deep mud and stepped to the rider's side. The man was propped up by a framework of branches across his shoulders and back and his eyes were wide open, but he was seeing nothing. A bullet, fired at close range, had blown away most of the left side of his skull, but not before he'd been tortured by fire and a knife.

Even contorted in death as they were, the man's lined features were unmistakable.

It was Lem Anderson.

"Look at his mouth, Marshal," Doc Holliday said. "It seems like something is stuffed in there."

Anderson's cheeks were puffed, his mouth open, and Matt saw what looked like crumpled paper shoved behind his teeth, into his throat.

Matt called out to a couple of the onlookers and told them to help him get the man off his horse. "We'll carry him inside," he said.

Thunder crashed, and in the glare of lightning, the marshal and the others lifted Anderson out of the saddle and into the saloon. They laid the dead man out on a table. Matt was aware of Kitty's horrified face as she watched from behind the bar.

Holliday stood close to Matt, rain running off his oilskins, and inclined his head as he studied the body. "I don't know him." He glanced around at the dozen or so men who were clustered around the table. "Any of you boys recognize him?"

Before anyone could respond, Matt said: "I know him."

Gingerly, the marshal removed the paper from Anderson's mouth, watched intently by Holliday and the other men. Kitty had stepped closer and she looked down at the dead man sprawled across the table, then at Matt.

"Who would do such a thing?" she asked.

His face grim, Matt answered. "I have a feeling we're going to find out."

He carefully spread out the damp paper in his hands. It was a page from a tally book, stained with blood and smudged by the rain, but the words were easy to read.

THIS IS WHAT HAPPENS TO TRAITORS.
SEND OUT FLYNN OR THERE WILL BE

A LOT WORSE TO COME.

The note was unsigned, but it could only have come from Lee Feeney. Matt walked to the door of the saloon. Behind him he heard an excited babble of conversation as Doc Holliday grabbed the paper and eagerly shared its contents with Kitty and the other men.

He stepped outside into the storm and looked through the rain to the bottom of Front Street. Feeney must have brought Anderson close, then let his horse loose. If it is unfamiliar with its surroundings, a frightened horse will walk toward people for the comfort and reassurance they bring, and the only people it saw on the street were Doc and Kate.

Beyond the last buildings, out there somewhere in the darkness, Feeney and his men were near. Matt could sense their closeness. But to go after them would be pointless. He would never find them in the gloom, and he might even invite an ambusher's bullet.

The door opened and Kitty stepped beside the Marshal, shivering slightly in her low-cut dress. "I just ordered a drink on the house," she said. "Those boys need it with a dead man lying there. What did they do to him?"

"Looks like he's been cut up and burned," Matt answered. "Feeney has an Apache breed with him and he knows how to make a man scream for a long time."

"Oh, Matt, that's just horrible."

Rain was trickling down Kitty's naked shoulders, and Matt held her close. "We'd better get you inside," he said. "You'll catch a cold for sure."

Festus was at the bar, enjoying Kitty's generosity, and Matt told him to drink up and find the undertaker.

Percy Crump appeared a few minutes later, looking like a bedraggled crow in a black tailcoat and collarless shirt. "Is this the deceased?" he asked.

"Do you see any other dead men?" Doc Holliday snapped, a glass of whiskey to his pale lips. The gambler had no liking for Crump, being himself closer to the attentions of an undertaker than most men.

"Oh dear, oh dear," Crump fussed, wringing his hands. "This one won't be easy, oh dear, no."

"Just bury him, Percy," Matt said, suddenly weary. "You don't have to make him look good."

"And the bill —"

"To the city as usual," the marshal said. "Mark it to the attention of Mayor Kelley."

Matt had one more task for Festus. He told him to go to the Dodge House and tell Ed Flynn that their ride to the canyon would have to wait. Before then he had to find out what had happened to John Farnborough . . . His wife had left a candle burning in the window for him.

The darkness of night had just begun to flee the day when Matt Dillon rode up on the bend of the Arkansas where he had left Farnborough and Anderson with the horse herd.

The rain had stopped, but the sky was the color of gunmetal and the wind blowing from the north held a chill. Stretching away from the marshal lay miles of flat grassland, green from the rain, here and there old buffalo wallows showing streaks of brown across their muddy bottoms. Low clouds hung close to the ground, veiling the way ahead, so that no horizon was in sight. Horse and rider moved silently through a tunnel of mist that shrouded their shape with shifting ribbons of gray.

After an hour, Matt rode between streams running off the lower reaches of the Pawnee, scattered cottonwoods and willows growing along their banks and further away wild plum and yucca.

He saw no sign of Farnborough.

The rain started again, spattering against Matt's slicker, and the bay showed its annoyance at being far from its dry barn by tossing its head, the bit jangling loud in the quiet.

The marshal patted the horse's neck, his eyes trying to penetrate the cheerless gloom ahead, a slate gray curtain of mist and rain that revealed nothing.

He rode on. Ten minutes later Matt topped a low rise and looked down into a sloping pasture of grama grass, streaked with bands of yellow wildflowers. It was a field of bones.

As far as the eye could see, the bleached skeletons of buffalo lay where they had been shot and skinned by hunters, the horned skulls gleaming wet in the rain like white boulders.

Matt sat his horse and estimated that at least sixty buffalo had been killed here several years before. The robes had been taken, and maybe a few of the tongues, but the huge bodies of the animals had been left to rot.

It was a silent place, the only sound the rustle of wind and the fall of the rain, a hushed requiem for the buffalo that had once roamed these plains in the millions.

A small sadness in him, Matt knew that their like would never be seen again, not in his lifetime or in any other.

He urged his horse down the slope, the bay picking its way fastidiously between pale rib cages and skulls. The ground leveled out again and Matt saw the tops of cottonwoods ahead of him through the mist. The rain had grown heavier, driven by a wind blowing cold and far from the icy rim of the earth, and a long distance away thunder rolled.

Head down, Matt rode among the trees by the edge of the creek, grateful for their meager shelter. He swung around a willow growing from the bank and just ahead of him he caught a glimpse of red in the undergrowth.

Matt stepped out of the saddle and drew his gun. On cat feet he walked toward the spot, his thumb on the hammer of the Colt. A man lay there, dressed in a tan-colored slicker, a red bandanna around his neck. The body was sprawled and undignified in death, the face ashen, turned upward to the teeming rain.

John Farnborough had been shot several times, all of the wounds in his chest. His gun was still clutched in his stiff fingers, evidence of a draw that had been way too slow.

Matt kneeled beside the rancher and put the back of his hand against the man's cheek. But the skin was cold and all the life that had been in John Farnborough was gone.

Matt saw the candle glowing in the ranch house window when he was still a ways off.

A bearded man standing in the door of the bunkhouse watched the marshal ride closer, then noticed the burden he was carrying on the back of his horse. Heedless of the rain, he ran toward Matt, calling out over his shoulder to others in the bunkhouse to join him.

"It's John," the marshal said as the bearded man stopped at his stirrup. "He's dead."

Three other hands had gathered around the bay, and now the four men lifted Farnborough's body from the horse and laid him gently on the ground. For the first time, they saw the bullet wounds.

"Who did this?" The eyes the bearded man lifted to Matt were cold as death.

"An outlaw named Lee Feeney," Matt answered, "and others."

"I've heard that name. Why would he kill

the boss, a decent man?"

"Decent doesn't enter into Feeney's thinking. He killed John because he wanted to prove to me what a bad man he is."

The ranch house door swung open, and a tall, thin woman with her hair pulled back in a severe bun stepped outside. Her dress was soon soaked as she walked through the pounding rain and stopped beside Matt.

"Is my man dead?" Jean Farnborough asked, her face as unmoving and pale as marble.

"Yes, ma'am," Matt said, touching his hat. "He was shot not far from here by the outlaw Lee Feeney and his men."

The woman nodded, a tremble on her lips. "Boys," she said, in a soft Irish brogue, "bring John inside and later I'll be washing his poor body." Her eyes lifted to Matt, who was still sitting his saddle. "Marshal Dillon, you'll be needful of coffee and a bait to eat. Step down and come into the house."

Matt followed the woman into the house, a long, low structure with a shingle roof and a porch in front. Inside, the place was spotless, the pine floor scrubbed, the rough wooden furniture buffed and polished to the color of old honey. An upright piano stood against one wall and there was a fine table in the middle of the floor, obviously

185

brought from somewhere back east when she and her husband had first settled on the plains.

Feeling big and awkward, as though he was taking up too much space in the room, Matt stood with his hat in his hands as Mrs. Farnborough cleared the table of knick-knacks.

"Take off his coat and lay him out on the table," she told the hands as they carried the body inside. "I'll do what needs to be done later. It would be himself who would take a stick to me if I didn't see the marshal fed first."

"Ma'am, there's no need for that," Matt said. "You need time to be alone."

The woman walked past him and blew out the candle. "The light is gone, Marshal," she said. "And the darkness will come soon enough. Now come into the kitchen."

"Miz Farnborough," the bearded man said, "should me and the boys saddle up?"

"You know your duty, Bob Murray. Is there any need for me to be reminding you of it?"

"No, ma'am, there isn't." Murray turned to the other hands, three men younger than he, typical tough, capable punchers. "Let's go, boys. We're riding."

"Bob Murray," the woman said, stopping

the man in his tracks, "come back riding your horse or draped over it, but don't fail to see that the reckoning has been paid."

The man called Murray touched his hat, his face grim. "As you say, Miz Farnborough. Just as you say."

Matt did not try to stop the men from going after Feeney, knowing that if he'd tried, they would not have listened.

The four punchers rode for the brand and their boss had been murdered. It was a point of honor that they avenge his death. They were following a tradition that dated back centuries to the armored and belted men who ate and slept in their lord's hall and vowed their allegiance only to him. For Farnborough's hands to have broken with that unwritten law would have been unthinkable.

Her back straight and stiff, Jean Farnborough watched from the window until her men were lost in mist and rain; then she turned to Matt.

"Marshal," she said, "there's coffee on the stove and an Irish stew I was keeping warm for himself. He knows you brought him home and he'll want you to have it."

Chapter 19
The Guns of
Ed Flynn

Matt Dillon angled across the rain-swept plains toward Dodge. He had seen no sign of other riders. The morning was gone and it was now well into afternoon but the light across the flat land had not changed. The day was still dreary and sunless and nothing moved in that vast wilderness but the rain and the wind.

The marshal turned in the saddle and watched as the three o'clock train out of Dodge rattled along the Santa Fe track, the locomotive belching black smoke. He kept his eyes on the train until it rounded a curve and the red lights of the caboose disappeared into the misty distance.

Alone again with his thoughts, Matt wondered where Feeney would strike next. The outlaw was rapidly upping the ante and his chips were dead men. He was trying to make Matt fold and throw him Ed Flynn, and bitterly the marshal realized that in

John Farnborough a man far better than Flynn had already been sacrificed. How many more decent men would have to die to save a man who was not worth saving?

As the day began to shade into evening, Matt saw the lights of Dodge appear through the gloom, and he urged the bay into a trot.

He had one last question for himself: In trying to save Flynn's life, was it his honor at stake or just his stubborn pride?

The marshal had no immediate answer, but with the killing of Farnborough weighing heavy on him, he vowed that no one else would die because of Flynn.

When Matt reached Front Street, he saw a crowd gathered at the front of the Dodge House. To his relief, Festus was there, talking to the desk clerk.

"Big happenings, Matthew," Festus said when the marshal swung out of the saddle. "Ol' Ed just bedded down two of Feeney's men."

Matt's eyes swept around the crowd — mostly early diners from across the tracks — the black umbrellas that mushroomed over their heads dripping rain. Ed Flynn was leaning in the hotel doorway, his thumbs tucked into his gun belts. He had a slight smile on his face, as if bemused by what was going on around him, though he seemed to be reveling in the wary looks from the men and the speculative glances of the women, measuring the famous gladiator from under fringed eyelids.

"What happened, Festus?" Matt asked, unwilling to talk to Flynn just yet.

"Well, the way Ed tells it, when you didn't meet him this morning, he decided to stay out of bed, anyhow. Then, about half an hour ago, he went down to the dining room for a bite to eat.

"Two men wearing slickers and mighty mean expressions walked in a couple of minutes later. They asked him if he was a low-down, murdering skunk by the name of Flynn. When Ed said he was and what of it, the two said they had a present from Lee Feeney and drawed down on him." Festus shrugged. "Matthew, they hadn't even cleared leather when Ed put a bullet into both of them — then two more just to make certain."

"Anybody hurt in the dining room from flying lead?" Matt asked.

The deputy shook his head. "Not a one. Ed generally hits what he's shooting at."

Matt nodded. "I'll go take a look inside, then talk to Flynn."

"I'll put up your hoss, Matthew," Festus

said. "He looks beat and, come to that, so do you."

Matt shrugged off his deputy's concern and said: "Switch my saddle to one of Moss Grimmick's rental horses and bring it back here," Matt said. "And bring along Flynn's mount."

"You ridin' again, Matthew?" Festus asked, surprised.

Matt nodded. "Yeah. Mr. Flynn is leaving town."

As the marshal edged past Flynn in the hotel doorway, the gunfighter said: "It was a fair fight, Matt. Maybe twenty people saw it and they'll tell it that way."

Matt ignored the man and stepped into the empty dining room.

The bodies of two men lay sprawled on the bloody floor near a table against the back wall. A skinny towhead still had a gun in his hand. The other's Colt had dropped from his fingers and was lying a few feet away from him. Both had wounds in the chest, and the towhead had also been shot low in the belly. The blue death shadows were already gathering on their ashen faces, but they had the hard-bitten look of gunmen who had been in shooting scrapes before and had killed their man.

It had obviously been self-defense as

Flynn claimed. A half-smoked cigarette and cup of coffee still lay on the table where he'd been sitting.

As Matt left the dining room, he met the desk clerk. "Better send for Percy Crump," he said. "And tell those people outside they'd best find another place to eat. It's a mess in there."

As the white-faced clerk left to find the undertaker, Matt stepped beside Flynn, who was still in the doorway, standing lean, tough and watchful. The man turned cold, insolent eyes on the marshal, tinged with something that could have been dislike.

"You read it," the man said. "Didn't it happen like I told you?"

"Seems that way." Matt nodded to where Festus was walking across the street toward them, leading the horses. "I'm getting you out of town tonight."

Anger flaring in him, Flynn jerked his head in the direction of the dining room. "Hell, because of that?"

"There were people in there when the shooting started," Matt said. "One of them could have caught a bullet."

"But nobody did."

"I know, but somebody else did, a rancher named John Farnborough, a man I knew and liked. Lee Feeney and his boys killed him."

"And you're blaming me for that?"

"Yes, I'm blaming you, Ed. If you'd never ridden into town John Farnborough would right now be hale and hearty, dozing off a meal of Irish stew." His blue eyes hard, the marshal added: "The cost of keeping you alive is getting way too high. That's why you're heading out of Dodge right now."

"You mean to go to that Horse Thief Canyon place you've been talking about?"

"I'm taking you there now, Ed. If I was you, I'd hole up there for a week and then ride on. Maybe by then I'll have arrested Feeney for John Farnborough's murder."

"And if you haven't?"

"Then you're on your own."

"What about that debt you owe me?"

"Ed," Matt said, his voice edged by his own anger, "I reckon John Farnborough paid that debt for me with his life. You never knew him, but he was a fine, upstanding man and a brave man." Then, cold as ice: "Ed, I grieve for his dying because he was worth any number of you."

The gunfighter looked like he'd been punched in the belly. "Now I know how things are with you."

Matt nodded, no give in him. "That's how

things are. And this much I know: I won't have anyone else die to save your sorry hide."

Flynn elbowed off the doorway, his face like thunder. "Then I'll need coffee and grub, tobacco and whiskey."

"I'll bring them out to you tomorrow, or send Festus. Don't worry. You won't starve."

"Damn you," Flynn said. "I feel like I'm being run out of town."

"You are, Ed," Matt said. "I just wish I'd done it the day you rode in here."

While Flynn went to his room to pick up his slicker and his other belongings, Matt stepped beside Festus. The two stood in the pouring rain, and the deputy's uneasy eyes were on Matt's face.

"Out with it, Festus," Matt said. "You got something stuck in your craw."

"Just you be careful out there, Matthew," the deputy said. "I seen ol' Ed's face an' he's an angry man. An angry man who shoots as good as him is a thing to be reckoned with."

"Had that very thought my ownself, Festus." The marshal smiled. "But then, Ed needs me. Otherwise he won't get his grub and whiskey."

Matt and Ed Flynn rode out of Dodge in

darkness. The rain had stopped for now and the clouds had parted, unveiling a hollow moon surrounded by a halo of pale pink. The wind was rising, blowing hard and cold, stirring the bluestem and Indian grass that in places grew to a height of five feet.

Flynn riding close behind him, the marshal rode into Duck Creek, splashed through shallow water for a mile or so, following the bed of the creek east, then climbed out and headed north again.

He doubted that he and Flynn had been seen leaving town and were being followed, but several times he drew rein and checked his back trail, listening for sounds. He heard nothing but the wind and the creak of his own saddle.

Saw Log Creek lay ahead of him; then he and Flynn must cross six miles of flat, open country before fetching up to the canyon.

Wishful for coffee but having none, Matt gave the paint its head, loping into a wall of blackness, only here and there touched by moonlight. Riding in icy silence, Flynn stayed close, his rangy palouse easily matching the speed of the paint.

A careful man, the marshal rode down into the bed of the Saw Log and followed the creek east for a couple miles, as he had done at Duck Creek. Finally he rode out of the creek and swung to the northwest. After a mile or so, he came upon a wild-horse trail and followed it until the narrow path ended at a small blue lake bordered by a few willows and cottonwoods.

Here Matt and Flynn watered their horses. The gap in the clouds had closed and the rain started again, kicking up startled Vs of water all over the surface of lake.

Ignoring the baleful presence of Flynn, the marshal, who had once spent much time in lonely places, turned his face to the rain, enjoying its sweet, clean fragrance, like the newly washed hair of a beautiful woman. He remembered that Kitty's hair smelled like that, like rain falling on wildflowers, and the memory of it made him smile.

"We riding or we going to sit here and grin all night?" Flynn asked, his face surly in the gloom.

"Not a patient man, are you, Ed?" Matt asked in turn. But he gathered up the reins of the paint and swung away from the lake.

The marshal rode up on the Horse Thief from the south. Sentinel Rock, a tall spire of weathered sandstone, marked the entrance to the canyon, red cedar and a few stunted wild oaks growing at its base.

Reining in the paint, Matt sat his saddle for a few moments and thoughtfully studied the dark-shadowed canyon. The rocky walls were steep, roughly cut, haphazardly shaped by rain and wind. In places, large sections of cliff had broken away by water seepage and its seasonal freezing and thawing.

Grass, mostly buffalo and grama, grew on top of the rusty brown-and-gray canyon walls and beyond its entrance the slanting shadows were black as pitch. There was no sound but the relentless rattle of the rain and the rustle of the wind.

"Not much of a home sweet home, is it?" Flynn asked, his voice loud and disgusted in the quiet.

"No, but that's why you'll be safe here," Matt answered. "Lee Feeney could ride for a month and never find this place."

The marshal kneed the paint forward, the little horse tossing its head, not liking the darkness. Matt rode into the canyon, Flynn behind him, under a sky that was again erupting into thunder.

Steep walls rose on either side of the two riders. There were shallow pools scattered around the canyon floor, many of them noisy with croaking bullfrogs. When lightning flashed, Matt caught sight of the tracks of deer and coyote, but it looked like no humans had been here for a long time.

Just a few years before, the canyon had

been a watering hole for buffalo, but now that the great shaggies were gone, deer and antelope had moved in to take their place.

Two hundred yards into the canyon, Matt found what he'd been looking for: a shallow opening to his left, about four feet above the canyon floor. A few scattered boulders that had fallen from the wall above lay close and gave easy access to the cave.

Matt turned in the saddle and said to Flynn: "You'll be sheltered from the wind and rain in there and be snug enough. If you want a fire, there's wood lying around in the cedar breaks near the canyon entrance and grazing enough for your horse."

In the gloom the marshal watched the man's eyes lift to the cave. "I have to spend a week in there, like an animal?" Flynn asked

Matt shrugged. "That's up to you, Ed. You could ride on, but no matter what direction you choose, you're liable to run into Feeney. Now I've got a charge of murder to hold him on, I'd suggest you wait until I make the arrest."

Lightning flashed within the canyon and the marshal caught Flynn's eye. "Feeney is down to the Jicarilla Kid and maybe a couple other men. You could get lucky and outgun them."

Flynn spoke again and Matt caught the bitterness in his voice. "You don't know the Kid. He's rattlesnake-fast with a six-gun. Maybe a few years ago, I could have shaded him, but now I'm not so sure."

"Odd words coming from you, Ed," Matt said, surprised.

"A man gets older, slows down some. I'm still plenty fast . . . faster than you and most other men, but that breed has me worried."

"Then stay here. I'll get grub out to you tomorrow."

"Seems like I don't have much choice."

Matt swung his horse around, but Flynn's voice stopped him. "Matt, remember what I told you. When all this is over, we'll meet again as enemies. You didn't do right by me, and I won't forget that."

"I did right by you, Ed," the marshal said. "I just realized quite recently that sometimes the man isn't worth the bill that has to be paid."

"Your words cut deep, Matt," Flynn said, hollow-voiced from the darkness. "And one day I'll surely remember and kill you for them."

Chapter 20
Bob Murray Takes
a Prisoner

It was still full dark when Matt Dillon rode into Dodge. He put up the paint, then went back to his office, stretched out on a cot in one of the cells and gratefully let sleep take him.

The changing light woke him. Matt lay on his back for a while, staring at the timber ceiling, listening to the morning sounds Festus always made, the shuffle of his booted feet and the clang of coffeepot meeting stove.

The sleep had refreshed Matt, and he finally swung his feet off the cot and stretched.

"Morning, Matthew," Festus said, carrying a cup of coffee in one hand and a sandwich in the other. "Brung you this. I had it made up at Ma's Kitchen," he said. "Bacon and a fried egg on fresh baked sourdough." The deputy's left eyebrow crawled up his forehead. "Miss Kitty asked me last night if'n you was eatin' reg'lar an' I said I reckoned you were missing your last three meals and she said come mornin' I was to get you breakfast an' see that you ate it."

But Matt had no problem on that score. The smell of the bacon made him realize he was ravenously hungry, and he ate quickly and in an appreciative silence.

He picked up a crumb that had fallen on his knee, popped it in his mouth and said: "That was real good, Festus. Thanks."

"Thank Miss Kitty, Matthew. She was the one who tole me to make sure you had some grub."

"Talking about grub, can you sack up some supplies for Ed Flynn and take them out to Horse Thief Canyon? And he wants tobacco and whiskey."

"Demanding kind of feller, ol' Ed, ain't he? Who's gonna foot the bill, Matthew?"

"I can't charge it to the mayor, so I guess it will have to be me."

For a few moments, Festus was silent as he tried to dab a loop on the thoughts running around his head. Then he said finally: "While Ed is safe out there at the canyon, you plan on going out after Feeney an' them?"

Matt nodded. "I aim to charge all of them

with the murder of John Farnborough."

"You mean arrest them?"

"That's my notion."

Festus shook his head. "Mathew, Lee Feeney won't stand to be arrested, and neither will the Jicarilla Kid."

"It's their call. I'll bring them in dead or alive."

"I heard that the Kid is good with a gun, maybe the best there is."

"Who told you that?"

"Ol' Charlie Granville. He says the Kid is pizen mean and real fast on the draw."

"Granville talks too much," Matt said, "even for a poet."

"He talks about bein' a poet all the time, but I've never seen him write a poem," Festus said, his face wrinkled in thought. He shook his head as though clearing his mind and said: "Matthew, John Farnborough was a highly respected man. You can round up a posse and go after Feeney. You'd get all kind of volunteers."

"I know that, Festus. But chances are that more good men would die. I have to go this alone."

"You an' me, you mean."

Matt smiled. "Old-timer, that goes without saying."

"Just so you know, Matthew," the deputy

said, pleased.

Around ten, Festus left for the canyon, and thirty minutes later, in a driving rain, Jean Farnborough's hands rode up to the marshal's office. They were a soaked, dispirited-looking bunch, but they had a prisoner with them, a sullen man with a sweeping mustache who had his hands tied to the saddle horn.

Matt stepped to the door and opened it wide, rain spattering against him. Bob Murray, bearded and grim, untied his prisoner and shoved him onto the boardwalk and then toward the door.

"Caught this one making a run for it, Marshal," Murray said. "He says his name is Chris Pierce and that he's one of Feeney's men. I was going to hang him right away, but he has a story to tell I thought you mought want to hear."

"Glad you didn't hang him," Matt said, ushering the men inside. "You'd be breaking the law, Murray."

The foreman shrugged. "Right, like I've never done that before."

The captured outlaw was in his midthirties, not much above medium height, with hard gray eyes that spoke of a close association with violence and death probably dating back to the War Between the States. He showed little fear, but he was watchful and silent, letting events come to him.

Matt decided to hit the man hard to try to unbalance him. His voice cold, he said: "I plan to charge you with the murder of a rancher named John Farnborough and one Lem Anderson. You'll get a fair trial and then I'll hang you." Matt hesitated a heartbeat, then added: "Any questions?"

The outlaw shifted uneasily on his feet as fingers of rain ran down his slicker and pooled on the floor. "I liked Lem and I had nothing to do with his death. It was Lee who ordered a drumhead court-martial and then sentenced him to be tortured and shot. It was the Kid who pulled the trigger on him, but that was after a long, long while."

"And John Farnborough?" Matt prompted.

"That was all Lee and the Kid's doing. When he tried to stop the breed torturing Lem, they both shot into him, said it would be a lesson to you. I mean when you found him dead, like. Lee wants you to give him the man who gunned his brother and the need to kill him is driving him half crazy. He's got it all planned on how the breed will keep Flynn alive for days while they work on him."

"So you admit you were there, but you had nothing to do with the killing of Farnborough or Anderson?" Matt asked.

"That's about the size of it."

"Somehow I find that real hard to believe."

Pierce's eyes were direct on the marshal's. "I admit I'm no saint. In the past I've gunned my share and never gave any of them a second thought. But I liked Lem Anderson, liked him just fine. One time him and me, we bunked together for a month in a line shack when we were riding for Charlie Goodnight."

"Did you like John Farnborough just fine?"

"I didn't know the man. If Lee had told me to shoot him, I would have done it. But it didn't happen that way. What I've told you is the truth."

Anger stained Murray's brown cheeks scarlet. "I knowed I should have hung you when I had the chance."

Matt let that go and asked: "Pierce, where were you headed when Murray here found you?"

"I was riding for the Nations. Me and another man by the name of Burns pulled out late last night — figured we'd had enough. When all this started, there were twenty of us, and now with Feeney and the

205

Kid, we're down to four. Burns said he was riding clear to the Nueces, where the climate was healthier, and maybe he got away clean. I don't know." The outlaw's eyes lifted to Matt. "Lawman, you've sure played hob."

"It was Feeney's doing," Matt said.

"And Ed Flynn's," the outlaw said.

"Pierce, if I charge you as an accessory to murder, you may not get the rope, but I guarantee for twenty years you'll be breaking big rocks into smaller rocks at the state penitentiary in Lansing. That is, if you don't end up in some hell in the Louisiana swamps."

For the first time, it looked like the outlaw had begun to realize the harsh fate that awaited him in the living death of a penitentiary. There was a wildness in his eyes that might have been panic as he said: "Twenty years in the big pasture is a hell of a thing for a man. Can you set me down easier, Marshal?"

Murray laughed. "All some badmen need is to be scared good and hard and they go back to being virtuous real quick."

"Lansing is a place to scare a man," Matt said. His cold eyes fell on Pierce. "Get up in court and testify against Lee Feeney and the Jicarilla Kid at their murder trial. I'm not promising anything, but do that and I'll try and get your sentence reduced."

Pierce's eyes were suddenly shuttered as he thought about the good and bad of what the big lawman had just offered him. Matt stepped in to help him decide.

"Take it or leave it," he said, a finality in his voice.

Dumbly, Pierce nodded, his chin on his chest. "I don't have much choice, do I?"

"Not much at all," Matt said.

The outlaw looked around him. "If Lee gets word that I aim to testify against him, he'll come looking for me. This two-by-twice jail won't stop him."

"You'll be protected," the marshal said. "I'll have someone here on guard at all times."

"He better be faster than the Jicarilla Kid — that's all I'm saying," Pierce said. "And I don't know anybody who is."

After Matt locked up Pierce, he stood on the boards in the rain, watching as Murray and his three young punchers swung into the saddle. When Murray was mounted, the marshal said: "If you find Feeney and the Kid, don't try to shoot it out. Just burn the breeze back here for help."

The foreman grinned in his beard. "Hell, there's just two o' them and four o' us."

"And four isn't near enough," Matt said.

CHAPTER 21
MATT IS HIT HARD

By early afternoon the rain was still falling heavily, and to Mayor Kelley's dismay, flooding had become a problem in Dodge.

Front Street looked like a sluggish brown river. Across the tracks, where the ground was lower, water had reached the porches of some of the houses. A sinkhole opened up behind the Alamo saloon, swallowing a brewery wagon, and down by the rail depot, floodwater had reached the second boards of the cattle pens.

There were drips from the roofs of every home, saloon and store in town, and Matt had placed buckets all over the office floor. They were already three-quarters full, the steady *plink-plink-plink* sounding like a badly tuned banjo.

Pierce complained bitterly about a drip falling onto his cot and Matt moved him to another cell. To the outlaw's disgust, his new accommodation offered little improvement.

Festus stepped into the office, bringing with him an angled sheet of rain. He pushed the door against the buffeting wind and finally got it shut.

"Ain't fit weather for man nor beast, Matthew," he said as he hung up his coat and slicker. "An' I'm sure hankering for a cup of hot coffee."

As his deputy poured himself coffee, Matt asked: "How is Flynn?"

Festus shrugged. "Madder'n heck about being stuck out there. He said for you to get ol' Lee quicker'n scat, an' the Jicarilla Kid even faster. He's sure spooked by that Kid. Says he's a devil."

"Anybody follow you out there?" Matt asked.

Festus took a seat at the desk and shook his head. "I don't think so. I checked my back trail a time or three, but with all this rain, it was hard to tell. A man could have an army riding behind an' never catch sight of it. Matthew, I swear I rode through thunderclouds that were squattin' right down on the grass, lightning flashing all around me an' Ruth. Scared us both out of a year's growth, I declare."

Thunder rolled across the sky and Matt waited until it was over before he said: "We have a prisoner. One of Feeney's men, a hardcase who calls himself Chris Pierce. John Farnborough's hands brought him in, said they caught him hightailing it for the Nations. He was real lucky he wasn't hung."

"Ol' Lee's boys quittin' him, Matthew?"

"The two that were left, Pierce and another man. Now there's only Feeney and the Kid out there." Matt rose, poured himself coffee and added: "I plan to charge Feeney and the Kid with the murders of John Farnborough and Lem Anderson. Pierce agreed to testify against them in return for a lighter sentence as an accessory to murder."

"Sure hope ol' Lee don't get wind o' that," Festus said.

Matt smiled. "So does Pierce."

Festus got to his feet and walked back to the cells. He returned after a few moments and said: "That hardcase is sure draggin' his tail feathers, Matthew. Looks downright glum to me."

"He's got reason to be. Whichever way the pickle squirts, he knows he's looking at some hard time in Lansing when this is over."

Festus whistled through his teeth. "I guess that don't do anything to sweeten a man's disposition. Knowed a feller one time who did three years in Lansing for bank robbery, said he'd taken a long ride into hell. Changed his ways when he got out, and last I heard, he was prospering in the hardware business an' teachin' in Sunday school."

Thunder slammed and the office was lit by a flash of lightning. Matt drained the last of his coffee and rose to his feet. "I have to be making my rounds, Festus. Mayor Kelley says he's real concerned about flooding and asked me to take a look at the worst of it. He says if the rain keeps up the town will have to change its name to Lake Dodge."

The deputy threw an uncertain glance to the streaming window and said halfheartedly: "Want me to come with you, Matthew?"

"No, you stay here and guard the prisoner. I don't plan on being long." Matt suddenly thought of something. "Has Doc Holliday left town yet?"

Festus shook his head. "Nah, Matthew, ol' Doc has took right poorly again, and him just startin' to feel better. He says this wet weather is a misery on his lungs, an' if'n he don't bite the ground this time, it will be a miracle, and that's what Kate says as well."

"Keep an eye on him, Festus. When he's back on his feet I want him out of Dodge."

"I'll do that, Matthew, but the way ol' Doc's hackin' an' coughin', I don't rightly know when that will be."

"The sooner the better," Matt said, his distaste for Holliday evident in his scowl.

For a few minutes, Matt stood and watched the efforts of a half dozen men and a mule skinner and his team as they tried to pull the brewery wagon out of the sinkhole behind the Alamo. For some reason, an old Chinese man in an oilskin cape was running around yelling advice. But since he spoke in a language they couldn't understand, nobody paid him any heed.

The straining mules were slipping and sliding in the mud and couldn't get any traction. Matt suggested somebody bring some straw from the livery stable and scatter it under their feet.

The old Chinese, who seemed to understand English better than he pretended, ran in the direction of the stable. He returned with an armful of straw, then another.

After the straw was scattered around the mules, the animals again strained in their collars at the urging of the cursing mule skinner. Slowly the wagon creaked inch by inch out of the hole. When it was once again standing on its four wheels, the mule skinner touched his ragged cloth cap to Matt.

"Obliged to ye, Marshal," the man said.

"The straw was a good idea."

Matt nodded to the Chinaman. "He work for you?"

"Never seen him afore. He just showed up and started jabbering in that heathen tongue of his." The man smiled. "Still, I owe him a drink, since he brung the straw."

The mule skinner waved to his rain-soaked helpers. "C'mon, boys, into the Alamo. You too, Hoo-flung-dung," he yelled, "an' be damned to ye for a heathen Chinee."

Matt watched the men file into the saloon, the old Chinaman still jabbering, his mouth stretched in a toothless grin. Then Matt turned and regained the boardwalk.

The rain hammering against him, the marshal walked head bent toward the cattle pens. At least he could tell Mayor Kelley that the beer wagon had been saved, though the sinkhole would take a lot of men a long time to fill it with rocks and dirt. Matt smiled, thinking of how the parsimonious Kelley would blanch at the thought of that expense.

All the low-lying stock pens were flooded to a depth of a couple feet, and deep pools had formed in front of the feed sheds, where hollows had been worn in the sand by the passage of hundreds of booted punchers. The train station, raised on a platform of timber, was high and dry, though rain cascaded from its steeply pitched roof.

A locomotive hitched to a short train — just a couple passenger carriages, a boxcar and a caboose — hissed steam at the platform. A ticket agent, huddled in long black oilskins, stepped out of the depot and walked to the locomotive. He tilted back his head and yelled something to the engineer, and a hand waved from the cabin in reply. After a glance at the threatening sky, the agent nodded and hustled back to the shelter of the depot.

Above Matt's head the hanging sign of a general store swung on its chains in the wind, and when he glanced inside, he saw a man behind the counter arranging women's boots on a shelf that bore the hand-printed guarantee SOLD AT COST.

There was no point in staying out in the rain any longer. Matt could tell the mayor that though there was flooding in places, there was no immediate danger of Dodge sinking under the deluge.

The marshal waved to the man in the hardware store, then quickly turned to head back to the office.

Accompanied by the flat statement of a rifle, a bullet shattered a pane of the store window where Matt's head had been just a split second before. The marshal dived for the boardwalk, rolled on his back and frantically tore open his slicker, ripping off buttons to get at his gun.

He saw them then. Lee Feeney and the Jicarilla Kid, both mounted, were splashing toward him through the liquid mud of the street, rifles at their shoulders. Feeney's Winchester flared orange. Matt felt the bullet burn across the top of his chest, shredding its way across slicker and shirt. He reached for his gun. It wasn't there. The Colt had fallen out of the holster when he made his jarring dive for the boards.

Matt scrambled to his feet, looking around for his gun. He was aware of the Jicarilla Kid firing. The bullet crashed into his right shoulder and he slammed hard against the store window, his weight smashing framing and the glass that tinkled around his feet.

Lee Feeney was a talking man, and it was his need to talk that saved the marshal's life.

The outlaw jerked his rifle from his shoulder, waved to the Kid to stop firing and screamed: "Damn you, Dillon, you brought this on yourself. This is for my brother!"

Suddenly bullets cut the air around the two outlaws. Matt glanced to his right and saw a horseman pounding down the street toward them, clots of mud flying five feet into the air from the churning hooves of his horse.

Feeney and the Kid were startled, their heads swiveling to face the new threat. Matt saw his gun lying against the wall of the store; he bent and scooped it up. His gun hand hung uselessly from his wounded shoulder and he fired with his left, fired again. Both misses. The store owner was suddenly in his doorway. He cut loose with a shotgun, missed and began to reload. Feeney and the Kid fired at the oncoming horseman. A bullet burned across Feeney's cheek, drawing blood. The outlaw cursed, decided that the odds were no longer in his favor and swung his mount away. He cantered over the railroad tracks toward the edge of town, the Jicarilla Kid following close.

The rescuing horseman reined his mount to a stop and emptied his gun at the fleeing outlaws. He scored no hits, but Feeney was done. As was the way of the guerrilla fighter, he'd bide his time and wait for another day when the deck wasn't stacked against him.

Matt stood swaying on his feet as Charles Granville swung out of the saddle and stepped up onto the boardwalk. "How badly are you wounded, Marshal?" he asked, his face concerned.

There was no point making light of it. "I'm hit hard, Granville," Matt answered. "My shoulder is broke and I can't feel my right arm."

"Then stay right where you are, Marshal," Granville said. "I'll bring Doc Adams before you lose any more blood."

CHAPTER 22
A VISIT FROM KITTY

"The bullet entered under your collarbone and exited just above the right shoulder blade, Matt. You're pretty torn up," Doc Adams said. "You'll have that right arm in a sling for two or three weeks, but the feeling in your hand should return in a few days."

"Doc, it's my gun hand."

The physician shrugged as he snapped his bag shut. "Then stay out of trouble."

The marshal was sitting in the back room of the general store, a basin of bloody water close to his elbow. He felt light-headed and weak and had to fight the urge to sleep.

"I'll help you back to your office or your room at the hotel, whatever you prefer," Granville said. "You had a close call, Marshal."

"I'm beholden to you, Granville," Matt said. "Recently it seems like I've been saying that a lot to people who saved my life."

The Englishman smiled. "You mean

people like Ed Flynn? Don't worry. Unlike him I won't hold it over you. I was only doing my duty as a concerned citizen." Granville shrugged. "Missed the blighters, though."

"You burned Feeney," Matt said. The fingers of his left hand strayed to his cheek. "Right here. How come you were on the street in the rain?"

"I love to ride in the rain, Marshal. Clears my mind for my verse."

"Someday I'd like to read one of your poems."

"And one day you shall," Granville said brusquely. "But now let me escort you back to . . . ?" His eyebrow raised in a question.

"The office will be fine. I can take it from there."

"Remember, Matt, that sling stays on until I say it comes off," Doc warned. "If you don't wear it, you could further damage your shoulder and maybe never get the feeling back in your hand."

Matt rose to his feet, his head reeling. "I'll bear that in mind," he managed.

"Don't just bear it in mind — do it!" Doc snapped. "I'll stop by your office tomorrow to check on the wound and see how you're feeling."

■ ■ ■ ■

Matt sank into the chair at his desk, grateful to be out of the rain and cold. His shoulder pained him considerably, and though he tried several times, he couldn't close the fingers of his numb right hand. He could still shoot with his left, but hitting a target would be a mighty uncertain thing, especially a target that was shooting back at him.

Festus fluttered around the marshal like a frantic mother hen until Matt decided enough was enough and sent him on an errand to pick up some shotgun shells from Newly O'Brien the gunsmith.

But the deputy had no sooner left than Matt traded one mother hen for another. Kitty stormed into the office, a frown on her beautiful face. "I've been so worried," she said. "I just heard you'd been shot."

Matt nodded. "Took a bullet in the shoulder, but it went right on through. Doc Adams says I'll be fine in a few days."

Kitty made a face. "A few days, my foot! I've already spoken to Doc, and he says your arm will be in that sling for at least three weeks." The woman frowned. "And he says you have no feeling in your right hand."

Matt shook his head. "You know, for an educated feller, Doc sure likes to hear himself talk."

"He didn't volunteer the information. I pried it out of him. Now you've got two dangerous outlaws gunning for you and you can't shoot back."

"I still have my left hand."

"And much good that will do you, shot all to pieces the way you are."

"Kitty, I have a shoulder wound and a bullet burn across my chest. I'd hardly say I was shot all to pieces."

The woman got the coffeepot and refilled Matt's cup. She stood beside him, holding the pot as she said: "Well, I've made up my mind. I want you on the next train out of Dodge. You can stay with my cousin Hattie in Philadelphia for a few weeks until you feel better. You remember Hattie — she's the one with the fainting spells and the female problems who's married to an accountant. He's always down with something, poor thing, and keeps right poorly. They have seven children, but the youngest one is a bit simple." Kitty smiled. "Still, they're very nice people."

Despite the pain in his shoulder, Matt laughed. "Kitty, by the sound of what you just said, I'd rather face a gang of dangerous outlaws than spend a single day with your relatives."

"Do you have a better idea?" Kitty looked hurt. "The way you are right now, you can't even defend yourself."

"I just sent Festus for more shells for the Greener. If it comes right down to it, I can use the scattergun."

Kitty stamped her foot. "Matt Dillon, you're so stubborn sometimes. At least swear in some deputies, like that Charles Granville person. From all I hear, he's very good with a gun."

"He's good all right, one of the best I've seen."

"And then there's Doc Holliday. He's still in town."

"No, I draw the line at Holliday," Matt said firmly. "He's a born troublemaker. He's a man who shoots first before he even thinks up the questions."

Kitty returned the coffeepot to the stove and took a chair opposite the marshal. "Matt, why did Lee Feeney try to kill you? I thought he only wanted Ed Flynn."

"I've been thinking about that myself. I've hit him pretty hard, cut his men down to just him and the Jicarilla Kid, and that's something Feeney won't forgive and forget. I'm betting he knows by this time that I plan to charge him with the murders of John Farnborough and Lem Anderson, so he has every reason to get rid of me." Matt smiled. "And if all that wasn't enough, he reckons I'm still protecting Flynn."

Kitty's eyes clouded. "Feeney gave that man Anderson a horrible death."

"Worst than most," Matt agreed.

"I hear you have one of Feeney's men as a prisoner."

"Festus tell you that?"

"Why, yes, this morning."

Matt's exasperation was obvious. "And this is why Feeney knows everything that's happening in Dodge. Festus or somebody else tells you and pretty soon every saddle tramp within earshot in the Long Branch hears it, as well. For a few dollars, a man who's riding the grub line will tell Feeney everything he wants to know."

"It's not Festus' fault, Matt. He's worried, just as I am."

Kitty's eyes moved to the window, where the day was just shading into night. She rose to her feet. "I have to get going. I promised Sam Noonan I would take over the bar and let him have a night off." She leaned toward the marshal and her fingers lightly touched the back of his hand. "Take care, Matt, for my sake. I don't want to lose you."

After Kitty left, the memory of her perfume lingered. Matt felt suddenly alone and, for the first time in his life, vulnerable. He tried to close the fingers of his gun hand . . . but they were swollen and stiff and refused to move.

CHAPTER 23
THE UNDERTAKER IS PROSPERING

"Doc Holliday says he wants to talk to you, Matthew," Festus said. "He claims it's important."

"I have nothing to say to him, except to ask him when he's leaving town," Matt said, staring into the night from the office window.

Rain was slanting along Front Street, driven by the wind, and above the roofs of the buildings, lightning flashed blue to the west. The town lamps were lit, throwing elongated Vs of orange light onto the muddy street. A wet and bedraggled coyote stepped warily along the boardwalk outside the Long Branch before vanishing into the gloom of an alley.

The night was full of sound: the kettledrum beat of the rain, the sighing of the wind and, from somewhere on the plains, the faraway wail of a weather-beaten train echoed its loneliness.

"Doc says the Jicarilla Kid is a man to contend with, Matthew," Festus said softly.

Matt smiled, but did not turn away from the window, his lean face reflecting in the glass, transparent, like the face of a ghost. "Holliday is telling me something I don't already know?"

"He says up close the Kid will be mighty sudden. Faster than you can believe."

"Then I won't let him get up close."

A silence stretched between the two lawmen, broken only by the steady plop of the rain into the buckets on the floor and the competing *tick-tock-tick* of the railroad clock on the wall. It showed ten o'clock.

"Doc says for you to talk to him about the Kid, Matthew," Festus said finally, his voice quiet, as though he was almost afraid to be heard. "He says he can help you."

Matt turned, irritated. "Festus, I don't need Holliday's help. Now let it go."

The deputy nodded, a small hurt in his eyes. "Anything you say, Matthew."

Guilt stinging him, the marshal got the pot from the stove and poured coffee into Festus' cup. "All right, I'll talk to him, maybe tomorrow, maybe the next day."

Festus smiled his relief. "You know ol' Doc is real slick with the Colt, Matthew, and in a fight, he don't give a damn whether

226

he takes a bullet or not. A man like that can teach you things, maybe so."

"He can teach me how to die." Matt's smile was without humor. "Doc's been practicing for years."

A restlessness in him, the marshal stepped to the window and again looked outside. "I wonder how Flynn's making out?" he asked, more to himself than Festus. "That cave in the canyon can't be too comfortable in all this rain."

"Maybe he's moved on," Festus suggested. "He had grub, and the chances of ol' Lee catching him now are mighty slim."

Matt nodded. "Feeney would have to be in the right place at the right time — that's for sure. But Flynn hasn't been told that Feeney has no more riders left, and his fear of the Jicarilla Kid might keep him at the canyon. He told me he doesn't think he can shade him."

Festus was shocked. "Ed Flynn scared o' the Kid? I don't believe it. Why, there ain't nobody west of the Mississippi faster with a gun than ol' Ed."

"Could be, at one time, but he says he's slowed considerable." Matt shrugged. "We all get older, I guess. Maybe that's why he wants to head west and see the ocean-sea before it's too late."

"Want me to ride out there and tell him there's only Feeney and the Kid left and that there's a mighty good chance he has an open road to the mountains afore the big snows hit?" Festus asked.

"No, I reckon I'll do that myself. If he's as scared of the Kid as he says he is, he might need a power of persuading."

The deputy's eyes flashed concern. "Matthew, you can't ride with that shoulder."

"I'm sure going to try. I'd rather take my chances out in the open than holed up here in Dodge waiting for Lee Feeney to take another shot at me."

Matt told Festus to spend the night in the cell next to the prisoner while he slept in his room at the Dodge House, figuring that a bed softer than a straw mattress might favor his shoulder.

He took his Colt from the holster and shoved it into the waistband of his pants, where it was handier for a left-hand draw. Then he threw his slicker over his shoulders. It wasn't a long walk to the hotel and he would stay reasonably dry.

As the marshal thudded along the muddy boards, a turbulent wind slapped the slicker around his boot tops and the downpour beat hard into his face. The hissing sky flared electric blue, momentarily edging swollen clouds with silver, and around him, reflected lightning flickered on the fronts of the buildings, rain running down the warped pine boards.

The gas lamps of the Alamo were being dimmed as the marshal passed, and from inside, a piano chimed a single discordant chord as the lid was shut.

On the other side of Front Street, the lights of the Dodge House emerged through the blowing curtain of rain. Matt stepped down from the boardwalk and angled across deep mud to the hotel.

A gun roared and an exclamation mark of mud kicked up at the marshal's feet. A split second later another bullet cut the air next to his right ear. This time Matt saw the gun flash in the alley opposite. Awkward and slow with his left hand, he drew and fired at the rifle flare, fired again.

Boots pounded on the boardwalk. Festus was running toward him, his Colt in his hand. Across the street, from somewhere at the other end of the alley, a gun fired, then fired several times more.

Festus stopped beside the marshal, his eyes lost in pools of shadow. "Where are they, Matthew?"

"Over there in the alley," Matt said. "But

I think somebody else shot at them."

"I'll go look," Festus said. But he stopped as Charles Granville stepped out of the darkness of the alley, his smoking Colt hanging in his hand.

"Missed them, Marshal," he yelled while he was still a distance away. "There were two of them and they ran. Must have had their horses close by."

"Did you see them?" Matt asked as Granville got closer.

The Englishman shook his head. "Too dark to see anything but shadows. I fired at the brigands but I don't think I scored a hit."

"How did you get here so fast, Granville?" Matt asked, an as-yet-unformed suspicion rising in him.

The man smiled. "I was returning from the outhouse at the back of the hotel. Too much coffee, you see."

Granville was hatless, wearing only a shirt, boots and pants, and his coat was draped over his shoulders. The Englishman could have fired from the alley, then, when Festus arrived, pretended to shoot at bushwhackers, but Matt decided to give him the benefit of the doubt.

"Well, thanks again, Granville," the marshal said. "When I'm being shot at, you have a habit of arriving in the nick of time."

"Just luck, Marshal, though I doubt this was a serious attempt on your life. Feeney must have known that his chances of hitting you in all this darkness and rain were slim. He could have gotten closer of course, but he would have needed to expose himself to your fire, and he's too cautious for that. Or at least he was."

"What do you mean by that?"

"I mean, even in the dark he could see well enough to know you can't use your gun hand."

Matt opened his mouth to speak again, but the sound of a flurry of shots snatched the words from his lips.

"Matthew! That came from the jail!" Festus yelled.

Followed by Festus and Granville, Matt headed for the boardwalk, where the going would be easier. He stepped up on the boards and walked quickly toward the office, his gun up and ready.

He was too late.

A couple horsemen were already splattering through the mud as they headed for the edge of town, whipping their mounts into a fast canter with the reins.

Beside Matt, Granville fired. But the riders were soon lost in darkness and distance, and only the mocking hiss of the rain remained.

Chris Pierce lay on his back in the middle of his cell, his open eyes still registering the last terrifying moments of his life and his affront at the manner of his dying.

He had been shot at least six times in the head and chest, and lay in a widening pool of blood, bright scarlet against the gray cement of the floor.

Festus unlocked the cell door, and it was Granville who kneeled beside the young outlaw. After a few moments, he rose to his feet and said to Matt: "He was dead when he hit the floor. Any one of the bullets could have killed him, and he's been shot half a dozen times."

The marshal swore bitterly under his breath and Granville said: "Under the circumstances, don't swallow your tongue, Marshal. Use both barrels and air out your lungs."

Matt shook his head in frustration. His witness was gone and, with him, his best chance of dragging Lee Feeney and the Jicarilla Kid to the hangman.

Feeney and the Kid had been watching the office and had seized their opportunity when Matt left for the hotel. They'd shot at him to keep him occupied and had quickly doubled back to the jail and murdered Pierce. It had been the work of a moment, giving them plenty of time to get away.

"Matthew, we can still get Feeney before a judge," Festus said, as though he had been reading the marshal's mind. "He's tried to kill you twicet, an' me and Charlie are witnesses to that."

"Without Pierce's testimony, he'd walk," Matt said. "Any smart lawyer could convince a jury that positive identification is impossible through the smoke of a gunfight, to say nothing of rain and darkness. We know Feeney tried to kill me, but knowing and proving are two different things."

"I have to go along with you there, Marshal," Granville said. "The only way to deal with a man like Feeney is to draw down on him and kill him like the mad dog he is."

Festus threw an accusing glance at the Englishman. "Hell of advice to give a man who can't use his gun hand, Charlie."

"I'll get by," Matt said, suddenly spent. He told Festus to fetch Percy Crump. "Seems like the only person prospering in Dodge this fall is the undertaker," he said.

CHAPTER 24
THUS PERISH THE
LAWLESS

Matt Dillon took the trail to Horse Thief Canyon before first light. The raw pain of his wound and a short, restless sleep had drained him and he nodded in the saddle after he splashed through Duck Creek and rode across a land pummeled by wind and rain.

An hour later, as night gave way to the dawn, he reached Saw Log Creek, found an easy crossing between the cottonwoods and swung due north toward the lower tributaries of Spring Creek.

Over the last thirty minutes, the temperature had dropped and the rain had changed to a wet sleet. Matt shivered and turned up the collar of his slicker, pulling it closer around his neck.

Matt glanced at the black iron of the sky. The sleet was a bleak harbinger of winter, and if Ed Flynn wanted to find a trail across the mountains, he would have to leave that day. Otherwise the big snows would soon close the passes.

Getting rid of Flynn would solve one of Matt's problems, and then he'd only have to contend with Feeney and the Jicarilla Kid. But even by themselves, those two were a handful, and handicapped as he was by a stiff right arm, the outcome of any gunfight would be a mighty uncertain thing.

The marshal topped a rise still covered with the pink blossoms of crazy weed, then dropped down through a narrow draw and over another shallow hill. After this, the lonely land smoothed out again, cut through by many narrow streams, broken up by stands of prickly pear and yucca. The silent sleet fell thin and white on the grass but every now and then a gusting wind drove it cold and stinging into Matt's face, slamming his breath back into his chest.

He was cold and tired and his shoulder ached, torn muscle and chipped bone refusing to let him forget the bullet. He smiled into the sleet storm, thinking of Doc Adams. Doc probably figured he was resting in bed, not riding across a land grown suddenly hostile as it changed from a hard fall into a harder winter.

There would be time for rest later — if he lived that long. Otherwise — the muscles around Matt's eyes grew tight as his smile faded — his unending sleep would be sound.

Annoyed with himself for being so maudlin, Matt spurred the bay into a canter as the canyon loomed into sight through a gray morning light shredded by sleet. The canyon was still painted with slanting blue shadows and only the very tops of the sandstone walls were visible.

Matt drew rein at the canyon mouth and stood in the stirrups, his eyes trying to penetrate the gloom. He figured that under the circumstances Flynn might be a shade trigger-happy, and he decided to take it slow and easy, like he was visiting kinfolk.

"Ed, it's me, Matt Dillon!" he yelled.

For a few moments the echoes of his own voice mocked him, then bounded away into silence. Was the man asleep?

"Ed, it's Matt Dillon! I'm coming in!"

The marshal gathered up the reins of the bay but stopped as he heard the muffled footfalls of a horse within the canyon. The animal was coming toward him.

Matt slid his left hand inside his slicker and his fingers closed on the walnut butt of his Colt.

The horse, unhurried, was getting closer.

Easing out his gun, the marshal held it

across his chest, his thumb on the hammer.

Flynn's Appaloosa stepped out of the canyon, then stopped in the entrance, its head up watching him. The big horse sensed no threat and turned away. It walked among the cedars and wild oaks growing at the base of the wall and began to graze.

Where was Flynn?

Matt rode into the canyon and swung out of the saddle before he reached the cave. "Ed?" he called out. No answer. His Colt up and ready, the marshal walked deeper into the canyon, the only sound a steady drip of water from one of the walls onto rock and the thudding of his heart in his ears.

Matt stopped, his head lifted, sensing the morning. A dour light was now touching the interior of the canyon and sleet tumbled around him. To his right something timid scurried in the grass and ferns growing around some fallen talus rocks, and then fell silent.

The canyon felt as though it was crowding in on itself, the walls pressing close, and the air was harsh and cold and hard to breathe.

Matt's mouth was dry as he walked warily toward the cave. After a few steps he stopped and called again: "Ed Flynn, it's me, Matt Dillon."

A flock of cawing crows exploded from stunted cedars growing on the canyon rim and, startled, Matt swung his gun in their direction, the hairs on the back of his neck stiffening.

The crows flapped into the air like scraps of charred paper rising from a fire, and Matt did not know if they were noisily cussing one another or him.

After his hurriedly hammering heart settled down, he again stepped toward the cave.

Ed Flynn lay on his back, the top half of his body hanging over the lip of the cave floor. His eyes were wide open, staring into nothingness, and there was a neat bullet hole in the middle of his forehead.

The man's guns were still in their holsters, so he had made no attempt to draw. He had known and trusted his attacker, so that canceled out Lee Feeney and the Jicarilla Kid.

Only when Matt stepped back from the body did he see the words scratched onto the rock to the right of the cave. The killer had used a rock that left a white mark on the red sandstone to write:

THUS PERISH THE LAWLESS

The lean planes of Matt's face hardened as an ill-defined suspicion that had begun when Granville shot the wounded man at Feeney's camp took shape as reality.

The words were something a man who had taken it upon himself to single-handedly end the rampant lawlessness of the frontier would write. He would see himself as a crusader for right, a knight-errant in shining armor who hunted down and punished the wicked wherever he found them.

And such a man might call himself Tancred, a mighty warrior and the greatest of all the crusading knights.

Charles Granville was obviously mentally unbalanced, and that made him all the more dangerous.

He had questioned the marshal closely about Ed Flynn, and now Matt realized that the Englishman's purpose had been to gauge Flynn's guilt or innocence.

Granville had found Flynn guilty and had come out to Horse Thief Canyon and acted as his judge, jury and executioner. He must have been returning from his mission at the canyon when he rescued Matt from Feeney and the Kid.

Normally a suspicious man, Flynn knew Granville and for some reason trusted him, perhaps thinking he was bringing a message from Dodge. And that momentary lapse in the habit of a lifetime had cost the old gunfighter his life.

Matt shoved his Colt back in his waistband, reached out and closed Flynn's eyes. Not a praying man, he nevertheless glanced at the gray sky and whispered the hope that somewhere, somehow, Ed Flynn had crossed the mountains and was now gazing out across a vast ocean, the smell of the sea in his nose and the white sand of the shore gritty between his toes.

Flynn had once saved him from death, in a different time and place, and even after all that had happened, Matt Dillon could not allow himself to become a forgetting man.

It was as yet early afternoon when Matt rode into Dodge. He put up his bay and Flynn's Appaloosa in the livery, then stepped across to the Dodge House. His right hand useless, he needed an edge against a man as fast as Granville, and he carried his drawn gun against his leg.

"Mr. Granville is gone, Marshal," the clerk said. "He rode out early this morning and he didn't say when he'd be back."

"Did he say where he was going?"

"No, he didn't." The clerk saw Matt's gun and his eyes widened. "Is Mr. Granville in some kind of trouble?"

Matt's smile was thin. "You could say that. When he comes back, you come running and tell me, you hear."

"I sure will, Marshal." The man shook his head. "If this don't beat all, and Mr. Granville being such a nice gent an' all."

CHAPTER 25
PICKING UP BONES

By nightfall, Granville had not returned to Dodge, and Matt voiced his concern to Festus as they sat at the marshal's desk under a guttering pool of orange light cast by the overhead oil lamp.

"He might be out there going after Feeney and the Kid, or he figures his work here is done and he's lit a shuck for parts unknown to chase down other badmen."

Festus shook his head. "I still can't believe Charlie done for ol' Ed. Only a buzzard feeds on his friends."

"They weren't friends, Festus. As far as Granville was concerned, Ed Flynn was no better than an outlaw and that made him his bitter enemy."

The deputy smiled like a well-fed wolf. "Maybe Charlie will catch up to Feeney and the Kid, and they'll end up killing each other. That would sure let us off the hook."

"It would at that," Matt said absently,

knowing how unlikely it was to happen.

The marshal had bought a child's rubber ball at the general store, and he was squeezing it, working his fingers.

"That helping any?" Festus asked.

"A little, but they're still too stiff and sore to draw a gun. Even if I got the Colt out of the leather, I'd be sure to drop it."

"We going out after Charlie, Matthew?" Festus asked, his face doubtful.

"Where do we look first?" Matt asked in turn. "Sometimes it's better to just sit your horse and do nothing than wear him out chasing shadows. The Farnborough hands are still searching, so we might get word of the whereabouts of Granville and Feeney soon enough."

But it was news of the Jicarilla Kid that arrived less than an hour later, and none of it was good.

A wagon piled high with bleached buffalo bones creaked along Front Street just before midnight, two men up on the seat, a dead man nodding between them.

As Matt himself had witnessed, the slaughter of the buffalo had left their bones scattered all over the plains. But now some enterprising men, including farmers facing hard times, were gathering up the bones and shipping them east to be ground up for china and fertilizer at five dollars a ton. The white skeletons of the great animals were rapidly vanishing from the prairie and soon only their ghosts would remain, spirits having no commercial value.

The bone pickers started hollering when they were still a distance from the marshal's office. Matt and Festus walked to the door and stepped onto the boardwalk.

The bearded oldster who was handling the lines took them in one hand and cupped the other to his mouth. "Murder, Marshal!" he yelled. "A poor boy gunned down!"

Matt waited until the wagon churned through the mud and creaked to a halt, the eight mules in the traces hanging their heads from exhaustion.

Festus helped the oldster lift the dead man from the seat and Matt said: "Bring him inside."

Festus and the oldster were helped by the other picker — a younger man in a buffalo coat with a tangle of yellow hair hanging over his shoulders — the dead boy was carried into the office and laid gently on the floor.

Matt took a knee beside the youngster. The kid looked like a raw farm boy, his face round and freckled, a few wisps of hair on his top lip. The marshal guessed his age to be seventeen, no older than that. The boy had an old gun belt buckled around his waist but the holster was empty.

Matt unbuttoned the kid's mackinaw, pulling it away from a collarless shirt that was black with dried blood. The boy had been shot twice in the chest, the bullet holes not more than an inch apart.

"His name was Jacob Higgins," the older man said. "He was my grandson."

Matt's eyes lifted to the man, who was round shouldered with big, work-worn hands, a gray beard stranded with black spread over the front of his coat. "Who did this?" Matt asked.

"Said his name was the Jicarilla Kid, told us to remember it so we could tell others how it happened."

"How did it happen?" the marshal asked, rising to his feet.

The oldster turned to the younger man. "This here is Long-haired Dan Dolan. He has an Irish way with words and can tell it better than me."

The name immediately registered with Festus. "Would you be the Long-haired Dan Dolan who kilt Howie Truckman over to Fort Benton way a spell back?"

Dolan looked from Festus to Matt, his eyes defiant. "I would. He came at me with his gun drawn and I cut down on him. A man who's a sore loser shouldn't play poker."

"I heard tell that Truckman was real slick with the iron and had killed a few," Festus said.

Dolan's laugh was harsh and without humor. "Mister, after what I saw today, he didn't come near to being slick, and now I know that neither do I."

"Tell it, Dolan," Matt said. "What happened?"

"We'd filled the wagon with bones, and since it was getting on to dark, we figured we'd make camp and drive to the railhead come morning. The coffee was just on the bile when two men rode right into camp, didn't even ask a by-your-leave. I was about to have some hard words with them, but Grandpa Higgins here told me to let it go, that them two had the gunman's look about them and could be almighty dangerous."

"Then they picked on the youngster here?" Festus asked.

"I'm getting to that," Dolan said, a slight Irish lilt to his voice. "Well, we fed them two salt pork and coffee. Then this Jicarilla Kid feller starts picking on the boy. He said he looked like a damned stupid sodbuster and smelled like a hog, stuff like that."

"The other man," Matt said, "he didn't try to stop it?"

"Him? Nah, he gave his name as Feeney, and he just sat there watching, a little smile on his face, like he found the whole thing real amusing. That Apache or half-breed or whatever he was, he kept needling young Jacob, calling him a rube and asking if his ma was his pa's sister. The boy was getting so mad I saw tears in his eyes. Finally he couldn't take it anymore and grabbed for his gun."

Dolan was silent for a few moments, remembering how it had been. Then he said, "That Jicarilla Kid let the boy clear leather before he drew and shot him. He shot him once while he was standing, then again when he was falling." The bone picker shook his head. "I've never seen a man shuck a gun that fast. It was almost like he wasn't human, that he was some kind of demon. And when it was done and Jacob was lying dead on the grass, them two mounted up and rode away laughing, like the killing of a sixteen-year-old boy had been a good joke."

"You've killed your man," Matt said. "You outdrew a named man who was good with the iron. How come you didn't make a play?"

That stung Dolan and it showed. Two kinds of men did not prosper in the West and were shunned by all: liars and cowards. A man of his time and place, Matt Dillon would not tolerate either. He'd had his say.

"I was heeled all right," Dolan said, "but my gun was under my coat. Feeney drawed almost as fast as the Kid and he had me covered."

"Pays a man to be careful, I guess," Matt said, as Dolan refused to meet his eyes.

A silence hung in the room for a few moments. Then the old man said: "Don't blame Dolan, Marshal, nor me neither. Them two had us cold." He shook his head. "Now I have to tell Jacob's ma what happened. It will be a mighty hard business. She trusted me to look after her boy."

"Mr. Higgins," Festus said, "I know this ain't calculated to help much, but you can give the boy a decent buryin' with a preacher an' all, right here in Dodge."

"Thank you kindly, Deputy," Higgins said. "But we'll dump our buffalo bones here at the railhead, then carry Jacob home to the Nations. It wouldn't rest easy on his ma's mind knowing her son was lying far away in foreign soil."

"Mr. Higgins," Matt said, "I intend to hunt down Lee Feeney and the Jicarilla Kid and bring them to justice. I'll see them both hung from the same gallows."

His voice edged with barely suppressed anger, Dolan spoke. "Marshal, that's big talk, and talk is cheap, especially coming from a one-armed man. I seen what that Kid can do with a gun, and from where I stand, you just don't stack up."

"Let me worry about that, Dolan," Matt said sharply, his own irritation flaring. And to Higgins: "You can leave the boy's body here while you drop your load at the rail depot. We'll lay him out in one of the cells."

Higgins shook his head. "That was kindly meant, Marshal, but I'll take Jacob with us. I failed to take care of him in life, but maybe I can do right by him in death." A single tear ran down the old man's cheek and into his beard. "I never reckoned so before, but now I'm thinking that I've lived too long." He managed a wan smile. "It's a hell of a thing."

The long night crowded damp, cold and dark around Dodge as Matt stood at his office window and looked into the street. Sleet was slanting in a keening wind, each drop the size of a nickel, reflecting white and fleeting in the glare of the streetlamps. An uneasy silence lay on the town, fragile as glass, ready to shatter at the slightest sound.

Behind him Matt heard the soft *slap-slap* of Festus' mop as he cleaned up the dead boy's blood from the floor, and a log fell inside the cherry red stove with a faint crash.

The sleet and cold would bring them in, Matt decided.

Out there on the open plains, Feeney and the Kid could not long endure the weather's change for the worse.

They would be driven into Dodge, he was sure of it . . . and he would be waiting.

CHAPTER 26
THE PINKERTON
RETURNS

Standing on the boardwalk the following morning, Matt Dillon heard the train that was about to present him with a whole new set of problems pull into the station. The hour was early, not yet eight, but freight and farm wagons were already crowding the street, their huge, steel-rimmed wheels sinking deep into the mud, making it look like a plowed field.

A few townspeople were already walking the boards on their way to work, their heads bent against the driving sleet. The cuffs of the men's pants and the hems of the women's dresses were brown with mud, and the lucky few who had umbrellas sheltered behind them as they pushed into the wind.

The mercury thermometer nailed to the wall outside the marshal's office registered a couple degrees above freezing, and the temperature could drop as the day progressed. There was no sun, the sky was a uniform gray and the air tasted like raw iron.

Matt's attention was attracted to the procession heading in his direction along the boardwalk. In the lead walked a small, thin man in a long coat and a plug hat, carrying two carpetbags. Behind him was a woman with a baby in her arms, and behind her, strung out in a line, were seven other children, none of them older than ten.

The man was Silas Vernon, the Pinkerton detective, and the woman was the wife of Uriah Scroggins.

Vernon touched his hat to Matt and said: "Marshal, a pleasure to see you again." He waved a hand to the woman. "As you can see, I finally caught up with Mrs. Emily Scroggins. Ran her to earth in Wichita, of all places." He slapped the carpetbag. "And I've recovered the stolen money, less a couple of thousand that she and her late husband had already spent."

Matt nodded to the door of the office. "Let's go inside."

Vernon's face showed concern as he saw Matt's arm. "Marshal, you've been wounded."

"Goes with the badge," Matt said, not caring to feed the man's curiosity.

Once inside the office, the baby in Mrs. Scroggins' arms began to cry and shriek at the top of its lungs, and a couple of the younger children joined in, setting off a caterwauling that shook the walls of the office.

Mrs. Scroggins, a thin, mousy and care-worn woman, tried her best to hush them but to no avail.

Vernon was shouting above the din. "She was sidetracked to Wichita. Otherwise I would have missed her! Bridge support down farther along the track! Her train was delayed for twenty-four hours! I was lucky!"

The crying of the children was now in full throttle and had been joined by others and Matt yelled to the detective: "What do you want done with her?"

Vernon cupped a hand behind his ear. "Eh?"

"What do you want —" Matt gave up. He turned and his eyes found his deputy, who was looking at the kids with a dazed expression on his face, like a man who had just been hit by a club. "Festus!" he hollered above the clamoring cacophony of shrieks and wails. "Do something!"

Festus shrugged and spread his hands, and his mouth formed the word: "What?"

Matt fished in his pocket, found a dollar and spun it to the deputy. "Take them for candy or soda pop!"

The deputy shook his head, signaling that he hadn't heard.

Matt rose to his feel and yelled into Festus' ear. "Take 'em all for candy or soda pop!"

Now Festus smiled his understanding. He rounded up the kids and yelled, in a voice that Matt decided was worthy of a politician or the opera stage: "Young'uns, we're all a-goin' for candy sticks!"

One by one the crying children came to a snuffling halt and one of the younger children reached up, her brown eyes huge, and took the deputy's hand.

"Go, Festus," Matt said urgently. "While the getting is good."

After the deputy ushered his brood through the door like a mother hen, only the screaming baby remained. "She's hungry," Mrs. Scroggins said. "I can feed her if you gentlemen don't mind."

"I don't mind a bit," Matt said quickly, his ears ringing. "Go right ahead."

The woman unbuttoned her dress, put the child to her breast and a blessed silence fell in the room.

"Now, Vernon, what do you want" — Matt realized he was still hollering and he modified his tone — "done with Mrs. Scroggins?"

"Emily Scroggins by name, Emily Scroggins by nature." The woman smiled.

"I'd like you to hold her for the authorities in the Arizona Territory, Marshal. Either that, or take her there yourself."

Matt was horrified at that suggestion and suddenly his shoulder began to throb. "Why don't you take her?"

The Pinkerton shrugged. "I don't have that authority. I have no power of arrest. This woman could just walk away from me at any time between here and the Arizona Territory unless I could convince the local law to detain her. It was a town policeman in Abilene who put Mrs. Scroggins and her brood on the train for me." The man smiled. "Truth to tell, Officer Earp only did it because he seemed quite anxious to be rid of us."

"What's the charge against her, Vernon?" Matt asked.

"Why, isn't that obvious? She's an accessory to the embezzlement of thirty thousand dollars from the Cattleman's Bank of Broken Bow in the Arizona Territory."

Emily Scroggins smiled. "Oh, no, Mr. Vernon, that was all Uriah's doing. He wanted to make me happy, you see." She dabbed a small lace handkerchief to her eyes. "My poor Uriah, he was always so considerate

255

and caring."

"Madam," Vernon said, his face stern, "he wasn't very considerate to the people of Broken Bow. Many lost their life savings, and when he heard the news, one hard-pressed rancher even committed suicide."

"And Uriah was very upset about that. The day after we arrived in Dodge, he said to me, he said: 'Emily, my love, one day I will make amends and return the money to the bank with interest.'" The handkerchief again saw use, and the woman sniffed. "That's the kind of man my Uriah was, always thinking about others and not himself." Mrs. Scroggins' light brown eyes searched Matt's face. "Marshal, did you ever discover who murdered my husband?"

"Not yet, ma'am. But I'm working on it."

"Uriah wouldn't harm a fly," the woman said. "Why would someone want to kill him?"

"Maybe because he robbed a bank and destroyed a town and the lives of its citizens," Vernon said, his face stiff.

Mrs. Scroggins had no answer for that, but it set Matt to thinking. "Mr. Vernon, did you remember the name of the man who killed himself?"

The Pinkerton studied the marshal, drawing a blank. Then he said: "I forgot all about you asking me that." Suddenly his face changed and he slapped the desk with the flat of his hand. "But wait. I do remember! Yes, his name was Granville, Thomas Granville. He was a Welshman, I think. No, no, he wasn't Welsh. He was English. Came from a good family, I believe."

Matt sat up and took notice. "Do you recollect if he had a brother?"

"That I do remember quite well. There was talk of a brother who came after the funeral. He sold off Thomas Granville's ranch and cattle for what little they would bring and recovered the suicide weapon from the local sheriff. I understand it was an engraved Colt in forty-five caliber and quite valuable."

Matt's eyes swung to Emily Scroggins, who was buttoning up her dress, her baby sound asleep in her arm. "Ma'am," he said, his voice edged with the urgency he felt, "I believe your life may be in danger."

The woman's small mouth opened in a startled O. "But who would want to kill me, Marshal?"

"A man called Charles Granville. He's the brother of the rancher who committed suicide after the Broken Bow bank collapsed. I believe Granville murdered your husband as an act of revenge and he may well try to do the same to you."

"But . . . but Mr. Vernon has recovered the money."

Matt shook his head. "That might make a difference to a court, but not to Granville. The man believes he's on a crusade to rid the West of the lawless, and that includes people like your husband . . . and you."

"He'd . . . he'd kill a woman, a mother of eight children, with one at her breast?"

"Mrs. Scroggins," Matt said, taking it slowly so she'd understand, "Charles Granville is mentally unbalanced. Maybe the death of his brother did that. I don't know. But I believe he's capable of killing you — and your children."

Now the full horror of her situation hit home and the color drained from the woman's face. "My poor children! Marshal, what can I do?"

Matt realized that Mrs. Scroggins was not an intelligent woman, and as though he was talking to a child, he said slowly: "Before I answer that, I want you to promise me something on your word of honor."

"Anything, Marshal. I'll promise anything if it will save the lives of my children."

"I want you to promise me you will accompany Mr. Vernon to Arizona and surrender yourself to the authorities there."

"Yes, yes, I promise on my word of honor." She turned to the Pinkerton, her voice pleading. "Mr. Vernon, you know I will. Oh, please say you know I will."

"Vernon, how does that set with you?" Matt asked.

The Pinkerton thought things through, then answered: "I can go along with that. When I return the money and at least one of the guilty parties, I've accomplished what I was hired to do."

Matt glanced at the clock on the wall. "A train leaves for points west at five tonight. Mrs. Scroggins and her children can stay here under guard until then."

"Marshal Dillon, what will become of me?" the woman asked. "Do they hang women in the Arizona Territory?"

"The money, or most of it, is being returned. The jury will weigh that and the fact that your husband was murdered," Matt said. "I believe that since you're a mother of eight children, the court will go easy on you."

"Jail time? I couldn't bear to be parted from my children."

The marshal shook his head. "I don't know, Mrs. Scroggins. I suspect the chances are you'll be acquitted and get proposals of marriage from every single man on the jury, and maybe the judge."

The woman dabbed at her eyes. "Oh, thank you, Marshal. Now I feel much better." Her eyes were suddenly calculating. "I just wonder who could take the place of my dear Uriah. He'd have to be tall, dark and handsome with a gallant mustache. I can tell you that."

When the Scroggins brood returned, exploding into the office with faces sticky from candy canes, Matt told Festus to take the coffeepot off the stove or one of them would be sure to pull it over on himself. Above the din, he filled the deputy in on his plan for Mrs. Scroggins and told him to guard the woman until train time.

Then Matt Dillon shrugged into his slicker, grabbed the Greener from the rack, and beat a hasty retreat . . . ignoring Festus' pleading look.

Chapter 27
Doc Holliday
Makes an Offer

The sleet had changed back to an icy rain as Matt walked along the boardwalk, then angled across Front Street toward the Dodge House. He saw Doc Holliday, looking pale and sick, urgently beckon to him from the doorway of the Alamo Saloon, but he ignored the man.

Matt couldn't stand Holliday at any time, and Doc was even more disagreeable before he'd had his morning coffee and bourbon.

The desk clerk told the marshal that Granville had still not returned, and the marshal took the key, unlocked the man's room and stepped inside.

The bed was made up and the wardrobe door hung open. It was empty. Granville was gone and it looked like he would not be coming back.

Matt dropped off the room key, walked out of the hotel and stood under the canvas awning above the front door that sheltered him from the worst of the rain.

Gray clouds hung low over Dodge and thunder was sulking just to the north, lacing the sky with lightning. Matt held the Greener in his good hand and looked up and down the street, empty but for a single freight wagon standing outside Hardy's general store.

He was reluctant to return to the office to face Mrs. Scroggins and her squalling brood, and he watched Silas Vernon pick his way across the muddy street to seek refuge in the Long Branch.

A feeling of helplessness swept over the marshal. Somewhere out on the plains were Feeney and the Jicarilla Kid, and he could only wait for them to make their next move. He was sure that Granville was also close by, and that the noisy arrival of Mrs. Scroggins with her eight children and a Pinkerton had not gone unnoticed.

Where was the man?

Matt's eyes swept the rooftops and lingered long on the narrow alleys. He was certain that Granville had not left and was here in town. But where?

Granville's horse was at the livery stable, but when Matt ran a hand over the animal's flank it was still wet. The horse had been ridden recently. Granville must have slipped back into town unnoticed, probably while Matt was talking to Vernon and Mrs. Scroggins.

There was only one reason for Granville to stay close — and that was the woman.

Awkwardly, using only one hand, Matt saddled his bay and rode down the middle of Front Street, his shotgun across the pommel, his eyes everywhere. Before he reached the bridge over the Arkansas, he swung east, then made a circuit of the town, drawing rein now and then to study the scattered shacks and storage sheds behind the stores and saloons.

An hour later he returned to the bridge, having seen nothing but the mesh of the rain and the flash of lightning in the sky.

Matt was still sitting his bay when two riders trailing a couple horses reached the opposite end of the bridge and started across. The man in front was Bob Murray and the horses were carrying dead men across their saddles. Just behind the Farnborough foreman was a younger puncher, bent over in the saddle, his face gray. As he got closer, Matt saw that the young rider was clutching his stomach, blood seeping scarlet between his fingers.

Murray reined up when he was close to Matt and said: "We ran into Feeney south of here." The man's bleak eyes lifted to Matt's, rain lashing into his face. "You were right, Marshal. Four wasn't near enough." The foreman inclined his head. "Ben Selby here is gut-shot and can't live. The other two are dead."

"When?" Matt asked.

"Two hours ago, maybe a little more. It happened south of the Mulberry. Feeney had made camp along a stream among some willows, and we saw his smoke from a ways off. We got up real close and charged the camp, but they must have seen us coming because they were waiting for us. The Jicarilla Kid" — he waved a hand behind him — "killed them two and Feeney put a bullet into Ben."

Murray shook his head. "Marshal, Feeney had the drop on me and I thought I was a dead man. But instead of cutting my suspenders, he told me to pick up my dead and take a message to you."

"Bob," Selby groaned, "I'm hurtin' real bad. My belly's on fire."

"I'm getting you to a doctor, Ben," Murray said.

"It's too late for me, ain't it?" the man called Ben said.

Murray nodded, his face like stone, a man trying to appear harder than he was. "You're gut-shot, Ben," he said. "You know there's no coming back from that."

"Then God help me," the wounded man gasped.

"Murray, you'd better get that man to Doc Adams," Matt said. "Doc can give him something to help with the pain."

"Don't you want to hear the message, Marshal?" Murray asked. "It ain't long in the telling."

"Let me hear it."

"Feeney says he knows Ed Flynn is dead and he says you robbed him of his reckoning. He says he and the Kid will ride into Dodge real soon and call you out." The man shrugged. "That's what he said."

Murray's eyes moved to the sling on the marshal's arm under his unbuttoned slicker. "Better have some good men close when it happens, Marshal. Me, I'm done. I'm pulling my freight while I still can. There's nobody alive can stand up to Feeney and that damn Apache of his."

Matt nodded. "Take your man to Doc."

Murray waved a hand. "Good luck, Marshal."

The foreman swung his horse away, and Matt watched him and Selby ride along Front Street until they faded into the shifting haze of the falling rain.

Matt sat his horse for several minutes, thinking. He could go back to his office and wait for Feeney to come to him. Or he could take the fight to the outlaw, probably the last thing the man expected.

Of the two options, the marshal much preferred the latter. He was not one to take a step back from any man, especially a low-life like Feeney. The outlaw knew the marshal had been hit hard in the fight against him and the Kid, and he might expect that his message would make Matt run scared — and scared men got careless.

But had Feeney known Matt better he would have understood two facts very important to his own survival — that the marshal would take his hits and keep on coming . . . and that he didn't scare worth a damn.

Matt rode south across the plains, his eyes scanning the rain-scarred land for any sign of Feeney and the Jicarilla Kid. In the distance, lightning forked from low-hanging clouds and around him the long grass tossed in the wind. The day was cold and raw, and Matt's wounded shoulder throbbed.

Just before noon he took shelter in a grove of cottonwoods and managed to start a small fire among the sheltering roots of an ancient windfall. He got a cup and a small package of tea from his saddlebags and sipped the hot brew gratefully, feeling it slowly warm him. Then he swung into the saddle again and continued south.

So far he had seen no sign of life on the plains and the only sounds were the footfalls of his horse and the rustle of the grass.

He found Feeney's camp among the willows by a stream running off Mulberry Creek. A few scattered shell cases told the story of the outlaws' fight with Murray and his punchers, and there were still traces of blood on the grass.

Matt laid the barrel of his shotgun over his shoulder and looked around him in all directions. Nothing but wind and rain. Feeney and the Kid were long gone.

Due to the weather, there were no tracks and Matt felt a sense of defeat. He'd hoped to have it out with Feeney, trusting to the Greener to give him an edge, but that wasn't going to happen. Not today at least.

Matt stepped into the saddle and swung north.

He'd been riding for an hour when he saw a lone horseman coming toward him through the gloomy screen of cloud and rain. Matt's far-seeing eyes tried to make out who the man was, but only when he got closer could he make out a gaunt figure, an umbrella opened above his head, astride a rawboned roan with an awkward, shuffling gait.

The rider wore a long tan-colored overcoat and a derby hat, and his eyes and sunken, emaciated cheeks were in shadow. But there was no mistaking the man's stooped, high-shouldered seat in the saddle and the way he constantly scanned the land around him.

It was Doc Holliday, more dead than alive, riding across plains when he should have been in bed dying like a gentleman.

Matt drew rein and let Holliday come to him. The gambler's face was a ghastly gray, and when he got within talking distance, Matt saw a hot fever in his red-rimmed eyes.

Holliday reined up his horse and said: "If the mountain won't come to Mohammad, then Mohammad must go to the mountain." Doc winked. "I've been following your trail since you left Dodge."

"What do you want, Doc?" Matt asked. "You look like hell."

Holliday smiled. "Ah, Marshal, you were ever the master of understatement. In fact, I'm starting to feel a little better. You should have seen me when I was really sick."

"I did, Doc. That was when I asked you when you and Kate were leaving Dodge."

Holliday uncomfortably shifted position in the saddle and adjusted the angle of his umbrella to keep off the rain that was now riding a west wind.

"And, as I recall, about Tancred, the noble crusading knight. As to my leaving, the answer is soon, Marshal Dillon, soon. Kate, always the optimist, expects we'll be able to leave your fair city in a couple of days."

"It can't be soon enough for me," Matt said, fixing Holliday with cold eyes.

"You just don't like me, do you?" Holliday said.

"Not a bit. You're a troublemaker, Doc, and I don't like troublemakers in my town." The marshal gathered the reins. "Now, unless you've got anything else to say to me, give me the road."

"Wait," Holliday said. "I didn't ride all the way out here to pass the time of day. I must have words with you." The gambler looked around him. "We can't converse in all this rain. Let's go over there among the trees."

To Matt's right, cottonwoods and stands of prickly pear were growing around tumbled sandstone rocks, a relic of some ancient volcanic eruption. A narrow stream ran close by and beyond that a few wild oaks.

The marshal nodded. "All right, we'll talk. But make it fast, Doc. I've got things to do."

Holliday grinned. "A marshal's work is never done. Nobody knows that better than me."

The two men dismounted in the shelter of the cottonwoods and Holliday carefully placed his umbrella over his saddle to keep it dry. He stood with his back against a tree, lit a slim black cheroot and studied the glowing end with apparent great interest before he said: "I understand that you'll soon be facing a showdown with Lee Feeney" — Doc hesitated before his cold blue eyes lifted to Matt's — "and the Jicarilla Kid."

The marshal didn't bother to ask where Doc got his information. News, especially bad news, traveled fast in Dodge. Instead he said: "What's it to you?"

Holliday ignored the question. "I know Feeney. In a gunfight he'll try to get every advantage he can, and that includes shooting a man in the back. But the Kid now, he'll come right at you."

"You know him as well?"

"In the past our paths have crossed a time or two. I saw him kill a man in Shanessy's Saloon in Fort Griffin, that Texas dung heap. I'd say that breed was the fastest man with a gun I ever saw."

Matt's impatience was growing. "Why are you telling me this?"

Holliday took his time replying. He found a flat bottle of whiskey in his coat pocket, offered it to Matt and, when the lawman refused, he took a long swig, his prominent Adam's apple bobbing.

The gambler drew the back of his thin hand across his mouth, put the bottle away and said: "I'm telling you this because there are only two men I know who can perhaps shade the Jicarilla Kid. You, Marshal, when you have the full use of your gun hand — and me."

"You still haven't answered my question, Doc. Why are you telling me all this?"

"Because, damn it all, I'm offering you my help. How long will it be before you can use your right hand — two, three weeks? If all I'm hearing is true, Marshal, Feeney and the Kid won't wait that long."

Matt was taken aback. "Why would you want to help me?"

Holliday shrugged, his smile thin. "Because I like you, Marshal. I believe you to be a decent and honorable man, and in my circle of acquaintances, such men as you are few."

Matt opened his mouth to speak, but

Holliday held up a fragile hand to quiet him. "And there's another reason. That time in Fort Griffin, after the shooting, the Kid looked around the saloon and asked if anyone else wanted what he had to offer. I kept my mouth shut — something I've regretted ever since. Now I have a score to settle with that damned Apache."

Irritated, Matt said: "Holliday, let me lay this on the line for you. Maybe someday, in some other town, a lawman will ask for your help, but I'm not the one. My troubles are not yours. The day I ask you to stand by me in a gunfight will be the day hell freezes over."

Chapter 28
Ambush in the Rain

Doc Holliday seemed unfazed by Matt's refusal of his offer. "What I said still stands, Marshal," he said. "All you need do is ask."

Thunder rumbled and lightning flashed and the rain seemed heavier. "We'd better get going," Matt said. He glanced at the blazing sky. "We'll be lucky if we reach Dodge alive."

Holliday laughed. "You're safe with me, Marshal. Death has passed me over too many times to strike me down with lightning."

Rain hammered on Doc's umbrella as the two riders headed north through the storm, Doc regaling Matt with excerpts from the *Canterbury Tales*. The marshal later admitted to himself that, despite his dislike of Holliday, he had been amused by the man's rendition of the bawdy "Miller's Tale," though at least half of the old English words went flying right over his head.

Before they parted ways at the livery stable, Doc touched Matt's arm. "Remember," he said, "when Feeney and the Kid get here and it's all on the line, my offer still goes."

"Don't sit at the window looking for me, Doc," the marshal said. "I won't be coming."

The little gambler shrugged. "Adverse circumstances sometimes have a way of altering the way a man thinks. I'll be waiting."

Matt, reluctant to return to the office and share Festus' noisy purgatory, crossed the street and stepped into the Long Branch, instead.

There were only a few men in the saloon and Kitty was behind the bar. As soon as she saw Matt, she said: "I heard about poor Mrs. Scroggins. What's to become of her and her children?"

Matt smiled. "She asked me that very question. I told her that a jury of Western men would go easy on a woman with eight kids. Besides, the Pinkerton got most of the stolen money back and that will make a difference."

"When is she leaving for Arizona?"

"She's leaving Dodge on the five o'clock train west. After that, it will be up to the

Pinkerton to get her to where he figures she needs to be."

Kitty was talking again, but Matt wasn't listening. He was thinking about Granville. Did the man now know about Mrs. Scroggins? The woman's arrival had not gone unnoticed and tongues were no doubt wagging all over town. If the Englishman was around somewhere, then he had heard by this time.

". . . and it's very unfair, at least that's what I think."

"Sorry, Kitty," Matt said. "What's unfair?"

"Matt Dillon, you haven't been listening to a word I've said," Kitty said, a scowl on her pretty face.

The marshal smiled. "Sorry. I was busy thinking." He glanced round the saloon. All the men sitting at tables were townsmen and known to him. "You haven't seen Charles Granville, have you?" he asked.

"Why, yes, I have. He was here not thirty minutes ago. He drank a cup of coffee and then left."

Then the Englishman was still in town. Matt touched his hat to Kitty, leaving her puzzled behind him, and walked onto the boardwalk.

Where was Granville?

■ ■ ■ ■

Matt stepped along the boards, then dropped off and walked into an alley. Behind the saloon and storefronts, most of the scattered shacks and cabins lay empty after the cowboys left. During the cattle season, they were rented out to the girls who worked the line, overnighting railroaders or to the assorted drifters and hangers-on who followed the herds north.

Granville could be holed up in any one of them.

Matt reached down with his left hand and eased the Colt in his waistband. He was in no shape to meet Granville in a gunfight, but the man professed to be an upholder of the law, and if that was really how he felt, he was unlikely to resist arrest.

Or so the marshal fondly hoped.

After reaching the end of the alley, Matt stopped, looking around him. Diagonally to his left rose a three-story warehouse with several freight wagons parked close to its loading dock. Ahead of him was a stable for the mule teams that hauled the wagons and a small corral, with a rusting steam engine of some sort pushed into one of the corners, long strands of bunchgrass growing around it.

To the right was a sprawled collection of shacks, mostly built of tar paper on flimsy wooden frames, tin chimneys held in place by wires sticking out of their angled roofs. None of the chimneys trailed smoke and the four-paned windows on the sides of the shacks looked at the marshal with dusty blank eyes.

Above Matt's head thunder crashed and lightning sizzled, its blinding light banishing the gloom for a single moment. The pouring rain thrashed against his hat and slicker and underfoot his boots squelched in mud.

He would try the stable first.

A couple dozen mules stood in stalls on each side of the barn, a long, low building with a peaked canvas roof. Gun in hand, Matt walked softly to the end of the barn, where tack and bales of hay were stored. He saw nothing but some rats busily scratching around in a corner.

This would have been an obvious place for Granville to hide out, but Matt knew that the man was too smart to choose the obvious.

Now he'd have to do it the hard way.

One by one, the marshal began to check out the shacks, peering through windows and trying doors. Matt's efforts met with no success, and he walked toward a couple cabins separate from the rest, as though they'd decided to wander into the plains and had lost their way.

He had stuck the Colt back into his waistband, needing a free hand to test doorknobs, and was unprepared when a bullet kicked up mud at his feet, then another.

A drift of smoke came from a broken cabin window just ahead of him and man's voice yelled: "Don't make me have to kill you, Marshal! Stand right where you are."

Matt was facing a cold deck and he knew it. By the time he drew his gun and fired, Granville could put a couple aimed shots into him.

Desperately the marshal tried a bluff. "Granville, you're under arrest," he said, the wind and rain driving his words back at him.

A laugh came from the cabin window. "I don't think I'll permit myself to be arrested today, Marshal. There's still much work to be done." A moment's silence, then: "It troubles me that the thieving Scroggins woman and her vicious brood still walk the Earth while my brother lies cold in his grave. And there are many others just like them. It may take me the rest of my life, but I plan to exterminate them all."

"Granville —"

"Call me Tancred."

"Granville, harm a hair on that woman's head and I will personally see you hang."

The Englishman laughed again, a harsh sound without humor. "I do believe you'd like to see me hang as it is. Surely you haven't forgotten Uriah Scroggins and Ed Flynn, lowlifes though they were?"

"You will face trial for both those murders," Matt said, feeling as naked and vulnerable out here in the open as a newborn babe.

"Marshal," Granville yelled, "with the fingertips of your hand, lift out your gun and drop it to the ground. Make sure it's done slow and easy. I'm rather an excitable chap."

Matt thought about it. Could he draw and fire and put a bullet into Granville's head where it was just visible behind the window?

The Englishman answered that question. "Don't even attempt a draw, Marshal. I can kill you before your gun comes level."

Granville had him buffaloed and Matt knew it. He did as the man asked and his Colt slapped into the deep mud at his feet.

The door of the cabin opened and Granville stood in plain sight, his fancy gun in his hand. "I'm so dashed sorry to inconvenience you in this way, Marshal, but I have no choice, you see." The man's gun spat flame and Matt felt like his right thigh had been hit by a sledgehammer. His leg buckled under him and he fell facedown into the mud.

"That will keep you abed until my work is done," Granville said. "Again, I'm so sorry, old fellow. No hard feelings, I hope."

Then the Englishman turned and walked quickly toward the rear of the mule barn. Frantically Matt reached into the mud and felt around for his gun. But by the time he found it, Granville was gone.

The marshal got to his feet, the gun in his hand dripping mud. Pain from his wounded leg slammed at him, and he felt light-headed and sick. He limped toward the shack where Granville had been hiding and leaned against its clapboard wall, fighting off waves of nausea.

Pulling the bottom of his shirt out of his pants, Matt used it to clean the worst of the mud off his gun. He tried the action a couple times, then elbowed off the cabin wall and staggered after Granville. The devil was driving him and he was filled with a cold, killing rage.

Matt reached the wall behind the mule barn, stumbled and fell, picked himself up and fell again, this time stretching his full length on the ground. The pain in his shoulder was a living thing, gnawing at him mercilessly. His entire right leg throbbed and he felt blood squelch in his boot.

Struggling to his feet, the marshal staggered on, his eyes searching every nook and cranny of the dark buildings around him. Thunder roared and lightning flashed and the rain pummeled him, the wind smashing each gasping breath back down his throat.

Willing himself to stay on his feet, Matt left the barn and its muddy corral behind him and lurched toward a ruined sawmill with a caved-in roof that stood close to the rear of a boarded-up dance hall. He stumbled toward the mill, his gun up and ready in his left hand. Right then he wanted to kill Charles Granville real bad.

He was halfway to the sawmill when he stepped on an empty bottle buried in the mud and his ankle gave way. He fell hard, his wounded shoulder taking the worst of it, and a shrieking pain jolted through him. Matt tried to rise but a sudden darkness descended on him and he plunged headlong into a bottomless abyss. . . .

■ ■ ■ ■

Matt opened his eyes and saw Festus Haggen's concerned face swimming above him. "Matthew, you're still alive," the deputy said.

"More or less," Matt answered. He struggled to rise, but Festus gently pushed him back into the mud. Lightning shimmered, illuminating one side of the deputy's homely features, leaving the other half in shadow.

"You've been shot in the leg, Matthew," he said.

Matt nodded. "I think I already know that, Festus."

"Who done for you, Matthew? Was it ol' Lee?"

"It was Granville. He aims to kill Mrs. Scroggins and her children. He wanted me out of the way."

"Looks like he succeeded, Matthew. You're all shot to pieces."

Matt managed a wry smile. "Thank you, Festus. That makes me feel a whole lot better." He raised his left arm. "Help me to my feet. I've got to get to Doc Adams."

"You'd never make it, even with me helping you." The deputy waved a hand. "I managed to borry a handcart from that old Chinaman who's been hanging around town. Him and his three sons are here to help you into it." Festus turned his head, looking behind him. "Ain't that right, Wong . . . Wung . . . Wan . . . whatever your name is?"

Matt heard a laugh. Then strong hands were lifting him to his feet, and he was carried across the muddy ground and laid on the bed of what looked, to him, like a fruit cart.

This, the marshal thought to himself as he was pushed and pulled along Front Street in the direction of Doc's surgery, *is a mighty undignified way to travel.*

A few townspeople stood on the boards, some of them politely trying to hide smiles, as Festus and the old Chinese man hauled on the handles of the cart and his three sons pushed from the back.

The ride was a jolting misery, and by the time the cart stopped outside Doc's office, Matt's leg was on fire with pain and he worried about blacking out again.

Doc Adams came to the door, drying his hands on a towel, and saw the marshal being helped from the handcart.

"Take it easy there," he snapped. "That man is hurt bad."

CHAPTER 29
AN OFFER OF HELP

"As to the state of your health, Matt," Doc Adams said, "the left side of your body is as hale and hearty as always. But it's the right side that concerns me."

Doc washed his hands in a basin of water, then vigorously began to dry them. "The bullet missed the bone and went right through the fleshy part of your thigh, but it's a bad wound. Add to that the shoulder that hasn't yet begun to heal and you'll be off your feet for at least a couple of weeks, I'm afraid."

Matt looked down at his split pants and the fat bandage on his leg, then glanced at the clock on Doc's wall. It was past noon. "There will be plenty of time for rest later, Doc," he said. "I have things to do."

"You mean go after Granville?"

"I won't need to go after him. I have a feeling he'll come to me." Matt told Doc about Mrs. Scroggins and Granville's threats against her life. "And Lee Feeney is still out there somewhere, biding his time," he added.

Doc looked irritated. "Then, for heaven's sake, man, swear in some deputies. There are plenty of men in this town who can handle a gun."

"And if I do that, there will plenty of grieving widows," Matt said. "Doc, you're right. There are good men in this town, men with sand, but they don't have what it takes to go against Granville and Feeney, to say nothing of the Jicarilla Kid. Those three are skilled gunfighters, and Feeney and the Kid are named men. Have you ever seen what gunfighters can do to a bunch of deputized citizens? I have, and I can tell you that it's not pretty. The streets of Dodge would be filled with dead men, men you and I know and respect." Matt shook his head. "No, Doc, what I have to do, I have to do alone."

"Along with Festus, I hope."

"That goes without saying. Festus wears a star. He knows what's expected of him."

Doc Adams was a realist and his cool, appraising eyes revealed that he knew there would be no talking Matt into a feather bed. Not that day. "I could give you laudanum," he said. "It would ease the pain."

Matt shook his head and smiled. "No,

thanks, Doc. I have to stay alert. Laudanum would slow me down."

"As though it would make any difference! Matt, you're already slowed by that shot-up leg and shoulder."

With a tremendous effort of will, the marshal rose from his chair and struggled to his feet. The pain in his leg was intense, pounding at him, and for a moment, he was deathly afraid that he'd be unable to stand.

"You need crutches," Doc said matter-of-factly. "Keep the weight off that leg."

"No, not crutches. They're real awkward to get rid of when shooting starts. I could use a cane, though, if you have one."

"Stay there," Doc ordered.

As the physician hustled into another room, Matt sank back gratefully onto his chair. The thought came to him then that standing might be impossible. If that turned out to be the case, he could not protect Mrs. Scroggins from Granville — or face Feeney and the Kid.

"This might do the trick," Doc said, reentering the surgery. He held an elegant ebony cane with a silver top. "A few years back a gambler gave me this in lieu of payment after I took a bullet out of him. Watch!" Doc pulled on the handle and slid out a long, wicked-looking blade. "It's a sword cane, made in Paris, France, and it just might come in handy."

Matt smiled. "It might at that, Doc. I can use it to pick up the papers that fall off my desk."

Doc slid the blade back into the stick. "It's the best I can do, Matt. Crutches I have in plenty, but this is my only cane."

"It's fine, Doc," Matt said. He struggled to his feet again and Doc passed him the cane. The marshal freed his right arm from the sling, leaned on the cane and tried taking the weight off his leg. It helped, but his entire arm throbbed from his hand all the way to his wounded shoulder. He would not be able to do this for long. After a while the pain would become unbearable.

Doc saw the strain on Matt's face and drew his own conclusions. "Are you sure you don't want crutches?"

The marshal shook his head. "I'll manage. Bat Masterson uses one all the time."

Doc made a face. "It was Bat Masterson who gave me that one."

When Matt stepped out of Doc's surgery, Festus and his faithful Chinese helpers were waiting for him. "You want the cart, Matthew?" the deputy asked, his face hopeful.

"No," Matt said. "I've had enough of that

for one day." He turned to the old Chinese man and said: "Thank you for your help."

The oldster grinned and bowed; then he and his three sons trundled the cart back along the street.

Matt watched them go. Then suddenly he remembered Mrs. Scroggins. "Festus, who's guarding the office?" he asked, alarm rising in him.

"That Pinkerton feller is there," Festus said. "When I came lookin' for you, I told him to bolt the door and keep the Greener handy."

"Go back there, Festus," Matt said. "Go right now. I'll catch up . . . eventually."

"Matthew, I can he'p you. Make it easier."

"No, I want you at the office." Matt took a step, then another, the deputy watching him with pained eyes. "Go, Festus," he said. "I'll be all right."

Reluctantly the deputy left. Matt watched until the rain crowded around him and even his yellow slicker was lost in the gloom.

Matt leaned on his cane and lifted his eyes to the boardwalk, calculating the distance to the marshal's office. A hundred yards, no longer, but it would feel like a journey of a hundred miles.

After struggling through the mud of the street, the marshal reached the boards and the walking became easier, the thudding cane an incongruous counterpoint to the soft chime of his spurs. He was stopped often by passersby asking solicitous questions about his wounds, and replied politely to each one, giving away as little information as possible.

The meeting usually ended with a slap on the back from men and a peck on the cheek from women. But nobody was fooled. Everyone Matt spoke to knew that something was in the air, something bad that would no doubt end in gunfire and death.

Newly O'Brien, the gunsmith, familiar with the ways of firearms and the men who used them, was standing in the doorway of his store as Matt hobbled toward him.

He threw an appraising glance at Matt's bandaged leg and the bloodstained arm sling hanging loose from his shoulder and said: "Hell, Matt, you've been in the wars."

The marshal stopped and said: "You could say that, Newly."

"What in God's name is happening?"

Matt knew he could tell it straight to the no-nonsense O'Brien, and he did.

When the marshal had finished talking, the gunsmith stepped closer and said: "Matt, it sounds to me like you're facing a stacked deck. Just say the word and I'll side you, me, Quint Asper and a few others I could name, all of them good men."

"I appreciate that, Newly, but Festus and I will handle this alone." He smiled. "If it all goes bad, and Festus and I are down, feel free to arrest Feeney and the Jicarilla Kid and hang them from the trellis bridge across Dead Coyote Wash. They'll have bullets in them, I promise, and won't feel like giving you too much trouble."

"Matt, that's shutting the barn door after the mule has bolted," O'Brien said. "I want to be there when the shooting starts, and so will Asper and the others."

"Newly, you're an honorable man, and a brave man," Matt said. "But I don't want dead citizens on the street. When it's over, you can pick up the pieces."

"Matt, in case you haven't noticed, you're an honored citizen of Dodge your ownself."

"I also wear the badge of a United States marshal and that makes the difference." Matt's eyes softened. "Stay out of it, Newly. I appreciate your concern, but this fight is not yours. I guess I brought it down on myself when I allowed Ed Flynn to stay instead of running him out of town."

"But, Marshal —"

"No, Newly," Matt said, the memories of years gone crowding back to him, "I won't have other men die for my mistake, my misguided sense of what was honor and what was not."

Matt hobbled on, conscious of O'Brien looking after him. The gunsmith, a simple man who saw every issue in black and white, could not understand the complex shades of gray that chased through the marshal's mind. Matt could barely understand them himself. But it was enough for him to know that in sheltering Ed Flynn he had made a bad blunder, and it was now up to him, and him alone, to rectify it.

When Matt walked into his office, he entered a scene of chaos. The Scroggins children were chasing one another around the office, darting in and out of the cells, yelling and screaming. The Scroggins baby was wailing on its mother's lap while Mrs. Scroggins considered her brood with a serene smile on her lips, like a homely and slightly seedy Madonna.

Festus was pinned to a wall, a hunted look in his eyes, and Silas Vernon was scowling, as though he wished to be anywhere else in the world but here.

And there were still four more hours until train time.

Matt touched his hat to Emily Scroggins,

then waded through running children and sank gratefully into his chair at the desk. He saw Festus looking at him with pleading, hound-dog eyes, and smiled inwardly. Matt decided that he'd never in his life seen a man look so unhappy.

Realizing that talking above the din was impossible, the marshal beckoned Festus over and said: "Why don't you and Vernon go get something to eat? Come back in a couple of hours. Then I'll get a bite."

Festus slapped his thigh and did a little jig. "Hot dang, Matthew, that's the ticket!"

As though fearful that Matt would change his mind, the deputy scurried to Vernon and the two had a hurried talk, then left immediately, Festus grabbing his slicker from the rack at a run.

Matt laughed, and despite the pain in his leg and shoulder, it felt good. Hearing that laugh, Mrs. Scroggins rose to her feet, her baby now silent at her breast, and perched on the very corner of the chair opposite the marshal.

There were black circles under the woman's eyes, and she looked tired and drawn. "Marshal Dillon, do you think my children will be safe after we leave for the train station this evening?" she asked.

A child started screaming, chasing another, and Matt waited a minute before he answered. "I plan to put you and the kids on the train with Vernon," he said. "I'll stay on the platform and Festus will be on guard along the track. We'll remain in position until the train pulls out." The marshal smiled. "No one will get on that train without Festus or me seeing them."

"But, Marshal, you're so wounded, I —"

"Let me worry about that, Mrs. Scroggins," Matt interrupted. "Just get your children into the car with the Pinkerton as fast as you can when I give the word."

The woman dabbed her eyes. "You're such a dear, sweet man, Marshal Dillon, and so brave. You remind me of my poor Uriah."

Mrs. Scroggins obviously meant that statement as a compliment, but Matt derived no pleasure from the comparison. The woman was talking again.

"Marshal, I don't mind telling you that I'm very afraid, not so much for myself, but for my children. Can that Charles Granville person really be as evil as you say?"

Matt winced as a running boy slammed into his wounded leg, then bounded away yelling like an Indian.

"They're such a handful — children, I mean — aren't they, though?" Mrs. Scroggins said, looking adoringly at her brood as she slowly shook her head.

Matt gritted his teeth and managed a grimace that at a pinch might have passed for a smile. "Just a bunch of little angels."

"You were about to tell me about Mr. Granville, Marshal," the woman said, smiling in turn, pleased by the tall lawman's comment.

"Not much to tell," Matt said. "He's not evil in the true sense of the word, but he blames you and your late husband for his brother's death and that makes him very dangerous. Granville is a man to contend with."

"Then he will kill me if he gets a chance. And my children."

"Without a moment's hesitation," Matt said. He saw the woman's stricken face and instantly regretted what he'd just said. But there was no use pretending that the danger did not exist. From the moment they left the office until she was safely on the train, Mrs. Scroggins would have to be on guard, mentally and physically.

After Festus and Vernon returned, Matt struggled to the restaurant and ate a leisurely lunch and lingered long over his coffee. There was no danger of Granville trying to force his way into the office. Crazy or not, the Englishman would not try to burst through the door and walk into Festus' scattergun and Vernon's rifle.

But Matt didn't know where the man was, and he was aware that his walk to the restaurant could have placed him in considerable danger. The chances were that Granville would make his move at the rail depot, almost deserted at this time of the year when few people traveled, but that was far from certain.

Matt took his watch from his vest pocket. It was after four. He had less than an hour until the train left.

CHAPTER 30
GRANVILLE GETS THE POINT

When Matt stepped out of the restaurant, the buildings opposite were veiled in rain, the alleys vague rectangles of shadow. Thunder rumbled and lightning reached out from the black clouds with skeletal hands.

The marshal eased the Colt in his waistband and thumped along the boardwalk, his eyes restlessly searching around him. A few people hurried past, their eyes downcast, intent on reaching their destinations, and a wet and bedraggled calico cat sheltering in the alcove of a store doorway regarded Matt with disdainful green eyes.

He reached the marshal's office without incident and stepped inside. The clock on the wall read four fifteen. "Vernon," Matt said, his voice rising above the din, "it's time."

The Pinkerton turned anguished eyes to the marshal. He waved a hand that encompassed Mrs. Scroggins and her brood. "God help me," he said, "I'll have this all the way to the Arizona Territory."

Matt nodded. "It comes with the job, Vernon." He smiled. "Besides, don't the Pinkertons say they never sleep?"

"When Alan Pinkerton said that, he'd never met Mrs. Scroggins."

Festus helped round up the children, and after a struggle, he and the woman managed to button them into their coats.

Matt took the Greener from the rack, checked the loads, and cradled the shotgun in his left arm. "Vernon, are you armed?" he asked.

The Pinkerton nodded. "I have a thirty-eight in my pocket."

"Shove it into your waistband," Matt said. "If it all goes bad, leave the shooting to Festus and me, but keep that gun handy. You may need it to protect —" he was about to say "Mrs. Scroggins" but decided on — "your prisoner."

It was a good choice of words, because Vernon nodded grimly and did as he was told, stuffing a nickel-plated Smith & Wesson into his pants.

Festus levered a round into the chamber of the Winchester, then eased down the hammer. He nodded to the marshal and grinned, his chin set and determined. Matt set store by his deputy. No matter the odds, Festus was a man who would stand his ground, take his hits and keep on fighting. He had plenty of sand and then some.

The children had suddenly gone quiet, eagerly looking forward to their train journey. Matt looked at Mrs. Scroggins, who was white-lipped with fright. He smiled, trying to reassure her, and asked: "Are you ready?"

The woman nodded but said nothing.

"Then let's get it done," the marshal said.

The train was at the platform when Matt and the others reached the depot. It was raining hard, mixed with sleet, and thunder still grumbled. Water dripped from the gingerbread eaves of the station house, and the pine boards of the platform were muddy and rain slick.

A gold-painted locomotive jetted steam and its bell clanked, and behind it were two passenger cars, several closed boxcars and a red caboose.

The guard took Mrs. Scroggins' carpetbags, touched his cap and said: "You and the young'uns can board anytime, ma'am."

Matt nodded to the woman. "Get into the car, and don't come back out for any reason." He turned to the Pinkerton. "Vernon, you go with her and keep your eyes skinned for a tall man in a deerstalker hat. If he gets past Festus and me, he'll come looking for Mrs. Scroggins."

The man knew that the chips were down, because he immediately began to usher the kids into a car with steamed-up windows. A few people were already seated, looking curiously at the Scroggins brood and the lawmen through circles they'd wiped in the glass.

Festus dropped down onto the track and ducked between the passenger cars, to cover the other side of the train. Matt moved against the wall of the station house to take the weight from his leg and he watched Mrs. Scroggins follow her kids into the car. When the woman was inside, Vernon stood on the steps and waved to the marshal.

"Good luck," Matt yelled.

The Pinkerton smiled and waved a second time; then he too disappeared inside.

Matt was left alone on the platform, the rain and sleet lashing around him as the thunder crashed and lightning flickered. It was cold and getting colder. Where was Granville?

One thought nagged at Matt. The train would stop at a water tower twenty miles down the line. Could the Englishman be waiting there? He'd know that Matt was back in Dodge and only the Pinkerton stood between him and Mrs. Scroggins.

Matt decided that if Granville didn't show, he and Festus would ride the cushions to the water tower.

The marshal consulted his watch. It was ten until five, and the gloomy day was shading into night. Inside the station house, the agent lit an oil lamp, which immediately threw a rectangle of yellow light on the wet platform.

Again, where was Granville?

Two slow minutes ticked past. The locomotive chugged and puffed as it built up steam and the cars clashed as it rolled forward a couple feet. The guard was on the platform, looking down at the silver railroad watch in his hand. He snapped the case shut and glanced around him, checking for late-arriving passengers.

Water from the roof drummed on Matt's hat and slicker, and he shouldered away from the wall, the Greener hanging loose in his left hand.

Granville wasn't going to show.

Matt let his guard down for a moment, getting ready to call out to Festus to board the train, but in that moment, Charles Granville struck.

"I told you to stay in bed, Marshal. This is truly distressing."

The voice came from behind him. Matt turned as quickly as he could but was hampered by his wounded leg. He was almost facing the Englishman, bringing up the Greener fast, when Granville fired.

The bullet smashed into the shotgun where the stock met the side plate and Matt felt a numbing sting from his wrist to his elbow. The Greener suddenly seemed to take on a life of its own, wrenching out of his hand before thudding onto the platform.

Granville was running. As he sprinted past Matt, he pushed the tall lawman away from him. Favoring his wounded leg and badly off balance, Matt slammed against the wall, then fell to his right, his torn-up shoulder hitting the platform hard. He bit back a cry of pain and clawed for his Colt.

Festus had heard the shot and appeared from between two boxcars. He tossed his Winchester ahead of him and followed the rifle with a booted left foot as he tried to clamber onto the platform. Still at a run, Granville fired and Festus was hit, falling backward out of sight.

A fury rising in him, Matt scrambled to his feet. Using the cane, he stumbled after Granville. From somewhere behind him, he heard the guard yell: "Here, that won't do! This is railroad property!"

Matt ignored the man and Granville turned as he heard the thud of the cane. The marshal saw Mrs. Scroggins' face peering out the window, chalk white and scared.

Granville had reached the car steps, but he stopped, his face twisted into an ugly mask of hate. "Damn you!" he screamed. "Let me be."

Matt was within arm's length of Granville. He tried to thumb back the hammer of his Colt. It would not move! He'd not thought to clean the gun since his run-in with the Englishman, and the action was jammed solid with dried mud.

Granville's Colt was coming up fast. Matt moved quickly and brought his cane down hard on the Englishman's wrist. Granville let out a yelp of pain, but he did not drop the gun. He was bringing the Colt up again as Matt drove at him, smashing the man's shoulders against the corner of the car. The marshal took a step back and swung a hard left hook to Granville's chin. The Englishman's head snapped back, spit flying from his mouth, and he fell to his right onto the iron steps that led into the car.

Granville did not move for a long moment, his eyes glazed. Matt slid the long blade from the cane just as Granville recovered and quickly tried to bring his gun to bear.

Matt plunged the sword into the man's chest and Granville screamed, his mouth suddenly stained with blood. The Englishman fired, but the bullet missed, splitting the air next to Matt's head.

His face gray, Granville rose to his feet, the sword handle sticking out of his chest. He tried to level his gun again, but it suddenly seemed too heavy for him, and it fell from his fingers. He took a couple stumbling steps toward Matt, his mouth working, then got up on his toes and crashed onto his back.

The marshal stood over Granville, looking down at him, his eyes like ice. The man touched the blade in his chest and whispered: "This is how a noble knight should die, Marshal. By the sword."

Remembering Festus, Matt said: "A man who planned on killing a woman and children is a no good tinhorn, Granville. I'd say you're a fair piece away from being a noble knight."

"Hurtful words, Marshal," Granville gasped. Then all the years of his living seemed to crowd into his ashen face and his head slumped to one side and he died.

Matt pulled the sword from Granville's body and wiped it clean on the man's tweed overcoat. He slid the blade back into the cane and whispered aloud: "Bat Masterson, I owe you one."

The guard and a few of the men from the train had manhandled Festus onto the platform. When Matt reached him, the deputy was lying on his back. His eyes were closed and the rain and sleet were falling on his face.

It looked like Granville's bullet had hit Festus low on the left shoulder, and when Matt checked, there was an exit wound in the deputy's back, just under the shoulder blade. His shirt under his slicker was covered with blood, and his breathing was fast and shallow.

Matt pointed out to the guard and the other men a flat, four-wheeled cart used for luggage. "You men get Festus on the cart right now and take him to Doc Adams. He's losing blood."

"But, Marshal, the train is already late," the guard protested, his face anguished.

Anger flared in Matt. "I don't give a —" He held his tongue and forced himself to stay calm. "Just do as I say. The engineer can make up the lost time, I'm sure."

"Very well, Marshal," the guard said. "But

you can expect a sharp letter from the board of directors of the Atchison, Topeka and Santa Fe Railroad."

After Festus was lifted onto the cart, Matt shrugged out of his slicker and spread it over his deputy. Festus' eyes flickered open and he smiled weakly. "Did you get ol' Charlie, Matthew?"

"Yes, he's dead. Now you lay quiet, old-timer. We're taking you to Doc Adams."

"Read to Charlie from the book, did ye?"

"I sure did." Matt smiled. "I guess you could say he finally got the point."

Chapter 31
Lee Feeney Sets a Time

Emily Scroggins and Silas Vernon left the car and stood beside Matt on the platform. The woman turned haunted eyes to Granville's body and asked: "That was him? That was Charles Granville?"

Matt nodded. "Yes, he was Granville. He claimed he was a poet, but I don't know about that."

Tears sprang into Mrs. Scroggins' eyes. "If Uriah hadn't taken that money, none of this would have happened. There's been so much blood, so many dead men."

"A man should consider the consequences of his actions, I guess," Matt said. "When your husband stole that money, he played hob with the lives of a lot of people."

"I wish I could go back and undo it, and change everything that happened."

"You can't go back and rewrite the past, Mrs. Scroggins," Matt said. "Right now you should be thinking about the future and the raising of those kids of yours."

Vernon put an arm around the woman's slim shoulders. "Better get back on the train, Mrs. Scroggins." He smiled. "Or may I call you Emily?"

"Of course you can . . . Silas." The woman's red eyes lifted to Matt's face. "Thank you, Marshal. Thank you saving my children and me."

Matt touched his hat. "Good luck in Arizona, Mrs. Scroggins."

The marshal watched Vernon and the woman board the train. His shirt was already soaked by sleet and rain and he shivered. He was making his slow, painful way back to the office when Percy Crump hurried past him.

"No need to run, Percy," Matt called out after him. "Charles Granville isn't going anywhere."

"Matt, Festus is in serious-enough condition that I don't want to move him. I plan to bed down right here in the surgery to keep an eye on him."

The marshal's troubled eyes read Doc's face, seeking reassurance. "He'll make it, though, won't he?"

Doc shrugged. "It's a bad wound and I think the bullet may have nicked a lung."

The physician smiled. "But Festus is as tough as an old boot, and if I was a betting man, I'd give him better than fifty-fifty."

"Can I see him?"

"Sure. I gave him something for the pain, but don't wear him out with a lot of idle chitchat. And while I'm on the subject, keep those caterwauling women from across the tracks away from here."

Matt smiled. "I'll try, but it won't be easy."

Festus was a hero to the fashionable young belles over on the lace-curtain side of town, since he often regaled the girls and their mothers with wild tales of his derring-do against bloodthirsty Indians and desperate outlaws.

When news of his condition spread, Doc would be inundated with a bevy of misty-eyed women anxious to comfort their fallen champion.

Festus was lying on a narrow steel cot, and under his tan, his face was ashen. Dark shadows had gathered under his eyes and settled in the hollows of his cheeks.

Matt placed a hand lightly on his deputy's chest. "Are you awake, old-timer?"

After a few moments, Festus' eyes flickered open. "Oh, it's you, Matthew." He managed a smile. "Doc fixed me up real good."

"I know. He says you'll be well right quick."

Concern showed in Festus' eyes. "Matthew, you're soaked to the skin. Why are you out without your slicker and us with our rounds to make?"

"I just forgot it, I guess. I'll go back to the office and get it."

"See you do, Matthew. Remember, we've got to go talk to old man Tanner about his Missoura mule that was stole."

They'd talked to Tanner a month before and had later found his runaway mule feeding on wild gooseberries in a draw off the Arkansas, a frayed rope halter still around its neck.

Whatever Doc had given Festus for pain was making the deputy's mind wander and Matt said: "You just lie there quiet, old-timer, and get some sleep."

Festus nodded. "I do feel some tired." His eyes lifted to Matt's. "I forgot, Matthew. Lee Feeney!" Festus struggled to rise. "I got to get up an' he'p you round up that skunk."

"You stay right where you're at." Matt smiled, gently pushing Festus back onto the pillow. "I think Feeney has lit a shuck. Once you're on your feet again, we'll go looking for him."

"Are you sure, Matthew?"

"Sure, I'm sure. Feeney can wait until you're better."

Festus' eyes closed. "Matthew, I think I'll take a little nap. I'm so . . . so doggoned tired that I . . ."

The deputy's chest rose and fell with his breathing and sleep took him and Matt walked softly out of the room.

Doc was waiting for him in the hallway, Matt's slicker in his arm. "Here, you better put this on. As it is, you'll probably catch your death of cold." The physician's eyes caught and held the marshal's. "One of the men from the train told me what happened to Granville. Hell of a way for a man to die."

Matt nodded. "Maybe so, but when you come right down to it, there's no good way."

"And there's still Feeney," Doc said

"Yes, there's still Feeney" — the big marshal hesitated a moment, leaning heavily on his cane — "and the Jicarilla Kid."

"What are you planning to do, Matt?" Doc asked, the deep lines on his rugged face betraying his concern.

"Doc" — Matt shook his head — "right now I have no idea."

Night had fallen on Dodge and the lamps on the streets and in the saloons were lit against the darkness. The wind drove cold and hard from the north, throwing sleet against the buildings, covering their sides in a rime of icy white. The smell of wood smoke drifted everywhere as log fires burned and the few people on the boardwalks were wrapped to the eyes in woollen mufflers, their noses pinched and red. Out in the plains the coyotes were calling, the gray sleet in their fur giving them the look of lonesome ghosts.

Matt was drowsing in his chair when a rider drew rein at the office and climbed stiffly from the saddle. As is the habit of men who live with danger, the marshal came instantly awake when he heard booted feet on the boards, the Colt on the desktop close to hand.

Knuckles rapped on the door. Then it swung open, and a tall, thin man in a canvas slicker stepped inside. The man wiped melting sleet off his drooping mustache with the back of his hand and said: "You the marshal?"

Matt nodded, his eyes measuring the stranger. "I'm Marshal Dillon. What can I do for you?"

"There's nothing you can do fer me. Name's Porter an' I'm jes' a poor puncher passin' through."

"Then why are you here?"

"Got a message fer you. From a ranny who calls hisself Lee Feeney."

"Where did you meet Feeney?" Matt asked, leaning forward in his chair.

"Back a ways, on the trail. He won't be where I met him no more."

"What's the message?"

"He give me five dollars to tell you that he'll be in the Long Branch at noon tomorrow." As though to head off other questions, the man added: "That's all he tole me an' that's all I know or wanted to know."

Matt nodded. "Help yourself to coffee."

"Much obliged, Marshal, but I'm a hungry man. Beef an' beans is what I need."

"There's a restaurant down the street a ways that's still open."

"I know. I passed it an' smelled the cookin'. Smelled mighty good." The man called Porter touched his hat. "Well, good evenin' to you, Marshal. I hope the message I brung wasn't bad news."

After the drifter left, Matt sat at his desk, thinking. Feeney, with his flair for melodrama, had set the time for the showdown at noon. There was no stepping back from it or hoping it would just go away. If he didn't meet Feeney at the appointed time, the man would come looking for him. All he'd be doing was postponing the inevitable.

Feeling suddenly alone, Matt picked up his Colt and tried cycling the action with his gun hand. His fingers were still stiff and refused to respond to his will. At best, if he walked into the saloon with his gun drawn and cocked, he'd get off one shot with his right. His trigger finger and thumb were stiff and he would not have time for another.

Unless . . .

The marshal stood, swaying unsteadily on his feet, his wounded leg protesting painfully. He held the Colt in his right hand, pretended to shoot, then tried a border shift. The gun spun through the air, then slapped into his left palm, but at an awkward angle. He had to quickly adjust the heavy revolver in his hand before he could thumb back the hammer.

He'd be slow, very slow, on the shoot. Maybe Feeney would allow him that much time, but the Jicarilla Kid would not.

Matt tried the shift again . . . and again . . . and again. . . .

Finally he tossed the Colt on the desk and sat down heavily, defeat weighing on him. At gunfighting range, against two skilled shootists, he would be dead before he fired a second shot from his left hand.

His eyes angled to the gun rack and the Greener. The shotgun might even the odds,

313

but against the flashing speed of the Jicarilla Kid even the scattergun could be a mighty uncertain thing. His leg was painful and stiffening up badly and he'd need the cane to support himself. If he let it go to use the gun with both hands, he could very easily fall or at least be badly unbalanced and his aim would suffer.

Thinking it through, he knew he'd have to work the Greener with one hand, and it would not be his shooting hand. It was a prospect that did little to bolster the marshal's confidence.

The clock on the wall stood at ten o'clock. He had fourteen hours . . . maybe just that amount of time to live.

Matt unpinned the United States marshal's star from his vest and laid it beside the blue Colt. He studied them for long moments, thinking. He could saddle his horse, ride away from here and leave both star and gun behind. He could head for the mountains and find a secret place above the aspen where the junipers grew and the air was clean and thin. A man could find peace in a place like that, where the silence of the morning lay on the land like a blessing and even the ageless pines spoke in whispers.

It was a way. A good way. But in his heart, he knew it was not Matt Dillon's way. He was not a man to cut and run, and if he ever did, there would be no living with himself from that day forth.

Matt picked up the star, pinned it back on his vest and sat still as stone, listening to the night sounds of Dodge and the distant voices of the coyotes. Sleet tapped on the office window and the smell of hot coffee drifted from the blackened pot on the stove. The clock ticked slow seconds into the room, and the flame of the oil lamp above the desk flickered in a cold draft like a yellow moth. Matt closed his eyes, but sleep would not come to him.

The ebony cane with its ornate silver top lay on top of the desk. Bat Masterson must have paid a pretty penny for the cane, Matt decided idly, especially since it came all the way from Paris, France.

But then, Masterson was a professional gambler and money came easily to him, as it did to his shady friend Doc Holliday.

Doc Holliday!

Matt was suddenly wide-awake.

Chapter 32
Doc Holliday
Plans a Fight

Grim faced, United States marshal Matt Dillon stomped along the boardwalk like a man walking to his execution.

With each step he made an attempt to swallow his pride, but it was stubbornly sticking in his throat like a dry chicken bone. On any given day, Matt Dillon was an affable, easygoing man who took people as they came, but his dislike for Doc Holliday ran deep and had a long history.

The man was a troublemaker, a gambler who was only as honest as he had to be, and he had killed his share. As good with a blade as he was with the Colt, Holliday was a dangerous and quarrelsome drunk, and he was drunk most of the time. According to those who knew him, and not many did, Holliday was a man of intense hatreds and fierce loyalties, though he hated many and was loyal to few. He had pretensions to Southern gentility, yet openly associated with the dregs of society, tinhorn gamblers, shifty con men on the make, drifting outlaws and the painted cow-town bawds who worked the line.

It was said of Holliday that he had the gun speed of a striking rattler and the disposition of a bouncer in the worst dance hall in hell.

And it was to this man that Matt would appeal for help.

With Festus wounded and out of the fight, the marshal's back was to the wall. He might be able to handle Feeney and the Kid by himself, but shot up as he was, the odds were stacked against him.

Under the circumstances, Doc Holliday was the logical choice, but Matt would rather have asked the devil himself for help.

The marshal tapped on the door of Holliday's room and Kate's voice asked: "Who is it?"

"The Marshal," Matt said. "I need to talk to Doc."

After a minute the door opened and Kate ushered him inside, her face pale and strained. "That ride he took in the rain just about done for him," she whispered. "He's very ill."

From the bed, Doc snapped: "Who is it, Kate?"

"It's Marshal Dillon."

"Then, for God's sake, let him in."

Matt felt a pang of concern. Holliday couldn't even see across the room. How useful would he be in a gunfight?

Holliday waved the stone-faced marshal into a chair beside the bed and said: "How nice to see you again, Marshal. And you all smiling, like y'all were visiting sick kinfolk."

The lamplight shadowed the deep hollows and lines of Holliday's face and imparted a yellowish tinge to the man's gray skin. He was not yet thirty but looked eighty.

"I want to accept your offer of help, Doc," Matt said, and each reluctant word that wrenched from him tasted like rotten meat in his mouth.

"I heard you'd been shot again," Holliday said, "by that Charles Granville ranny. Heard you bedded him down with the sword cane you're carrying."

Matt nodded. "You heard right."

Holliday shrugged. "Sword, gun, knife, a club even — a man uses whatever is to hand to get the job done."

Matt said it again. "I need your help, Doc."

"He can't help you, Marshal," Kate said, stepping beside the bed, the silk of her scarlet robe rustling. Her inch-long fingernails were the same color. "Doc followed you out in the rain and you turned him down, treated him like some lowlife. And now he's dying, and you come to him for help?"

"Let it be, Kate," Doc said. He bent over in the bed as deep, hacking coughs racked him. Kate hurriedly handed him a handkerchief, and when the coughing spasm had passed, the handkerchief he took from his mouth was stained with blood.

"Kate is a protective woman, Marshal," Holliday said, each word a tortured gasp. "She doesn't understand what passes between men."

"Doc, you can hardly stand and you can barely see across the room," Kate said. "You're in no shape to be siding with the law in a shooting scrape."

"Maybe Kate's right, Doc," Matt said. "You're sick and you need rest."

Holliday ignored that and asked: "Where and when do you plan on meeting Feeney and his damned Apache?"

"Noon tomorrow. Right here in Dodge at the Long Branch."

"No, not the Long Branch," Holliday said, shaking his head. "That's way too close-up and personal. The shooting would be too fast. We must lure them away from the saloon to a place where the Kid's draw won't be a major factor. With me sick and you all shot to pieces, we'll need time to get our work in."

"Doc . . ." Kate's voice was anguished.

"Enough, woman," Holliday said. "Who knows? the Jicarilla Kid might be the one."

"The one, Doc? The one for what?" Kate asked. She had gathered up a part of her robe and was wringing the crimson silk like a demented washerwoman.

"My dear Kate, isn't that patently obvious, even to a woman of limited intelligence like yourself? I mean the one who releases me from this hell of living."

"Doc, if you go out in that street, I'll leave on the morning stage." Kate was sobbing. "I won't see you carried to Percy Crump shot though and through, your face as white as a sheet and your nose as sharp as a pen."

Holliday managed a weak smile. "Your Shakespearean reference aside, you won't leave me, Kate. We're two of a kind and we need each other. Together we wallow in our joint misery and together we cheerfully claw the black slime at the very depths of depravity. We're like Siamese twins joined at the breast, you and I, and there is no separating us."

Kate's face was pale and very still. "This

time I will, Doc. I swear it. I don't want to be around to see you die like a dog in the street."

"Better like a dog in the street than a rabbit in a feather bed, my dear." Doc's eyes moved to Matt. "Marshal, there is a corral close to the livery stable. We will lead Feeney and the Kid there. I will meet you outside your office at ten minutes before noon. When we reach the corral, we'll choose partners and open the ball."

"Doc, are you sure you can make it?" Matt asked.

"He can't make it," Kate snapped. "He's dying."

"I'll be there, Marshal," Holliday said, ignoring the woman. "You can depend on it."

Matt rose to his feet, leaning on his cane. The hotel room smelled of Kate's perfume, cigar smoke, whiskey and sickness. "I'll see you then, Doc," he said.

The marshal stepped to the door but Kate headed him off, her eyes blazing. "You've killed him, you know," she whispered. "Killed him just as surely as if you'd put a bullet in his brain."

"I gave Doc his chance to step away from it, Kate," Matt said. "He didn't take it."

"Pride. It was pride that made him stick."

She shook her head. "I know you swallowed your pride to come here, Marshal. You are proud, Doc is proud and that pride will be the death of you both." The woman drew herself up to her full height, her head back. "Well, I too have my pride. I'll leave tomorrow. I won't wait around to shed tears over the dead."

Matt walked back to his office, his steps slow and painful. Sleet slapped at his face and the icy wind was merciless. The wooden signs outside the stores banged and creaked, their painted words framed by thin white frost. There was no one on the street and shadows angled everywhere, dark and mysterious.

When he was opposite the Long Branch he stopped. It was almost midnight, but the saloon was ablaze with lights, open for business, though a few late-working railroaders and sleepless townsmen would be the only customers.

Matt considered talking to Kitty, warning her about what was to come tomorrow. He decided against it. She would only worry or even try to talk him out of it. It was best to leave it until the gunfire told her all she needed to know.

When he got to his office, Matt poured

himself coffee, then sat at his desk. He thoroughly cleaned and oiled his Colt and got a fresh box of shells from a drawer. He inspected each round carefully, rejecting a few. Then, one by one, he filled all six chambers of the revolver.

He had no need to bother with the Greener. Festus cared for the scattergun like it was his own child and kept it ready to go at all times.

Matt lifted his right hand to his face and willed his fingers to work. But no matter how he tried, they stiffly refused, and for some reason, the effort made his shoulder wound ache.

He pushed his chair back from the desk and stretched out his long legs, closing his eyes. He was tired to the point of exhaustion, and within a few minutes, sleep took hold of him.

Outside, the wind drove sleet against the window and from somewhere a loose door constantly slammed open and shut. The coyotes had moved closer to town and were yipping their hunger. The calico cat padded past the office door and then stood still, looking up at the lighted rectangle of the window, amber fire in its eyes. After a few minutes, the cat moved on, sleet white on its whiskers. A bat, driven by hunger, flitted over the roof of the office on noiseless wings and then disappeared into the darkness like it had never been.

Matt drowsed in sleep. The railroad clock on the wall ticked away seconds, then minutes, then hours. At three in the morning, the oil lamp above the desk fluttered and went out, a tendril of black smoke rising into the air. An hour later the sleet turned to snow, the temperature plunged and the wind died down. Fragile flakes fell on Dodge, making no sound, settling on the roofs of the buildings so they looked like weary, creaking old men in white nightcaps who had wandered into the night and lost their way.

In the dark, ticking quiet, Matt Dillon slumbered . . . and dreamed of far blue mountains and ageless whispering pines.

Chapter 33
Kate Takes Her Leave of Dodge

When Matt woke, the clock on the wall scolded him, telling him it was nine o'clock and the morning would soon be gone. His leg stiff and aching, the marshal rose from his chair and stepped to the window.

Outside the snow had done its best to transform the shabby, warped saloons and stores of Dodge into things of beauty, but its efforts were an abject failure. The town, with all its warts and weathered ugliness, looked like an ancient crone in a white wedding dress.

Matt added water to the pot, then a handful of coffee. He threw some wood into the stove, then slid the pot on the heating plate to boil.

Dressed in his hat and slicker, leaning on his cane, he stood on the boardwalk, the snow drifting around him. Farther up the street the Lee-Reynolds stage stood at the depot, six rawboned mules in the traces.

He watched as Kate Elder, carrying a carpetbag, stepped along the boards to the stage. She saw Matt and frowned, obviously blaming him for a doomed relationship that had been destined to fail from its very beginning.

Kate threw one final glance at the marshal, a look that held both anger and dislike, and stepped into the stage. A few minutes later, the stage rattled out of town and Kate Elder began her long trip into obscurity.

The coffee was on the boil and Matt poured himself a cup. He was about to help himself to another when the door opened and Doc Holliday stepped inside.

The gambler was wearing a long gray coat and a bowler hat of the same color, and he held a silver-topped cane in his hand.

Matt groaned inwardly. He and Holliday were going to be a sight, both of them unsteady on their feet, tapping along with canes as they staggered out to meet two of the deadliest gunmen in the West.

Keeping his thoughts to himself, Matt held up the pot. "Coffee?"

"Don't mind if I do."

Matt poured a cup and set it on the desk for Holliday. "Couldn't sleep, huh?" he asked.

Holliday hung his coat on a hook, the

right pocket sagging from the weight of his gun. "Who sleeps?" he said. "Sometimes I fall into a deathlike coma for an hour or two, but that's my limit."

He sat at the desk and produced a silver flask. He poured a generous amount into his coffee, then looked at Matt, his eyebrows raised in a question.

The marshal shook his head. "Too early in the morning for me, Doc."

Holliday shrugged. "Before the late unpleasantness, it was the habit of the Southern gentlemen to begin his day with three fingers of good Kentucky bourbon. It's a tradition I've happily kept alive."

"Won't throw your shooting off, will it, Doc?" the marshal asked. He was not making small talk. He was genuinely concerned.

Holliday laughed, revealing remarkably white and even teeth. *His dental training,* Matt guessed.

"I tried shooting sober once," Holliday said. "But I never did get the hang of it." He tried his coffee. "Good," he said. He looked at Matt. "How is the gun hand this morning?"

There was no use in pretending otherwise, so the marshal answered honestly: "I can't shoot with my right. Not today."

"Oh dear," Holliday said. "Then we're in

for an interesting time of it, aren't we?"

"Doc, do you think you can take the Jicarilla Kid?"

"I don't know. He's fast, very quick on the draw and shoot."

"And you? How fast are you, Doc? I've heard stories but stories don't cut the mustard."

Holliday laughed again and didn't answer until he'd drained his cup and poured another. When he resumed his seat at the desk, he said: "I'm still alive, Marshal. That should tell you something." The gambler smiled. "Anyhoo, it doesn't matter how fast a man is, if the other man is so much as a hair faster."

Matt stirred in his chair, suddenly uncomfortable. "It isn't going to be easy, is it?"

Holliday shook his head. "No, Marshal Dillon, it won't be easy. Feeney is good, but that damned Apache kid is hell on wheels."

"Maybe I can bluff them, talk them into surrendering."

Holliday choked on his coffee, gasped, then managed, smiling: "Marshal, you don't try to run a bluff when your poke is empty! Sure you can talk, but when all the talking is done, the shooting will start."

Matt nodded, resigned to what was to happen. "I guess you're not telling me anything I don't already know."

"We lead Feeney and the Kid to Grimmick's corral and then we get to our work," Doc said. "After the smoke clears, it will be either them or us coughing up our lungs into the mud."

"Doc," Matt said, smiling, "it's a downright pleasure to talk to you."

The slow morning dragged past. The snow got heavier and the air grew colder.

At eleven thirty, Matt struggled into his slicker and settled his hat on his head. He shoved his Colt into his waistband and took the Greener from the rack.

"They've arrived," Doc said from the window. His voice was so casual, he could have been talking about a couple circuit preachers.

Matt stepped beside him.

A couple ponies were tied to the hitching rail of the Long Branch, and Feeney and the Kid stood outside the door, both of them dressed in long canvas slickers, Feeney with a yellow muffler wound around his neck, the ends trailing almost to his feet.

"I'd say those two are loaded for bear," Holliday said. "And I don't think there's an inch of backup in either of them." He smiled. "I fancy Ed Flynn's sitting in hell at this very moment, laughing fit to bust at the fix he's put you in, Marshal."

Matt nodded. "Ed was a laughing man, some of the time."

Doc put on his coat and hat and eased his gun in the leather-lined pocket. "How do you want to play it?" he asked. "The corral?"

"I guess it's better than no plan at all," Matt answered. "We'll step outside, then walk to the corral along the boardwalk, just like we're two old friends going for a morning stroll."

"And we're not?" Holliday asked, a mischievous smile on the thin pale lips under his mustache. "Old friends, I mean."

"Doc, I'll give it to you straight. I appreciate the help, but you're not my friend."

To Matt's surprise, Holliday laughed, genuinely amused. "Marshal, you're not the first lawman to tell me that. For some reason beyond my comprehension, star strutters just don't cotton to me much."

Matt shook his head, a smile tugging at his own lips. "I wonder why." His eyes measured the gambler, who looked ashen and sick. "Are you ready?"

"Hell, I've been ready since I spoke to you last night."

"Then shall we take partners for the cotillion?"

CHAPTER 34
DAY OF THE
GUNFIGHTER

Matt stepped out onto the boardwalk, Holliday at his heels. Both of them were leaning on their canes.

Feeney saw them immediately. His head turned and he whispered urgently to the Jicarilla Kid. The Kid grinned and cleared his slicker from his guns. Beside him, Feeney pointedly looked at his watch.

"You're early, Marshal," he yelled. "You in such an all-fired hurry to die?"

Matt ignored the man. The Kid's eyes were on Doc Holliday. He said something to Feeney and a surprised look crossed the outlaw's face.

"Doc," he hollered, "my fight ain't with you. Step away from it, man."

Holliday's voice was weak, but it carried across the silent, snow-flecked street. "I'm siding the marshal, Lee. Besides, I never did like that damned half-breed you've got with you."

"Holliday," the Kid yelled, his face black with anger, "I'll kill you for that."

"You're a good one if you do!" Holliday grinned.

"Right, Doc," Matt whispered, "turn and head toward the corral."

The move startled Feeney. He'd expected that Matt would close the range and have it out on the street. A few minutes ticked past as Feeney hesitated. Then he and the Kid moved off the boards and crossed the street, following the marshal and Holliday.

Out of the corner of his mouth, Doc asked: "Hell, do you think they'll give us time to reach the corral?"

Matt nodded, each stiff step its own moment of pain. "They won't open the ball until we stop, and they know we've got to stop soon."

Holliday coughed into his closed fist. "Damn this cold air. It's playing hob with my lungs."

The snow was falling thick and fast as the livery stable came into sight. Dark gray clouds hung low in the sky, yet the light was so clear that everything, including the prairie beyond the town limits, stood out in sharp detail, like cut glass. The air smelled of iron and wood smoke, and from somewhere drifted the tang of frying bacon.

It was a morning to make a man feel alive, a morning to make his dying all the harder.

Matt slowed as they reached the stable. He angled to his right, and he and Holliday took up a position at the far side of the corral. A thick corner post and the wooden poles that formed the corral would give them some protection from bullets, and it offered a fair field of fire.

Near to where Holliday stood was a zinc horse trough, about three feet high, and the gambler stepped behind it. He slid his Colt from his pocket and coughed into the back of his gun hand, his thin shoulders shaking.

"You all right, Doc?" Matt asked, worried.

"I'll be fine," Doc gasped. There were flecks of blood on his lips.

Feeney and the Kid split up when they spotted Matt and Holliday at the other side of the corral. The Kid was angling to his right, his gun ready in his hand.

Matt felt a quiet satisfaction. Doc had been right. The move to the corral had negated the Kid's fast draw, though the gunman was still fast and accurate on the shoot and highly dangerous.

"Marshal, this would never have happened if you'd given me Ed Flynn," Feeney yelled. "Now you're going to die for a no-good lowlife. How does it feel?"

Matt knew Feeney was playing for time, allowing the Kid to get into a flanking position.

But the time for talking was long past and, with it, the time for mercy. Matt raised the Greener to his waist, steadying the gun as best he could in his useless right hand. He triggered a shot at Feeney, then at the Kid.

The buckshot tore into the top of corral post where Feeney was standing and Matt heard the man yelp as splinters drove into his cheek. The Kid was crouching behind the wheel of a feed wagon parked near the corral. Matt had missed him clean.

"Lee, are you hit?" the Kid yelled.

"Just a scratch! Watch that damned scattergun!"

The Kid triggered at Matt a shot that cut the air next to his head; then he fired again. Feeney was shooting. Bullets flew close to Matt and one thudded into the post in front of him.

Doc Holliday had not fired a shot, but was out of the fight. He was curled up behind the horse trough, his frail body shuddering as violent, choking coughs tore out of his diseased lungs. The right side of Holliday's face was buried in the snow and blood from his open mouth was staining the spotless white a dark scarlet.

"Doc!" Matt yelled. "Get away from here!"

The gambler raised a thin hand, signaling that he'd heard the marshal, but he was unable to talk.

"In a fix now, ain't you, Marshal?" Feeney yelled. "Holliday's dying an' you're on your lonesome."

They were coming for him now.

Matt grabbed the Colt in his waistband and fired left-handed at Feeney, who was stepping along the side of the corral toward him. A miss. Feeney fired and a bullet burned across the thick meat of the marshal's left shoulder.

The Kid had jumped over the corral rail and was striding toward Matt, his gun in his hand and an eager grin on his face. He was primed and ready to kill.

Matt dropped to his belly, the trough hiding him for a moment from Feeney. Ignoring the stabbing pain in his leg, he fired at the Jicarilla Kid from under the bottom pole of the corral. He was using his left hand but the range was short. The bullet hit the Kid low in the belly and the man screamed and stopped. The Kid knew he had been hit hard, but now he staggered forward, his gun spurting flame.

A V of snow kicked up in front of Matt's

face, then another. His strength rapidly being sapped by his wound, the Kid was having trouble holding on to his gun and was shooting low.

Suddenly Feeney loomed above the marshal. Matt looked up and saw the man's gun pointed right at his head. "Damn you to hell, lawman!" Feeney yelled. "I'm going to scatter your brains."

The left side of the outlaw's head erupted in a fan of blood and bone as Doc Holliday fired from behind the trough. Holliday was still coughing, but the gun in his hand was rock steady.

Feeney was dead on his feet, but he took a single, shambling step and fell heavily on top of Matt. The marshal pushed the man off him and heard Holliday fire again.

The Jicarilla Kid had almost reached the post where Matt lay when Holliday's bullet hit him square in the chest. The gunman took a step back and stood still, the gun dropping from his fingers. His face was stiff with shock, his eyes wide and staring.

For a few moments, the Kid remained where he was; then, making a visible effort, he called out: "Doc Holliday!"

Doc, coughing, got to his feet. "What the hell do you want?"

"If I'd had any kind of an even break, I'd

have killed you," the Kid whispered, his voice fading with his life.

"Things are tough all over," Holliday said, and he pumped two fast shots into the man's chest.

The Jicarilla Kid staggered under the impact of the bullets and crashed onto his back. He gurgled deep in his throat, then lay still.

A greasy haze of gray gunsmoke hung over the corral, mingling with the falling snow. People were walking toward Matt and Holliday, their steps tentative and wary.

"Did you take another bullet, Marshal?" Holliday asked.

Matt shook his head. "One of the Kid's bullets burned me, is all."

"Damn close run thing," the gambler said. "For a minute, I thought I was out of the fight."

"So did I, Doc," Matt said. "Believe me, so did I."

Holliday let the empty shells fall from the cylinder of his Colt, then reloaded. It was the reflex action of the professional gunfighter.

A small crowd of people had gathered around the bodies of Feeney and the Kid, pointing and whispering, their measuring eyes now and then slanting to Matt and

Holliday.

Leaning heavily on his cane, Matt led the way through the press of people, Holliday following close behind. When they reached the boardwalk, Matt stopped and turned to the gambler, smiling.

"Thank you, Doc. I'd say you saved my life back there."

Holliday waved a careless hand. "Think nothing of it, Matt. Maybe you can do me a favor one day."

"Maybe someday I will." The marshal studied Holliday's thin white face with its blue shadow of beard. "How are you feeling, Doc?"

"Pretty fair, Matt. Gunsmoke always clears my lungs."

Matt nodded. "Do you have a carpetbag in your room at the Dodge House, a nice, big one?"

"Sure do. Want to borrow it?"

"No, I don't want to borrow it. I want you to fill it and then get on the next stage or train out of town. The choice is yours." Matt's face was hard, his blue eyes harder. "Doc, I don't want your kind in Dodge."

Matt knew that Festus would have heard the shooting and be worried. He crossed Front Street and rapped on the door to Doc

Adams' surgery.

Without waiting for the marshal to speak, the physician's eyes crinkled in a smile and he said: "He's going to be fine, Matt. If all my patients were as tough as Festus, I'd be the best doctor in the world. I'd have a hundred percent cure rate." A question formed on Doc's face. "Tell me about all the shooting. Then you can see him."

When Matt finished talking, Doc nodded. "Then it's over."

"Yes, it's over. But it left too many dead men behind."

Doc took a deep breath, like the world was slipping away from him. "Some things I just can't understand, Matt. All the shooting and killing, is it really necessary?"

The marshal shrugged. "A man can't step away from what he thinks is right, Doc. Maybe one day when the land is settled and the outlaws are all gone, towns will no longer need men like me, and the shooting and killing will stop."

Doc's eyes fixed on Matt's and didn't waver. "This land will always need men like you, Matt, and men like Festus. It will need your courage and your sense of what is right and just and what is not." The physician's smile was almost sad. "I don't ever want to see the day when you're no longer wanted or needed." As though he feared he was verging on the maudlin, Doc clapped his hands and said brusquely: "Now you can see my patient."

Festus was sitting in bed, propped up by pillows. When he saw Matt, he smiled. "Heard you talkin' out in the hallway, Matthew. Glad you took my advice about ol' Doc Holliday."

Matt let that go, sat on the bed and asked: "How are you feeling, old-timer?"

Snow was drifting outside the surgery window and a freight wagon creaked past, the driver's hunched shoulders covered in white.

"Weak as a day-old kittlin', Matthew." Festus rubbed his thumb and forefinger back and forth across his brow. "Know what Doc gave me for breakfast this morning, Matthew?" Before Matt could answer, he said: "A soft-boiled egg an' a sody cracker." Festus shook his head and rolled his eyes. "No wonder I'm so weak."

"Want me to bring you something?"

"No, Matthew, I couldn't face food right now." Festus brightened. "But now I study on it, maybe I could manage just a little bite of invalid food: maybe a steak an' six fried eggs and a mess o' biscuits. And, oh, some honey for the biscuits, like."

Matt smiled, rising to his feet. "I'll see what I can do."

Festus searched the marshal's face. "An', Matthew, get something to eat your ownself. You look all used up."

When Matt stomped along the boards to his office, Kitty was standing at the door waiting. She smiled when she saw him. "It's finished now, Matt, isn't it?"

The marshal smiled. "Good news travels fast."

"The word spread all over town before the gunsmoke even cleared." Her eyes were concerned. "Are you all right?"

"Just fine, Kitty. Just fine."

"And Doc Holliday?'

"He's feeling great. In fact, he says he's fit to travel." Matt waved a hand in the direction of the surgery. "I just spoke to Festus, and he's on the mend. In fact, he wants me to bring him some invalid food."

Kitty nodded. "I'm glad to hear that, but first you can take me to lunch."

"Sounds good. I could sure use some gr—" Matt stopped, then smiled. "I mean, it would be a pleasure to dine with you, Miss Kitty."

Kitty took his arm. "You're learning, Marshal Dillon," she said. "You're learning."

ABOUT THE AUTHOR

As a little boy growing up in a small fishing village in Scotland, **Joseph A. West** enjoyed many happy Saturday mornings at the local cinema in the company of Roy and Gene and Hoppy. His lifelong ambition was to become a cowboy, but he was sidetracked by a career in law enforcement and journalism. He now resides with his wife and daughter in Palm Beach, Florida, where he enjoys horse riding, cowboy action shooting, and studying Western history.

The employees of Thorndike Press hope you have enjoyed this Large Print book. All our Thorndike and Wheeler Large Print titles are designed for easy reading, and all our books are made to last. Other Thorndike Press Large Print books are available at your library, through selected bookstores, or directly from us.

For information about titles, please call:
  (800) 223-1244

or visit our Web site at:
  www.gale.com/thorndike
  www.gale.com/wheeler

To share your comments, please write:
  Publisher
  Thorndike Press
  295 Kennedy Memorial Drive
  Waterville, ME 04901